Michael Carson was born in
Merseyside, just after the second
world war. Educated at Catholic
schools, he then became a novice in a
religious order. After leaving
university, he took up a career as a
teacher of English as a foreign
language and has worked in various
countries including Saudi Arabia,
Brunei and Iran. *Sucking Sherbet
Lemons,* his first novel and his
second and third novels, *Friends and
Infidels* and *Coming Up Roses,*
are all published by Black Swan.
His fourth novel, *Stripping Penguins
Bare,* is now also published in
hardcover by Gollancz.

Author photograph by Pinsharp.

Also by Michael Carson
Coming Up Roses
Friends and Infidels

and published by Corgi Books

Sucking Sherbet Lemons

Michael Carson

BLACK SWAN

SUCKING SHERBET LEMONS
A BLACK SWAN BOOK 0 552 993484

Originally published in Great Britain
by Victor Gollancz Ltd.

PRINTING HISTORY
Victor Gollancz edition published 1988
Black Swan edition published 1989
Black Swan edition reprinted 1989 (three times)
Black Swan edition reprinted 1990 (twice)
Black Swan edition reprinted 1991 (twice)

This book is set in 11/12 pt Mallard
by Colset Private Limited, Singapore.

Black Swan Books are published by Transworld Publishers
Ltd., 61-63 Uxbridge Road, Ealing, London W5 5SA, in
Australia by Transworld Publishers (Aust.) Pty. Ltd.,
15-23 Helles Avenue, Moorebank, NSW 2170, and in
New Zealand by Transworld Publishers (N.Z.) Ltd.,
Cnr. Moselle and Waipareira Avenues, Henderson,
Auckland.

Made and printed in Great Britain by
The Guernsey Press Co. Ltd., Guernsey, Channel Islands.

For
Jerry Schultz
Michael Rosinski
Philip Harris

"Ah, touched in your bower of bone,
Are you! turned for an exquisite smart,
Have you! make words break from me here all alone,
Do you! – mother of being in me, heart.
O unteachably after evil, but uttering truth,
Why, tears! is it? tears; such a melting, a madrigal start!
Never-eldering revel and river of youth,
What can it be, this glee? the good you have there of your own?"

– from 'The Wreck of the Deutschland'
by Gerard Manley Hopkins

Contents

Part One
Wobbles

His satchel bouncing against his fat bottom in time to his stride, Benson walked home from school through the park. As he walked he kept a weather eye out for the rough boys from Sir William Grout's, while at the same time making certain that his Clarks 'E' width shoes were not touching any cracks in the paving stones.

In his green and gold striped blazer, Benson knew that he presented an easy target for the Secondary Modern hooligans in their dull navy and grey uniforms. They could be hiding behind any tree. And, if they were, and if they emerged to rag him and push him and throw his spectacular cap into the branches of the winter trees, there would be nothing else for him to do, but, like a Catholic budgie cornered and packed by Protestant starlings, expire with 'Jesus! Mary! Joseph! I give You my heart and my soul!' ejaculating from his quivering lips.

He pushed the possibility from his mind and concentrated on avoiding the cracks in the paving stones. What was at stake today were he to tread on one? Would dying sinners all over the world forget to repent and be lost? Would the whole future of the Catholic Church be placed in jeopardy and people become Protestants? Would Our Lady of Lourdes stop curing cripples? Would Mother be out and he'd have to wait on the cold ledge next to the step until she came home?

Deciding that the last horrific possibility would occur, Benson tripped warily towards the train station.

*   *   *

Benson did not think that he had trodden on even one of the cracks between the paving stones and was greatly put out to find the doors and windows of the house locked against him. He surveyed all three sides of the family home, pressing his nose against the leaded windows, and was doubly galled to see all the well-known objects in each room getting on very well without him.

The three doors at the back that belonged to the shed, the outside toilet, and the wash-house, were not locked. He opened each in turn and closed them again with a sound that was louder than strictly necessary. Benson felt he had to register his rising indignation somehow.

'How dare she! How dare she!' he exclaimed, making his way to the front of the house. 'If she won't give me a key of my own like David Mulligan has, the least she can do is be here when I get back from school! I mean, it's not as if my return is in any way unexpected. I always leave school at four on the dot and catch the four-twenty, or, if something really strange happens, the four-forty. It is all very predictable. Not too much to ask that someone be in!'

Back at the front of the house, he directed a look of infinite hurt and loss up the cul-de-sac, kicked the garage door a couple of times, and decided to inspect the back garden. Anything to avoid settling down on the cold step to await the approach of darkness and double pneumonia.

He fumed down the steps and into the greenhouse. It smelled of his dad. But, it being late February, there was neither warmth nor comfort there and he soon left it and returned to his customary waiting place on the ledge next to the front door step. There, after a few minutes of agonized indecision, he began to play Grocers' Shop.

The idea of Grocers' Shop was that invisible customers came to Benson's shop and gave him their weekly orders. Perhaps a customer might ask Grocer Benson for a dozen of his best eggs. To obtain this order, Benson had simply, seated as he was on the ledge, to lean back against the doorbell and strike two long rings, the code for 'best eggs', followed by twelve short rings to denote the number required. Over occasions past counting, exiled on the threshold of home, Benson had memorized a host of bell codes to cover all eventualities.

So, an imaginary Mrs Owen came to Benson's shop and complimented him on how fresh and good everything she had bought from him last week had been. And how cheap, considering the wonderful personal service which was, without doubt, the best in the area. 'We aim to please, Mrs Owen. Your satisfaction is our reward. This is a Catholic Grocers', Mrs Owen, and it is my sole aim in life to find salvation among the tins and bottles and bacon rashers.' Mrs Owen, though only a poor flailing Protestant, was impressed. Benson wiped his soul-white apron and beamed broadly.

He entered Mrs Owen's order into the unique bell system and imagined that behind the scenes a number of widows – he always employed widows, Catholic widows – were scuttling about collecting together the items for the order and neatly packing them into a brown cardboard box. 'It will be delivered of course!' he told Mrs Owen, who left his shop nodding with admiration and satisfaction and determined to contact the Catholic Truth Society that very day to take instruction in the True Faith. Then, at the end of Time, there she and Benson would stand before The Divine Throne and Mrs Owen in her dazzling heavenly crown would exclaim: 'I owe it all to Mr Benson here!' and The Lord and His Blessed Mother would smile and nod and offer endless supplies of Mars Bars that didn't make you fat and bottles of Cream Soda that didn't make you wet the bed . . .

But that was all in the life to come and in this one Benson was becoming cold and uncomfortable. Ringing in all the codes was also giving him a headache.

He gazed up the road for any sign of his mother making her way towards the house. He willed her appearance and closed his eyes for five seconds in the firm belief that, upon opening them, there she would be, full of apologies and with a quarter of sherbet lemons to sweeten her return and make amends for her sin against The Holy Grocer and Holy Punctuality. But when he opened his eyes the road was deserted.

The lamplighter came down the road on his bicycle, carrying his pole in one hand. He approached the gas-lamp at the bottom of the road and hooked it on, not for one moment losing control of his bicycle.

'Good evening!' Benson called out to the lamplighter. The man grumbled a reply, taking care not to drop the cigarette between his lips. Then, with a deftness that never failed to stir Benson, he turned his bike and went off up the road, where he hooked on the other lamp, and disappeared.

'It's lighting up time,' thought Benson and he kicked some pebble-dashing off the wall. 'If I weren't a good Catholic,' he told himself, 'I'd give that mother of mine a piece of my mind when she gets back.'

Rosemary Jenkins came down the road on her drop-handlebar bike. It made a noise like a motorbike because Rosemary's big brother had attached a piece of card-board clamped with a clothes peg to the back wheel so that it caught the spokes and clicked satisfyingly when the wheels revolved.

'Hello Rosemary!' shouted Benson. 'It's past lighting up time and you haven't got your lights on!'

'Hello Wobbles!' replied Rosemary. This remark seemed enough to Rosemary to both greet Benson and counter his jibe about her lack of lights. She disappeared with her now slow-ticking bicycle down the side of her house before Benson could think of a suitable response.

Instead he thought: 'I will not get angry and insult her back. Anyway it's too late now. She's gone. And it would be unchristian. I have, after all, been called to A Higher Way and must turn the other cheek even to Protestants and Methodists and other Pagans.'

He manoeuvred himself with difficulty from the stone ledge on to the doorstep: 'I am wasting valuable time! Brother O'Toole says that time is gold and we shall be called to account for every second of it. Golly! This moment could be my last. The Angel of Death could be about to give me a tap on the shoulder!' He looked round for her in the murky dusk but forgot and looked for Mum instead: 'Where is she? I should have finished my tea and be doing my homework by now.'

He sat down heavily on the front door step but finding the cold of it soon percolated through his bottom, stood up straight like the slim Roman soldier in Brother O'Toole's English class.

That day Brother O'Toole had brought in some post-cards of a picture called 'Faithful Unto Death'. It showed a Roman soldier guarding the door of a house. The soldier stood to attention but gazed upwards to his right, a look of some anxiety upon his handsome face. Behind him in the room gobs of fire were falling and three people were panicking as the fire cascaded down on them. But the soldier did not move. Encroaching fiery destruction glinted on his breastplate and belt. He held his spear and continued to do his duty.

Benson waited at the front door and attempted to emulate the soldier. Brother O'Toole had told the class that the picture had been inspired by the destruction of Pompeii. Apparently the body of a soldier had been found there, and, like the soldier in the picture, the mummified body, preserved in long-cooled lava, had been standing loyally to attention.

'Now what does this picture tell us, boys?' Brother O'Toole had asked.

The picture had been passed round but Benson had only had a quick glance at it before it was seized from his hands by curious classmates. Still, even the shortest glance had told him what was happening. He put up his hand.

'The soldier has a job to do and he is doing it. The people behind him are afraid because the volcano is erupting all over them. That's why the picture is called "Faithful Unto Death", because the soldier is faithful and he is definitely going to die.'

'Good lad!' Brother O'Toole had said.

15

Now Benson stood until he started to get pins-and-needles, and still Mum had not put in an appearance. He thought how hard it would be to remain faithful unto death. It was all he could manage to remain faithful unto Mum's return.

Reluctantly he gave up the good fight, and, placing his satchel on the step to insulate him from the cold, sat down. He took out his red Catechism from the inside pocket of his blazer and commenced testing himself at random:

'Who made you?'

'Well, I know that one! That one's a cinch! God made me.'

'In whose image and likeness did God make you?'

'God made me in His own image and likeness,' rattled off Benson, wondering for an instant if God was also rather too 'well-made' but quickly blocking out the thought as a wicked temptation from the Devil.

He picked another Catechism question at random:

'What does the ninth Commandment forbid?'

'The ninth Commandment forbids all wilful consent to impure thoughts and desires, and all wilful pleasure in the irregular motions of the flesh,' answered Benson, pricked by unease as quick as a sin stains the sheet of the soul.

'What are the twelve fruits of the Holy Ghost?'

'Er . . .' replied Benson.

He started consigning the twelve fruits of the Holy Ghost to memory in the encircling gloom.

The Religion examination was in three weeks. If he won the certificate again, it would make it the third time in a row and Mum had promised that she would get all three certificates framed in passe-partout by the nuns and hang them in the lounge.

The Jenkins' porch lamp was turned on by Mr Jenkins, viewed as a shadow through the mottled glass of the front door. That meant it must now be night. The coloured glass in the lamp reminded Benson of Rowntree's fruit gums, which he could never make last for an hour like some boys could, and during the day promised a wonderful light. But when it actually came to being switched on, it was something of a let-down. No gashes of crimson, blue, green and yellow painted the front square of lawn, just a warm pastel glow. Benson had pestered his parents to buy one that would really light up the night and make their porch 'like church', but up to now they had resisted his entreaties.

It was getting distinctly chilly. A damp, penetrating wind blew off the Irish sea, swerved around the Jenkins' house and cuffed Benson squarely in the face. He shivered and offered up his sufferings for the Holy Souls in Purgatory. He repeated the twelve fruits of the Holy Ghost to himself, but increasingly without enthusiasm or even gratitude.

A part of him thought if the Holy Ghost could go to the trouble of dropping those wonderful twelve fruits upon the Earth in general and Benson in particular, the least Benson could do was learn by heart what he had to thank Him for. But the other half of him was cold and miserable and unable to take any consolation whatsoever in the twelve fruits.

Anyway, God the Holy Ghost was a bit of a mystery for Benson. He was always the last member of The Trinity to be mentioned and by far the most mysterious. God the Father was easy enough. He was an old man with a beard who had been fond of the Jews and sent His Son to make good Catholics of the World. God the Son was Jesus and Jesus was nice and human and had long straight hair, a bit like Lilian's at *The Maypole*, and was good with children. But God the Holy Ghost was a dove. He had hovered over Mary at the Annunciation and done the same thing over the Apostles at Pentecost but Benson could not see why God the Father and God the Son could not do any of the things They had got God the Holy Ghost to do.

Benson suddenly recalled himself: 'What if I were to die here on the step? What if the Angel of Death approached me here in her black nightie and beckoned my soul to follow? It had happened to the Little Match-girl after all. He wondered if he would rise straight to heaven like a cork to the surface of water, or if he would have to go to Purgatory for a spell to burn off the sins of his past life. No, for sure, they were being frozen off here and now as he waited in the purgatory of the door-step for the return of Mum.

But then he reminded himself that he was not suffering for his own sake but for the sake of the Holy Souls. And top of the list of Holy Souls would have to come Grandma Benson who had given him threepenny bits for as long as he could remember and had then stopped.

A light went on in the front room of Mrs Brown's house. The room was suddenly bathed in a harsh white light. But only for a second, until Mrs Brown, her left arm out wide, then her right, drew the heavy curtains across the window and completely shut in the light.

Mrs Brown was a widow and lived alone. She had never had children and Mum said a lump was the reason. But she did have a stuffed monkey which hung by its tail from a standard lamp in the back room and held a banana in its fist. And nearby she had a wall cabinet with a little strip light that held her collection of miniature liqueurs. One of them had a gold leaf inside. Mrs Brown always showed it to Benson when he visited after letting him stroke the monkey. Then she would make him a cup of coffee in a mug with the Queen Mother on the front and George the Sixth on the back. Mrs Brown's coffee had a special taste, much better than home. But it took her a long time to make because her hand shook and she always seemed to be in danger of spilling the milk as she poured it.

Mrs Brown did not talk much either, which was a pity because Benson loved to watch the way her loose neck flesh wobbled. It was always left to him to make conver-sation which could be good too because Mrs Brown would nod or shake her head and that made her wobble almost as much as she wobbled when she talked.

Her hair was steely grey and looked like it was a bird's

nest put on upside down. Her face was very white, kept that way by a Stratton powder compact with a flight of ducks on the lid. She didn't go to church and Mum told Benson not to go to Mrs Brown's house if he wanted to sell flags for Canon McCarthy's babies.

Once, while passing her house, Mum had told him that Mrs Brown was anti-Catholic. Nothing else had been said until Mrs Brown had rung Mrs Benson and complained that Benson was calling her Auntie Catholic. Now, it was embarrassing for Benson to think about. Then, he had thought it a nice name. He had called lots of Mum's friends 'Auntie' though they were not really aunties.

Benson stood up and found that his left foot had gone to sleep:

'Sanctify my sufferings and save souls!' he commanded the starless sky.

Then he saw Mum making her way down the road loaded with shopping. He sat down at once on the step and feigned sleep.

'Been here long?' Mum asked apologetically, her blessed keys rattling.

'Er ... What? What?' said Benson, emerging from theatrical sleep. 'Mum, where have you *been*? I've been waiting here for *ages!*'

Mum opened the door and went into the house. Benson followed.

'Can't be helped. You know what it's like,' said Mum matter-of-factly.

Benson asked The Lord to forgive Mum's indifference. 'Yes, but . . .' he began.

But to be fair, he did know what it was like for Mum round at the shops. Her friends seemed ever to lie in wait behind trees, pillar-boxes and shopfronts aching to unload their news. He could not recall that Mum ever said that much back but he could remember a hundred occasions when he was smaller and pulled at Mum's coat to tug her away from the clutches of the highwaywomen in swagger-coats who stole Mum and son's time and fun at being out together, leaving them locked on pavements not doing what needed doing. But Mum had always remained faithful unto the slow death boredom brings, had smiled and stayed put while the sticky lava of hot gossip flowed over them.

Mum made her way down the hall in her swagger-coat. She sighed as she lifted the bags of groceries on to the table in the morning room.

'Can I help?' Benson asked.

'Too late now,' Mum replied without turning towards him. She reached into her black handbag with the clasp that Benson loved to trap his thumb in, and took out her puffer. She aimed this at her mouth, squeezed the bulb two or three times, and inhaled deeply.

'There! That's better!' she said.

'You'll be needing a new one soon, Mum,' Benson observed.

'It's got a few puffs in it yet, son.'

Then Mum sat down and lit a cigarette. 'Guess what eggs were!'

'Three shillings.'

'Three-and-six. And that was at *The Maypole*. Still, at least we can get them. Do you remember rationing, son?'

Benson stared at Mum, horror-struck that she could possibly think that he would ever forget the hell that was rationing. 'Of course I remember rationing, Mum! I only had sixpence a week in coupons to spend on sweets! You don't think I could forget that, do you?'

Mum smiled and fished into one of her bags. She produced a triangular paper bag.

'Only two ounces!' moaned Benson.

'That's right. More than enough. Now you get out from under my feet while I make the tea.'

Benson, thinking it all a bit thick, went off to the dining-room. There he drew the curtains, making sure that not a chink remained through which he might be observed. Then he rummaged in a pile of records by the gramophone until he found 'Coppelia'. He put it on to the turntable, unscrewed the old needle from the pick-up arm and reached into the tiny tin of new needles. The tin had a picture of His Master's Voice on the top. He inserted his index finger into the slippery pile of needles. The sensation was one of velvet rather than steel. He selected a new needle and screwed it into the arm.

The music started and Benson stood in front of the octagonal mirror which hung on the wall opposite the window.

He was a ballet-dancer. His arms were raised above his head and as the music played it lifted Benson out of himself and away from his chubby reflection into a world of princes and swans and superhuman physical effort. He pranced around the dining-room totally disembodied. When the record ended he bowed deeply to his invisible audience, who clearly wanted more. He would turn over the record and give them more. But first a sherbet lemon was called for.

After years of practice Benson had evolved and perfected several methods of eating sherbet lemons. Apart from the easily mastered methods of 'suck' or 'chew', he was also adept at storing the sweet between front teeth and upper lip. In public this gave to his face a grotesque appearance which he amplified by jutting out his jaw and making his eyes cross. He had once sent Teresa Higgins into hysterics by so doing. She had run off screaming and told her dad who had rung his dad. Teresa Higgins' dad was a plumber. They lived at the top of the road. Benson did not think that plumbers should be allowed to live in his road. After all, Mrs Brown's sister's husband had once been Lord Mayor of the County Borough.

But today he felt like putting his sherbet lemon to more pyrotechnic uses. His audience still gazed at him, rapt, from beyond the mirror. He would floor them by squirting the sherbet!

'Now I shall squirt the sherbet!' he told them. 'For this – my most difficult trick – I need total hush.'

He manoeuvred the sweet between his front teeth and

then bothered each end of the lemon-shaped sweet in turn with the tip of his tongue. When both ends were judged to have been sufficiently worn down, he stood in front of the mirror, pursed his lips around the body of the sweet and blew mightily. A great billow of white powder settled on to the polished surface of the sideboard directly below the mirror. The audience gasped and cheered Benson's versatility. He bowed, brushing the sherbet dust from the sideboard with a deft, theatrical gesture. Then he changed the needle and put on side two of 'Coppelia'.

There was a melancholy section on this side which Benson and his audience adored. It was preceded by a fast bit and he flung himself around the room and jumped from the seat of the easy chair on the left of the fireplace to the stool below the bowls of hyacinths. Then, as the sad section started, he leaned backwards until his back lay against the top of the sideboard, his head lying on its surface just a few inches from the mirror.

He rolled his eyes upwards towards the mirror, which had become a camera, and noted that the flesh on his face had pulled back from his nose and cheeks. Then, looking the picture of encroaching horizontal doom, Benson commenced an elaborate arm-dance to the music which culminated in his demise on the sideboard.

The music ended. A pregnant silence gripped the audience, which was at length broken by a sudden whoosh of applause. Benson chose not to acknowledge it. He would not step out of role. And he would make them wait for their encore, a piece of Rachmaninov from 'Sparkie's Magic Piano'.

Then, through the applause and cries of 'Bravo!', another sound impinged:

'Tea's ready!'

'I will return but my mother is sick unto death and I must go straight to her bedside. Please be patient,' Benson told the stunned and sorrowing crowds.

After tea the front doorbell rang.

Mum answered it. Eric Jenkins, Rosemary's twin brother, stood there fidgeting.

Eric Jenkins never went round to the back door, even though Mum told him to at every opportunity. She told him today, as a matter of form, but without much hope. Eric, smaller than his thirteen years might have a right to expect, proved stubborn in his routine and could not be cajoled to go to the more easily answered back door like Benson's other friends.

'Eric's here for you! At the *front* door!' Mum shouted upstairs to Benson.

Benson's heart sank.

He had been kneeling in front of his open wardrobe in his room putting the finishing touches to an altar, the centrepiece of which was a plaster statue of Saint Maria Goretti. This child Virgin and Martyr stood atop a copy of the complete works of William Shakespeare which had been covered with a gent's white linen hand-kerchief, one of three Benson had been able to raise little enthusiasm for when he had received them the previous Christmas from Auntie Muriel whose son was a White Father in Fiji. Around Maria Goretti he had ranged in obeisance a number of Holy Pictures. Medals hung from the ceiling of the niche and he had fashioned gold stars cut out from the paper inside Cadbury's Bournville wrappers.

Saint Maria Goretti held a special place in Benson's affections. She had been knifed to death at the age of sixteen while attempting to fend off a rapist. For this lethal defence of her honour, the culmination of a short life of quiet piety, she had been canonised by the Pope in Rome. Her body lay somewhere in Italy in a glass coffin and hadn't gone bad. Her killer, following many years in gaol, had been present at her canonisation and then had resided in a monastery. He too died in the odour of sanctity.

Only two years older than Benson when she died, he found Saint Maria Goretti extremely inspirational in his uphill struggle to preserve his own Holy Purity.

He had just added a torch with red cellophane wrapped round the business end to give the correct ambience to the altar when Mum announced Eric's arrival.

'O my God! Saint Maria Goretti! Pray for me! It's Eric Jenkins!' whispered Benson to the sadly smiling saint. 'Ask him what he wants!' he shouted.

'You ask him what he wants. I'm your mother, not the maid, and don't you forget it!'

'All right! Coming!' Benson shouted. Then he added to the crimson altar in the wardrobe, 'Sweet Jesus, save me! Saint Maria Goretti, intercede for me!'

He got up off his knees and went slowly downstairs to face the fidgeting temptation on the step.

'You've got a new scab on your knee!' said Benson, trying to avoid the inevitable.

'Yes, I fell off my bike. It doesn't half hurt,' said Eric, his voice squeaky with self-pity.

'Eric, I don't wish to be rude – we Catholics are not permitted to be rude, even to Methodists. It can under certain circumstances be a Mortal Sin. However, I must tell you that you are an Occasion of Sin for me and I really ought to avoid you for my soul's sake. It's nothing personal, you understand.'

'But you started it and Bruno wants a meeting tonight,' replied Eric.

'Bruno?'

'Yes, Bruno. He's in the garage now.'

Benson suddenly had a vision of tears cascading from the eyes of the statue of Saint Maria Goretti and soaking into the gent's handkerchief where they became the colour of blood. Were that to happen, he thought, it would be a miracle and the handkerchief would be a relic and might be put into a gold case for people to kiss. His road would be choked with charabancs and Mrs Brown would write to the Council.

But then he recalled himself to the problem in hand. 'You mean Bruno is *in the garage*!'

'Yes.'

'And he is waiting for us to have a meeting!'

'Yes,' replied Eric. 'A meeting.'

'You realise what that means, don't you, Eric?'

Eric shuffled and gazed at the worn doormat under Benson's gimlet glare.

Benson continued, 'Bruno, Eric, has gone to the garage with the *firm intention* of committing a *Mortal Sin*! You do realise what that means, don't you, Eric?'

Eric looked uncomfortable, like a tourist being harangued in a language he does not understand. He pulled at his fringe.

'It means,' continued Benson, 'that were Bruno to get run over on his way home, or were his heart to simply stop – and they do, Eric, every day they just stop – were this to happen, Eric, Bruno would go straight to eternal punishment in Hell.'

'Would he?' asked Eric.

'Of course he would!' rapped Benson. 'You know, Eric, I sometimes wonder if you Methodists are Christians at all. Bruno has gone to the garage to commit a sin which contains *serious matter*. He has gone there with the firm intention of *putting his soul to death*! Who let him in by the way?'

'I did,' said Eric unhappily.

'Then you are as bad as he is. You are an accomplice. The Catechism says: "In how many ways may we either cause or share the guilt of another's sin? We may either cause or share in the guilt of another's sin in nine ways: (1) By counsel, (2) By command, (3) By consent, (4) By provocation, (5) By praise or flattery, (6) By concealment, (7) By being a partner in the sin, (8) By silence, (9) By defending the ill done." Now I want you to examine your conscience most carefully, Eric. Have you not caused or shared in Bruno's sin?'

'Are you coming or aren't you?' asked Eric, addressing the doormat rather than Benson.

'No, I'm not! I told you last time that last time was the last time!' replied Benson with all the certainty at his command.

'But Bruno needs us, he says. He took it out and it's all hard!'

Benson felt dizzy. He knew that devils were hovering in legions around the front porch.

'It's huge!' said Eric. 'I think he's grown an inch since last week and he showed me hairs growing underneath as well as on top.'

'Saint Maria Goretti, pray for me,' intoned Benson silently.

'Come on, please! He'll kill me if you don't come. He will!'

Benson was silent for a long moment. Then he said, 'That would be adding further wickedness to what has already taken place. I will go to the garage, Eric. But I will go there only to exhort Bruno to change his ways before it is too late.'

But as he spoke he knew he was lost. Once inside the garage he would never be able to resist Bruno's whopper.

'Tell Bruno I shall be over shortly,' he told Eric, and with his heart pounding wildly he closed the door on the little Methodist.

Slowly, and in sorrow, Benson mounted the stairs and walked momentously along the landing to his bedroom. There he knelt in front of the statue in the wardrobe alcove. Avoiding the statue's eyes, he reached behind it and extinguished the torch. The glittering red-gold and red-silver medals floating in the air of the alcove disappeared into blackness – a blackness Benson knew was shared by his soul.

With a feeling made up of intense excitement and deepest mourning, Benson went to counsel Eric and Bruno in the garage.

Eric Jenkins had summoned Benson to attend the weekly meeting of 'The Rude Club'. He and Benson had been the founder members in the empty garage. The weekly ritual had consisted of a fondling of pre-pubescent parts while each boy intoned a litany of conjecture as to what the itchy attachments were really for.

It had been Benson's theory that the naughty parts had been placed there as a temptation, like the apple in the Garden of Eden or a cake on a table an hour before tea-time. But Eric had countered that his sister, Rosemary, did not have one and that it didn't seem fair. To which Benson had responded that every son and daughter of Adam had his or her own particular cross to bear; and that Rosemary, being in Benson's eyes very much a fallen daughter of Adam, would have hers too, even though it might not be as tangible as Eric's or Benson's.

If Benson was uncertain as to the exact use to which his rude parts should be put, he had been left in no doubt by the Brothers at school as to what uses they should *not* be put. He was not to take wilful pleasure in irregular motions of the flesh. That had been inculcated in no uncertain terms and he had communicated the heinous-ness of what they were doing to Eric. Eric, hopelessly mired in Methodism as he was, had asserted that they met regularly and not irregularly, but this had not pulled any weight with Benson, who, while completely certain about 'irregular motions', had little inkling what the regular motions could be.

What he did most nights between saying his night prayers and dropping off to sleep was definitely highly irregular and had to be confessed to the priest every Saturday. And each Saturday an assortment of priests told him that he must bridle his passions or he would become their slave and Benson said he would but didn't. And not bridling his passions imbued his night games with a disturbing sense of sin. He wanted to do it still. He did it still but he hated himself each time he did it, loathed the thought of his invisible soul turning from shining white to God-gone, decaying stench. So, added to his fears of punishment at school for homework undone, bullying for being fat, was added a lethal fear of the hell of red hot pokers to which his sin would take him were he to die in its thrall.

Each time he fell he prayed that he would be spared until he could immerse his soul in the acid bath of Confession. But in the interim he allowed himself full rein. Once blackened by Mortal Sin, the Catholic soul has no deeper to go. God, His Holy Mother and all the saints have turned away their faces in distaste. The worst has happened. He has already hit molten-rock-bottom. May as well lay sin on top of sin.

The meetings of The Rude Club had been lent extra spice by the arrival of Bruno who went to the Technical School and was not a Catholic, nor a Methodist, nor anything else that Benson could discern.

There was something foreign and exotic about Bruno, though when tackled about his ancestry, he always responded that his dad had fought in the war and his big brother was a Queen's Scout. But he was dark, and though about the same age as Benson, had far outgrown the Fairy Cycle he was never seen without. So large was he growing that he had to ride his bike with his knees out wide to avoid scuffing them on the handlebars.

And, most importantly, Bruno dangled while Eric and Benson merely peeped. He could also produce a grand finale to each meeting of The Rude Club which delighted, enthralled, appalled and entrapped his two less competent admirers.

Bruno knew everything there was to know about motions of the flesh, regular and irregular. He had once gestured to the fluid on the garage floor that had just sent the other two boys into fits of disgusted giggles, and announced:

'You can make babies from that.'

Eric and Benson had stared down at the unbabylike drops of liquid.

'Er . . . How do you mean?' asked Benson.

'Just what I say. You can make babies from that.' And he added: 'My dad told me.'

'Pull the other one, it's got bells on,' giggled Eric, though Benson was silent.

'You have to add an egg, of course,' said Bruno.

'How do you mean?' asked Benson again.

Bruno had sighed. 'You don't know anything, do you?

I'm not surprised really. Your mum and dad are probably waiting until you can make stuff like me before they tell you.'

'Tell us what?'

'About that stuff and the egg.'

Eric started to giggle again and Benson gave him a kick in the pants.

'What about that stuff and the egg?'

Bruno had pushed himself back into his short pants and continued in his deep monotone, 'Your mother's got the egg and the stuff gets into her and swims up her and meets the egg and they grow and nine months later a baby comes out of your mother's belly-button.'

'How do they get the baby out of the belly-button?' asked Eric.

Bruno had sighed the sigh of the teacher forced to cast pearls before plodders: 'The doctor unties the knot, takes the baby out and then ties up the knot again.' Then he added with a gesture of frustration, 'Honestly!'

Eric nodded.

'But how does that stuff get to your mother's egg?' asked Benson.

'Your mum and dad sleep together. It gets there while they're asleep.'

'But how does it get through the pyjamas of your dad and the nightie of your mum?'

Bruno did not reply.

'How does it get into your mother and where does she keep her egg?' asked Benson, sensing Bruno's growing discomfiture.

Bruno had shrugged.

'I think you're making this whole thing up, Bruno. My mum and dad would never have done anything like that to get me. My mum and dad prayed for me like good Catholics and God sent me to them out of His beneficence.'

Eric nodded. 'I agree,' he said.

Further encouraged by Eric's backing and Bruno's lack of response, Benson said, 'You know, that may be the way heathen foreigners get their babies but it's not the way we Christian Catholic English people get ours.'

'Not Christian Methodist English people neither,' added Eric.

Bruno started to sulk. He took his Fairy Cycle from where it was leaning against the wall of the garage and wheeled it to the door. He opened it, manoeuvred the bicycle through, and said flatly, 'Mine's bigger than yours and you can't make stuff.'

He disappeared and Benson turned to Eric. 'Well, maybe we can't make stuff but I'd rather be a good Catholic any day.'

'And I'd rather be a good Methodist.'

Then Eric and Benson had resumed taking pleasure in irregular motions of one another's flesh.

Tonight too the same thing happened. After initial remonstrations by a conscience-stricken Benson, The Rude Club meeting had got down to the business of the night.

Eric was right. Bruno was getting bigger. Benson wondered where it would all end. His fingers could not fit around Bruno and the peach-fuzz hair was darkening and thickening all around. This time the sight of Bruno reduced Benson to silence. He could not take his eyes off the other boy and became extremely irritated with Eric who would insist on making childish comments all the time.

In fact, that night Benson wished that Eric would go away and leave him alone with Bruno. He did not know quite why he wanted this, nor how things would be different and improved without the presence of Eric. But he did know that he wanted to concentrate on Bruno and on the part of him which was, every time he saw it, becoming more and more different from what he saw on himself, and which made Bruno, for all his Paganism and Pride, such an object of his abject admiration.

The next day Benson woke up late. He had wet the bed again.

Every night as part of his bedtime ritual Benson prayed that he would be able to stay dry through the night. His Guardian Angel, Tom, was the recipient of these prayers. Sometimes Tom listened and sometimes he didn't. Tom was not to be relied upon; though, of course, Benson knew that Tom always knew what was for the best.

This morning Benson did not have far to look for the reason why Guardian Angel Tom had turned a blind eye to his request for a dry bed. The meeting of The Rude Club must be the reason. If God and His Holy Mother had turned away Their faces from Benson then Guardian Angel Tom could not help but do likewise.

He washed himself all over hurriedly and got dressed. He stared miserably at the large circular stain on the sheet as Mum called him to breakfast for the third time. There was nothing to be done. He was late and any plan of concealment was therefore doomed.

Usually, if he woke and found his bed wet, Benson would strip the sheet off the bed, wash the wet part under the tap and put it back on the bed upside down, making sure that a dry face would present itself to Mum's investigative feel during the morning.

But today he did not have time. The bed-sheet mirrored his soul and his sin would surely find him out.

He ate his toast and drank his tea standing up. The clock ticked towards ten past eight, the latest time he could possibly leave the house and be sure of catching the twenty-two minutes past train, even if he ran as fast as his legs could carry him.

'Bed OK, son?' Mum asked.

'Er . . .' replied Benson, tentatively.

'I see,' said Mum curtly.

'Where's Dad?' asked Benson.

'He left ages ago. Called out during the night.'

'Anything important?'

'Shouldn't think so. They always call on your dad. Without your dad the whole police force would fall to pieces around us,' said Mum, speaking with a mixture of sarcasm and pride.

'Yes. Expect so.'

The wall-clock had reached eleven minutes past eight. He knew he would have to break all his previous records to make the train on time. He lurched into his blazer, picked up his lunch, crammed it into his satchel, kissed Mum and bolted out of the front door.

Benson sprinted up the road, round the corner and down the half-mile hill that led to the station. His thighs, exposed below his short trousers, wobbled and rubbed together as he ran and made a soft, swooshing sound which under normal circumstances made Benson acutely self-conscious. Today, however, he was too desperate to catch the train to worry about how his thighs either looked or sounded.

'Sweet Jesus! If I get the train I'll . . . I'll never never never ever go to The Rude Club again. I'll ban it. I'll do without cakes at Sunday tea and pray and sacrifice constantly for Bruno's conversion.'

His chest was tight and he felt that if he spat he would spit blood. Even in the cold of this February morning he was sweating profusely. His tie had worked itself round under his ear and the ends flew like a flag over his shoulder.

'What if I miss the train!' he thought. 'If I miss the train the evil man who said Pope Pius the Twelfth helped Hitler and didn't help the Jews will become more and more famous and poison the minds of millions of people to the Church; Eric and I will be found taking wilful pleasure in irregular motions of the flesh and be banished to the outer darkness where there shall be weeping and crashing of teeth; Canon McCarthy won't be able to collect enough money to keep his orphan babies and they'll have to go to Council orphanages; I'll wet the bed every night until I'm eighty . . .'

When he was still three hundred yards away from the station, Benson saw the train approach and draw into the platform. He was lost. They pulled a metal barrier across the entrance as soon as the train came in. He stopped running. It was quite pointless to continue.

Resigned, he searched in his pockets for the four-pence halfpenny return fare. By the time he got to the ticket office, the train had drawn away, leaving the platform empty.

'Half return to Central Station. Second Class,' Benson said to the ticket clerk, between puffs.

'You missed it!' remarked the ticket clerk, reaching for the ticket while he blew Woodbine smoke through the hole in the glass at Benson.

Had the ticket clerk been Eric, Benson would have attempted a witty riposte of a sarcastic nature, something he had learnt from close attention to the Assembly speeches of Brother Hooper. But he just said, 'Yes, I know,' and wandered on to the platform.

There he read an advertisement: 'Top People Take *The Times*!' Benson scowled, thinking it vain.

'Good people take *The Catholic Herald*!' he told it.

But Benson was not a good person. He stood on the bit of the platform where his favourite carriage always stopped and thought about all the millions of innocent people he had failed by missing the train.

Then, gazing down along the shining rails, he thought: 'Those rails are parallel. They will never meet.' He squinted down the line to where the rails met in the distance. 'It is merely an optical illusion. If the rails really came together then the train would fall off the rails and British Railways would be for it.'

He turned his attention to the electrified rail that ran next to the shining rail. It was rusty-looking, an ugly sister beside the other rail.

Benson had seen the connection, a pad like a carpenter's plane, running along it and sparking as the train approached. But, despite all the evidence of his senses and warnings from posters and his science teachers, he could not believe that the dull rusty rail was actually 'live'.

A year or so before, a boy from Benson's school had been struck dead by such a rail while crossing the line to get his Frido football. Benson had gone to his funeral. He had given up sugar in his tea for the repose of the boy's soul. But still he could not believe that something as really close to a boy's life as a Frido football could cause death. No, there must have been something else.

But Benson could believe that his soul was black, full of maggots and stench. And that somewhere unspecific but definitely real the Divine Being with the long hair and the gentle features had turned away from him and would not turn back until Saturday after Confession. Until then he must not take any chances. He could definitely not test his disbelief of the rusty rail.

Benson dawdled through the park towards school. It was now his object to make himself so late that he would at least miss the line at Assembly and be able, with luck, to slip into Brother O'Toole's English lesson in time for the attendance check.

As he walked he stepped on every crack in the paving stones. Not a one did he miss. Everything depended on his stepping on them all.

Then Mr Plunkett's blue Austin A40 passed him, slowed down and stopped. The car had a sign in the back window which said: 'The family that prays together stays together! Support the Father Peyton Rosary Crusade!'

Benson caught up with the car and Mr Plunkett leaned across and opened the door for him.

'Hop in, Benson.'

'Thank you, sir.'

Now he would definitely be in time to join the line of latecomers at Assembly. He did not wish to be ungrateful to Mr Plunkett but he did wish that he had left him to continue his dawdle to school unhindered.

'Late too, Benson?' observed Mr Plunkett as he started the car up.

'Yes, sir. The trains were late, sir,' lied Benson, without any feeling that it was a lie, so often had he used the excuse, and so much a part of his schoolboy survival kit had it become.

'Those trains!' smiled Mr Plunkett. 'They're almost as bad as the bridge. The bridge is my excuse, Benson.'

'Yes, sir.'

Mr Plunkett was the Art teacher and was very popular with everyone at St Bede's College. He seldom if ever strapped, never raised his voice, was never sarcastic, and, inexplicably, never had the least problem with discipline. His favourite form of admonition was: 'That's not like you!'. His only remonstrance when faced with failed artwork: 'Only observe! Use your powers of observation!'

Benson was useless at Art but nevertheless tried to use his powers of observation for Mr Plunkett's sake. He had been rewarded by having his potato-cutting of a Maltese Cross printed repeatedly on a twelve-inch handkerchief and mounted on the Art room wall.

Without any further conversation they reached the staff carpark at St Bede's. Mr Plunkett parked and wished Benson best of luck.

'Thank you, sir,' Benson said dejectedly.

Something in Benson's voice must have melted Mr Plunkett's heart, for he said, 'Why not sneak in with me to the Art room? You can help me fill the jam jars until they're finished with Assembly. Then you can get to your first class.'

Benson brightened. 'Thank you very much, sir!' Then a thought struck him. 'But what if someone catches me on the way to the classroom, sir?'

'Then you just say that I was to blame, that's all.'

Benson cheered up immediately. He followed Mr Plunkett up the stone steps to the Art room like a devoted puppy. Perhaps the day was not going to be such an unmitigated disaster after all.

'Only one jam jar between two, Benson. We're running short of them. I had Eddie Rudge yesterday. Kept back after school again. He managed to break half a dozen so we need to go a bit careful.'

Immediately Benson stepped into the breach. 'If you need jam jars, we've got piles at home.' He was dimly aware as he said it that he could get a halfpenny each for them if he took them back to the shop.

'We do! We do! Thank you very much. As many as we can get,' said Mr Plunkett.

Benson set about filling the jam jars with water from the sink in the corner of the Art room. He paused to admire his potato cutting of Maltese Crosses as he passed it, and wondered what he would create to follow that triumph.

When he had finished arranging the jam jars, he said, 'I'd better be going to class now, sir.'

'Yes, you had. And thank you for your help, Benson.'

'Thank you, sir.'

With confidence he walked along the top corridor of the long two-storey building, feeling safe and happy under the mantle of Mr Plunkett.

He joined his classmates from the left as they were streaming in from the right. One or two of the other boys gave him funny looks but most seemed not to notice.

He sat down at his desk and waited for his companion, Vincent Latos, to arrive. When he did, the two boys solemnly bade one another good morning by shaking hands. Then both opened their desks.

Vincent was a recent immigrant from Poland and still had a lot of trouble with his English. No doubt this contributed to his stiff, rather distant attitude towards Benson. He did not say much at all to any of the other boys in the class, for in his first few days at the school it had been fashionable to reply to anything Vincent said with, 'We had one but the wheel fell off.'

Benson had protested to his classmates about this treatment of an exotic guest and had been punched in the stomach by Hepher for his pains. But this had not prevented him from taking Vincent Latos to his bosom at once. He was rewarded on a daily basis because Vincent brought wonderful complex sandwiches with him to school in an Oxo tin; sandwiches crammed full of succulent morsels which Benson had never seen before. And Vincent was always happy to share his lunch with Benson.

36

Fat Benson and Foreign Latos kept a low profile at the back of 3B. Benson badly wanted to be liked, but, being fat and not good at anything in particular, found popularity to be a hopeless pursuit. He had to be nice to everyone merely to avoid being called 'Wobbles' and teased about his weight. He had to give his all in order to get even the minimum of civility in return. It was all very wearing and he was happy to be a peripheral figure at school, sat next to Vincent Latos who was fair and easy, if sometimes a little strict.

He was strict, for instance, about the order of both his and Benson's desk. Everything had to be just so inside and out. Benson was not so fussy about such things but took to the imposed discipline readily enough. Had the other boy only known, Benson would have gone to far greater lengths, endured far worse torments than tidiness, to keep his companion satisfied.

Benson reached forward and nudged Drury, the boy in front.

'What happened at Assembly?'

'Nothing much,' replied Drury, 'Hooper made Rourke cry about dinner money. What else?' Drury considered, while he rubbed the thick lenses of his spectacles, the bridge of which had been splinted with elastoplast, on his blazer. 'Someone from 4A has pinched something and 4A have to stay in tonight until he owns up. Oh yes. The Vocations Brother is coming tomorrow.'

'Yeah,' grinned Drury's desk partner, Mellon, 'that'll be good. We could miss double Maths if he comes in time.'

'You're right, Mellon,' said Benson, 'and we've got a lot of homework to do for Maths tomorrow. You done it?'

'No,' replied Mellon.

'Me neither,' said Benson. He wondered if he could risk not doing it in the hope that the Vocations Brother would come and give his talk at just the right time.

The Vocations Brother came to St Bede's every year to look for boys with vocations to be Brothers and who would go off to a place in Wiltshire for training. Benson had never paid much attention to his visits in the past, but it was the prospect of a talk taking up school time and, like a Roulette ball, landing on a lucky subject hour, that warmed Benson. To think that there might be a chance of missing the frightening boredom that was Maths with Brother Wood!

Benson nudged his books into tidy piles and worried about whether or not he should be worrying about something. He placed his bag of sandwiches in the left near-side of the desk which was where Vincent Latos always put his. No, there was no need. The day got off to a tranquil enough start with double English. No homework due for that, and, anyway, Brother O'Toole often forgot about it even if homework was due.

Brother O'Toole came in and the class stood up.

'Good Morning, sir!'

'Good Morning, boys! Be downseated,' said Brother O'Toole.

The class downsat.

Brother O'Toole patted the top of his bald head with his left hand as he waited for the hubbub to subside. This was the cue for the more brazen boys in 3B to do the same with their better-endowed heads. Left hands patted the tops of several heads. Brother O'Toole did not seem to notice. He never seemed to notice though the custom had been going on at St Bede's for the decade that Brother O'Toole had taught there.

'Now, before I take the register,' began Brother O'Toole, 'I'd like to tell you something that I recalled during my morning meditation. I was contemplating the Third Glorious Mystery of the Holy Rosary –' He stopped and asked O'Gorman, 'What is the Third Glorious Mystery of the Holy Rosary?'

'The Descent of the Holy Ghost on the Apostles, sir.'

Brother O'Toole did not acknowledge O'Gorman's answer, but continued, 'And as I was contemplating that blessed Mystery, a thought came to my mind. Back in 1912, before any of you were born, the Black and Tans came to our village. They were looking for an I.R.A. man, name of Docherty. At least that was their excuse. They were really there to raise a ruckus. Anyway, they burst in on old Mrs Flannagan who owned the sweet shop in our village. Now Mrs Flannagan was never one to become unhinged by the likes of the Black and Tans and she just asked the men, "Would it be sweets or tobacco you'd be wanting, me boyos?" Well, didn't the commander of the wicked band of English bandits take the good woman's innocent remark for cheek? He cocked his weapon – the heathen dog – and fired at the jars of sweets above Mrs Flannagan's head. I can see the look of shock on your faces, boys! It's hard to imagine, now that old Ireland's free, that such things could ever have taken place. But take place they did, God help us! You boys know very well what the English heathens did to our God-fearing race. You've heard about Cromwell and the Potato famine. But the Good Lord in heaven often made it plain as the nose on your face on which side He was on. The Holy Ghost descended that day in all His glory on Mrs Flannagan's sweet shop. And I'll tell you for how. Not only did the bullets not hurt one hair of Mrs Flannagan, even though shards of glass showered down all around her . . . not only that, but do you know what else?'

Brother O'Toole broke off and looked at each of the boys in turn. 'Do you know, O'Shea?'

'No, sir,' replied O'Shea.

'Oh, you don't don't you, O'Shea? Well you just take your finger down out of your nose and keep it out.'

'Yes, sir.'

'Do you know, Rudge?'

'No, sir,' replied Eddie Rudge.

'I will tell you what else, so. There was a statue of the Sacred Heart in the shop, placed on the top of the cigarette shelf. After the Black and Tans had left the shop, laughing, shouting obscene things and pinching chocolate and tobacco as they went, Mrs Flannagan – devout soul that she was, God rest her – went to give thanks before that statue and saw that a shard of glass as narrow as an arrow and a full six inches in length had struck the statue of the Sacred Heart. And can you guess where it struck the statue, boys?'

'In the head, sir,' volunteered O'Gorman.

'No, not in the head, O'Gorman.'

'In the leg,' tried Taggart.

'No, not in the leg.'

'In the eye,' chirped Rudge.

'No, Rudge, not in the eye! The very idea! Sure it is only you, Rudge, who could have thought of such a terrible thing. Sure it is a long way you are, Rudge, from being able to comprehend the workings of the Holy Ghost.'

Benson put his hand up and was called on by Brother O'Toole.

'In the heart, sir,' he answered piously.

'You're right, Benson. Good. In the heart. In the blessed heart of the Sacred Heart.'

Some of the boys turned and gave Benson a glare of reproach for spoiling their game. Though nobody had heard that particular version of the story before, it took none of them any effort to make the inspired guess, that, in all probability, the shard of glass would have pierced the Sacred Heart in the heart. Had Benson not intervened the class would have been able to go through a whole litany of anatomical parts while avoiding death to the game by aiming for the heart.

Brother O'Toole never appeared to notice these games. He congratulated Benson who sat down, stabbed by the looks of his classmates but basking in the light of Brother O'Toole's approval.

'In the heart,' continued Brother O'Toole, 'and what that told me, boys, as I walked through the Brothers' garden this morning at six of the a.m. – long before any of you heathens were awake, I fancy – was that the Holy Ghost descended not just the once on Pentecost Day all those years ago. No. He descends every day just as he descended on Mrs Flannagan's sweet shop during the Troubles. That statue you will be pleased to hear is now given pride of place in St Laurence's Church and the Faithful come from miles around to pray for favours and to see the wonders that He hath wrought. Now for your homework I want you to imagine that you are Mrs Flannagan. Tell the story I've just told you in your own words. Now open your "Julius Caesars", Act 2, Scene 2.'

The class did so, but too slowly for Brother O'Toole who said as he always did, 'Come on lads! We're taking longer to read this play than the Divine Bard took to pen it! As Gerard Manley Hopkins said: "I am soft sift in an hourglass". Let's get this done before our allotted span in this vale of tears runs out.'

Brother O'Toole was always asserting that the boys were 'soft sift in an hourglass' and the class always laughed. They laughed because Eddie Rudge had amended the line to 'I am soft snot in an hourglass'. Brother O'Toole heard the laughter and gave himself credit. But in this as in much else, he could not bring himself to plumb the perversities of the boys his vocation had caused him to minister to in the far away missionary land of England.

When the class was ready, he asked, 'Now what can you tell me about the story so far?'

Vincent Latos put up his hand, something he never usually did. Benson immediately felt alarmed for his companion. Nothing good could come out of Vincent speaking in front of the class. Waves of nauseous fear swept over him.

Brother O'Toole pointed to Vincent.

'Julius Caesar is ambition. He has come back in Rome and Pompey is on his chariot wheel. Brutus and Cassius are not like Caesar. They think he ambition. They will think to slaughter him. Former is honourable but latter is hungry and not trustable.'

Some of the less sensitive members of 3B giggled at Vincent's mistakes.

Brother O'Toole called on Eddie Rudge who had giggled most, 'All right, Vincent. Thank you very much. Now, you, Rudge. Perhaps you'll tell the class the story so far. In Polish.'

Everyone laughed at Eddie Rudge.

'Now in Act 2, Scene 2, we see Julius Caesar with his wife, Calpurnia. Now, boys, Calpurnia always reminds me of our first parent, Eve. She tries to persuade Julius Caesar to do what she wants him to do. How like a woman! She is also full of superstition and in this you can tell that the action of the play took place before Our Lord had come and swept away all human wickedness from the world. If one of those heathen Romans had a dream he always thought it had some implications for his life. They'd open up the liver of a goat and fancy they could find there something to help them predict the future. Imagine the folly of it, boys! But in those days it was all that the poor benighted people had to go on. I always think that things would have been different if Julius Caesar had been born a century later. Who knows, if he had he might have been St Julius and Brutus might have been St Brutus and we'd be reading about them in The Lives of the Saints rather than in the secular pages of Mr Shakespeare. Now who wants to be Julius Caesar?'

A forest of hands went up. Brother O'Toole chose David Mulligan who was good at games and had his own front door key.

'And Decius?'

O'Gorman was chosen.

'And Calpurnia?'

Nobody put up their hands.

'I'll have to choose, so! Benson, you'll make a good Calpurnia.'

More giggles.

'On second thought, you, Rudge, will be Calpurnia.'

Benson felt greatly relieved. He was always chosen to play women's parts. He had already been Portia to Drury's Brutus and, in the last play, had been Juliet most of the time and the Nurse when he had not been Juliet. While Brother O'Toole was well known for his absent-mindedness, Benson's repeated selection for female parts did not help either his ego or his reputation in 3B.

However, among the stuttering monotones of 3B, it had to be admitted that Benson's performances were of a higher calibre altogether. Were it not for the whisper-ing of 'Wobbles!' and 'Homo!' that punctuated his performance, the readings would have given Benson great pleasure.

As Rudge slaughtered the lines of Calpurnia Benson allowed himself the luxury of wondering how Julius Caesar's stuff got to Calpurnia's egg.

Benson arrived home without mishap. Mum was in the kitchen washing out towels and making tea at the same time.

'Can I make the table for you, Mum?' asked Benson helpfully.

'Go on then,' said Mum.

He set about collecting three sets of cutlery and lay-ing them out on the table. There were lots of knives, forks and spoons in the cutlery drawer, each in their own separate compartments. But they were of different sizes and much of the challenge of laying the table lay in the selection of cutlery of matching sizes for each place-setting.

He rummaged until he found two small settings – for himself and his mum – and one large one for his dad. He dimly remembered that a long time ago this cutlery had been located on top of the sideboard in a wooden canteen. He rolled the word around in his mouth. 'Canteen.' What a funny word for a cutlery case!

'What do you want when you get married?'

'I want a canteen of cutlery, please, if it isn't too much trouble.'

That would be what he would ask for, a canteen of cutlery.

But this cutlery had for some reason found itself demoted to the kitchen drawer and was now used for every day. He was not quite sure why. There did not seem to be much wrong with it. Perhaps the silver was coming off in places. And where had the canteen gone? It had disappeared as if it had never been. Oh, it's true, he thought, all flesh is glass.

'Where's Dad, Mum?'

Mum was coughing as she wrung out the towels energetically. Benson watched the flesh jiggle on her upper arms.

'He's not back yet,' she said, her voice strangled by the effort involved in wringing out the towels.

'Not back yet?'

'No, and don't you dare ask me why! I've not heard from him all day.'

'What about tea? Are we waiting?'

'We'll wait until half-six. If he doesn't come by then I'll put a lid on his plate and put it in the oven.'

'I'll get on with my homework.'

'Have you got much, love?'

'No, not much,' said Benson. He had already decided not to do his Maths homework, banking on his luck holding out and the Vocations Brother giving the class his talk during Maths. 'Can I do my homework here? You're good at compositions.'

Mum lit a cigarette and stood on a chair to put the towels on the drying rack that hung from the ceiling.

'I shouldn't help you at all,' she began but she didn't fool Benson for a minute. Mum loved exercising her flair for composition. She often did Benson's compositions for him, though for a while she had been scared off by a red remark made by Brother O'Toole on Benson's copybook: 'Do I smell mother here?' She had refused to provide any creative insights for a long while after that. Brother O'Toole must have missed Mum's mature touches because he wrote soon after, quoting Tennyson: 'O for the touch of a vanish'd hand, And the sound of a voice that is still.' Mum took this as a coded message from Brother O'Toole that she could resume her assistance.

'But you'll like this one,' Benson said persuasively. 'We have to imagine that we are Mrs Flannagan in a sweet shop. The Black and Tans come in and then . . .' And he retold Brother O'Toole's story.

Mum sat down and watched Benson as he opened his

composition book. 'What did I get for my last effort?' she asked him.

'Eight out of ten. Very good.'

'What are we going to call this composition?'

'How about "Mrs Flannagan's Day"?'

'No, we can do better than that. What about "The Day Sweet Jesus Came to My Sweet Shop"?'

'Yes, that's good!' Benson at once copied down the title with capital letters for every word except 'to'. He underlined the title using his comb which made an artistic wavy line.

Mum lit another cigarette. 'Ready?' she asked.

'Ready!' said Benson, his pen poised.

At a measured pace Mum dictated, 'It had been a slow day in the shop. An ounce of Erinmore to old Mr Hephernan; three gobstoppers bought by the tinker for his blathering kids – more as a kindness to the tinker's ears I'm thinking than for the benefit of the kids, sure it was to my way of thinking – a noisy bunch they are so they are. And haven't I always to keep my eyes peeled in case they make off with anything that isn't nailed down? Oh yes, and just before the Angelus in walks Mrs Pierce for her weekly half pound of sherbet lemons . . .'

'Did they have sherbet lemons in those days, Mum?' asked Benson, wishing suddenly that he had not chomped his way through his two ounces the night before. He recalled that Brother McNulty had told him that gluttony often led straight to impurity. That had certainly proved true last night.

'Yes, I'm sure they did. Look, you're making me lose the thread. Read back what we've done so far.'

Benson did so.

'. . . sherbet lemons. I was just about to close up the shop to have me lunch. I thought I'd treat meself to the trout Mr Murphy had brought me the night before. Sure I don't know where he gets them from but they're really delicious . . .'

'It's getting a bit long, Mum. Don't you think it's time for a new paragraph?'

'There you go again!' replied Mum, scowling, 'When I'm making a story I don't think about things like paragraphs! All you're doing is taking it down! You're the one who should be thinking about paragraphs!'

Benson started a new paragraph because Brother O'Toole liked lots of paragraphs and Benson knew that one had to try to please one's audience.

'It was then that they came into me shop,' said Mum, her cigarette describing dramatic arcs in the air, 'three young soldiers of the great and glorious British army; fathers of the sons who would one day, long after I was dead and in me grave, put Hitler and his filthy cronies into the hell they deserved . . .'

Benson pulled a critical face. 'I don't think Brother O'Toole will take to that, Mum.'

Mum ignored Benson and continued. 'I think these boys were a little the worse for the drink. It is only that which can explain their conduct. They asked me if I had seen a Mr Docherty. They felt that he could be of assistance to them in their enquiries. When I replied truthfully that no I had not, they got a little upset. The one with the red hair aimed his rifle and before I knew what was happening he had fired. I can't remember what happened next. There was glass all over the place. There was glass on my Penguin Biscuits. There was glass on my Mars Bars. There was glass on my Carr's Water Biscuits. There was glass on the floor and there was glass on the till. There was even glass on me but I wasn't hurt. The three soldiers were sorry for what they had done. They left hurriedly. When they had gone I went over to the Sacred Heart statue to make sure He was all right and to seek succour there. And what did I see? A slither of glass had pierced Our Lord's Heart. It was a message for sure. I went and fetched Father McNally. Do I feel bitter? I do not. I'm sure, had the soldiers known what had happened to the Sacred Heart, they would have been sorry. These things happen in the best-run armies. How's that?' asked Mum.

'I don't think Brother O'Toole will like some of the things you say, Mum.'

'Serves him right! Teaching English children to hate their own soldiers! Ought to be ashamed.'

Benson's mum had no Irish blood in her veins as far as she knew.

'I'm hungry, Mum.'

'Offer it up!' replied Mum.

There was no answer to that. Benson pursed his lips.

At quarter past six Benson heard the unmistakeable sound of Dad coming in. The key-click in the lock, the brief whoosh of draught-excluder over carpet, then a pause and the same whoosh, followed by a tick-tock note of the door closing.

'Hello, lady!' Dad called to Mum from the hall as he always did.

Then the hall wardrobe was unlocked, a longish operation taking many turns of the key. A silence and the sound of a policeman's coat settling down for a night off duty on its metal hanger.

'Hello, lady!' Again and the wardrobe door closing followed by a prolonged turning of the key, an operation which in a few seconds always drove his son mad with boredom. Then five paces down the hall. The morning room door was opened, the handle loose, requiring a knack Dad had.

'Sorry, lady!'

It had taken Benson a long time to make out what it was Dad was saying to Mum whenever he came in. It sounded like 'Maisie' but Mum wasn't called Maisie.

'We'd given you up,' said Mum.

Dad gave Mum a kiss on the cheek. 'Bloody awful business! Hello, son.'

Benson smiled at Dad.

'Sit down. Your tea's ready,' said Mum as Benson asked:

'What's the awful business, Dad?'

'It's too old for you,' said Dad.

'Oh, Dad!'

They ate stew for a while in silence, then Mum asked

if it was something serious that had kept him out so long.

'A H-O-M-O interfered with a kid last night. The kid's in a bad way,' Dad spelled out.

'Have you found who did it?'

Dad shook his head.

'What about the boy?'

'Later.'

'Do we know him?'

'Later.'

They continued eating in silence. When the rhubarb and custard had been eaten Benson volunteered to wash up and took the dirty plates to the kitchen sink.

'H-O-M-O. Homo. I know what a homo is,' he said to himself. 'I've seen it in the dictionary.'

Benson had often whiled away an idle hour by looking up such words in his Collins Gem. 'Bottom', 'breast', 'circumcision' and 'penis' yielded their meanings to his research. Hepher had once called Benson a homo because he had caught him looking at him in the showers after games. The name had caught on and a number of the rougher elements at St Bede's called him that whenever he fumbled a rugby ball, read out in class or pleased a teacher.

'A homo interfered with a kid last night.' Benson informed the washing up. And suddenly it struck him. 'I interfered with Eric and Bruno last night! I took wilful pleasure in irregular motions of the flesh! Maybe Eric confessed and his parents called the police! Maybe Bruno confessed! Maybe I'm the homo they're looking for!'

He stopped washing the dishes and listened to see if Mum and Dad were talking about it – but he couldn't make out what they were saying. It was only when he recommenced scouring the burnt stew pan that he heard:

'Buggered in Albert Park . . . You know. He was . . . S-O-D-O-M-Y!'

'Poor kid! where is he?'

'Hospital.'

'And you've been with him?'

'And with his parents.'

'Poor kid!'

'Sodomy' rang a bell with Benson – a faintly prurient bell:

Question: 'What are the four sins crying to heaven for vengeance?'

Answer: 'The four sins crying to heaven for vengeance are: 1. Wilful murder. 2. Oppression of the poor. 3. Defrauding labourers of their wages. 4. The sin of Sodom.'

He had learnt it in his Catechism. He still remembered the time that O'Gorman had asked Brother McNulty: 'What's the sin of Sodom, sir?'

Brother McNulty had given O'Gorman a look of complete contempt and passed on to the next question.

Then Benson heard Mum's next question:

'Do we know the boy?'

'Yes, we do. Bruno Tencer. That big boy with the little bike. Remember I told him he was a danger on it just last week on the way back from mass?'

'Yes, I do.'

'Well, him.'

Benson froze. Then he burned. There could be no mistaking it! A homo had got Bruno and done something to him that cried to heaven for vengeance. Now he was going hot and cold in rapid succession. He felt faint. He felt sick. He must be the homo. No, he couldn't be the homo. Then who was the homo? His dad had said that Bruno was in Albert Park when it happened and now he was in hospital. Surely something else must have happened after the meeting of The Rude Club! Or perhaps Bruno was just putting it on. He had left the garage in a temper. Maybe he had gone home and told his dad everything! If he had told his dad everything then the police would have come for him and taken him away! But maybe Dad knew and was not saying.

He saw himself being taken into the lounge by Dad:

'Do you know Bruno Tencer? I ask you that in my

capacity as a police inspector. You must forget that you are my son and I am your father. Do you know Bruno Tencer?'

'I . . . er . . . I . . .'

'Do you?' This in a voice of thunder.

'Yes.'

'And were you with him in the Jenkins' garage at seven o'clock on the night of February the eleventh?'

'Yes.'

'And did you commit a sin crying to heaven for vengeance with Bruno?'

'No . . . Yes . . . I . . .'

'You did, didn't you?'

It would be no good trying to find out what the sin that cries to heaven for vengeance could be. He had fiddled with Bruno's parts on more occasions than he cared to recall. Was that, then, the sin of Sodom?

Voices came from the garage crying vengeance to the heavens overhead. Archangels in nighties wielding great swords swept down to exact retribution from the sinners in the Jenkins' garage. No quarter! No mercy! His miserable soul would be picked up, plucked out of the garage, carried for a few blessed moments through the cool air of Earth and then plunged headfirst into an eternity of fire, boiling oil, prodding forks, laughing devils and bad company.

'Yes!'

Benson imagined himself hanging his head and admitting his sin.

'I disown you! You're no son of mine! No son of mine can be a homo! You're disgusting and you've brought shame on your family, your school, your country and your Church! We'd have had more children but your mum couldn't as you know. But even though you're the only one, better no son at all than a homo for a son!'

Then Benson saw himself led off in a police car. Mrs Brown looked out from behind her curtains but did not wave. He was going to where homos go.

*　　*　　*

But nothing of the sort happened.

Half an hour later Benson found himself sitting in the lounge watching 'Criss-Cross Quiz'.

He was still completely distracted, however. The devils of damnation had had no trouble at all in following him to the lounge.

Mum was answering all the questions as usual.

'Leonardo da Vinci!' Mum shouted at the television.

'Michelangelo,' said the contestant, whom Mum had rightly decided was as thick as two short planks from the moment the curtains had parted to reveal him to the world.

'No, I'm sorry! You're wrong! It was Leonardo da Vinci!' gurgled the quizmaster.

'You're not answering tonight, son,' remarked Mum.

'No.'

'Not feeling well?'

'I'm all right.'

Benson forced himself to concentrate on the next question.

'Manchester United,' he said without enthusiasm.

'Manchester United,' said the contestant.

'Manchester United is the correct answer!' exclaimed the quizmaster.

'I could do his job with one hand tied behind my back,' thought Benson.

'Well done son!' exclaimed Mum. 'Look! They're changing the subjects,' she added, as the noughts and crosses board rolled to the next round.

'Famous Names. You're usually good at that.'

The question was asked but Benson could not answer. Mum, after a decent interval, said: 'Clementine!'

Answer from the contestant came there none.

'Clementine!' exclaimed the quizmaster.

'Stumped both of you, didn't I?' Mum cooed happily.

'I'm just going into the dining-room to listen to some music, Mum,' he said as the advertisements came on. He left the room with 'The Esso sign means happy motoring' sung to the tune of 'The Toreador's Song' ringing in his ears. He scowled when he heard it. He was unable to hear the Toreador's Song without thinking of the Esso jingle. He felt it was an insult to great music somehow.

He put 'Coppelia' on the gramophone but it did not fit his unsettled state at all. So he changed the record and put on 'One Fine Day' from 'Madam Butterfly'.

At once Benson became the tragic Japanese heroine. He darted away from the mirror to grab his Maths exercise book from the table. This he turned into a fan which wafted a breeze from the sorrowful sea over his features, quickly orientalised by the stretching of his skin tightly across his forehead – which made his ears waggle – and narrowing his eyes. Then, thinking of John Wayne in a sea captain's uniform, he sang his own translation of the aria along with the record:

> 'One fine day I'll find you!
> At the seaside with the sun behind
>   you!
> Oh, how happy we shall be!
> We'll have Pop and Jap Fancies for
>   tea!'

It would have been a hard heart indeed who could have resisted Benson's passionate appeal for the return of his lover. The audience, silent for a long moment, erupted in a burst of applause the like of which the dining-room had never before witnessed. Benson acknowledged the rapture with modest, matter-of-fact bows.

Cheered by his tumultuous reception, he turned the record over and tried an aria from 'La Traviata', but he and his audience soon lost interest. It was too sloppy by half. He changed the needle and carefully put on 'Serenade' from 'The Fair Maid of Perth', Dad's favourite record.

For this he merely rested his bottom against the window sill like Perry Como might were he singing in the Benson's dining-room, and sang at the mirror with little movement or drama: 'Hear the voice of one who adores thee, Who now implores thee . . . lores thee . . . lores thee . . . lores thee . . .'

The record had stuck and broken the spell. Was it his fault? Dad was always telling him that records didn't grow on trees. Once again, fear and guilt swept over him like an oil slick up a beach. Once more he saw so many reasons why he should be anxious and feel damned.

Dad was in the greenhouse where he usually went for some peace and quiet. But would he talk to him about Bruno when he came in?

Benson took the record off the gramophone and wiped it on his shirt-cuff. Sighing, he opened the curtains wide, turned off the light and left the room.

He jittered in the hall for a moment, then dawdled into the kitchen to make himself a glass of lime juice. As he filled the glass with water he saw, in the light spreading outwards from the greenhouse, Dad talking to Mr Jenkins over the garden fence.

'Jesus! Mary! Joseph! Another accuser!' thought Benson, the lime juice turning to vinegar on his tongue.

He washed the glass guiltily, thinking of wet sheets and Mum. He put the glass back on its shelf and fled to the safety of the lounge, where Mum was watching a play starring Gwen Watford.

Benson liked Gwen Watford, second only to Rosalie Critchley. Gwen Watford was always nervous and upset and he found it therapeutic to see how bad other people could get.

Benson and Mum watched the play for about fifteen minutes. Once a television camera passed the window just as Gwen Watford had turned away from it, having said as she looked out over Florence: 'We are all dying, you know. Oh, not at the same time or in the same way; but slowly and surely, we are all dying.'

The audience in the lounge giggled, then laughed, as a boom microphone appeared in the top of the picture.

'If I worked in television,' asserted Benson, 'that sort of thing would not be allowed to happen.'

'Maybe,' agreed Mum, 'but I bet the director of the play doesn't wet the bed. First things first, son.'

Benson directed his 'that was uncalled for' look at Mum and turned back to the play.

There was Gwen Watford in bed with her television husband. Benson felt a well-known wave of embarrassment shoot through him.

'Maybe we should turn it off before there's any sloppy weather,' Mum said.

'They're only talking, Mum.'

'Yes, but as sure as eggs are eggs, it'll be sloppy weather any minute now.'

And, sure enough, Gwen Watford stopped talking and clinched with her television husband, almost as if she were determined to upset the audience in the lounge.

At that moment Dad came in. Benson sat frozen. Mum said nothing. For a moment Dad stood, hands in pockets, surveying the television. Then, quite suddenly, he strode across and turned it off. 'We don't want that rubbish in this house,' he said.

Then he looked hard at Benson, not making a move to sit down in the easy chair as he usually did. Benson looked back at his father and thought, 'I am not his son! I am adopted! I am really the son of Michael Redgrave and Rachel Kempson, left here with the nuns when they finished at the Playhouse!'

Dad glanced at Mum and Mum said, 'I'm going to see how the towels are doing. It'll be suppertime soon.'

Only when Mum had left the room did Dad sit down. But he did not sit down as he usually sat down. He did not take possession of the chair and engulf it. Instead he lowered himself gingerly as though he feared the chair might collapse under his weight. Then he laced his fingers together in front of him, gazing intently at them.

Benson feared the worst.

'You haven't had a talk from me for a long time,' began Dad.

That was true. The last time Benson remembered a serious talk with Dad was in the year he had taken his

Eleven Plus. Then Dad had said that, were he to fail the examination, he would have to go to the Secondary Modern. He could not afford to pay for him at St Bede's. The Secondary Modern was for rough, common boys. It was a fate worse than death as far as Benson was concerned. He had told Dad then that he would do his best not to fail, and, wonder of wonders, he had not. He still remembered clearly the morning the results had come. He had woken up to find Mum and Dad around his bed with an opened letter:

'Congratulations! You've passed!' They gave him a Brownie 127. It had been the happiest day of his life.

'Do you know a boy called Bruno?' asked Dad.

'Yes, he's a friend of me and Eric,' replied Benson.

'Well I've got some bad news to tell you about him. Last night on his way home a man interfered with Bruno in the park. Do you understand what that means?'

'Er . . .'

'Well, do you know where babies come from?' Dad sat back in his chair, but not comfortably. It was as if a book the size of a family Bible shared the seat with him.

'They come from Mum,' said Benson tentatively.

'Well, yes. But do you know how Mum comes to have them?'

Just as Dad could hardly bring himself to ask the question, so Benson could not even attempt a reply. He gazed at the rug in front of the fire and pulled faces at it.

'Well,' continued Dad rapidly, 'you've got that thing between your legs. Apart from letting you go for a wee-wee it also produces seed which go into Mum and help her to have a baby.'

Benson nodded.

'Well, what has happened to Bruno is this: there are some men who, instead of liking ladies and marrying them and having babies, lust after people of their own sex. These people are called homosexuals. Well, last night one of these men took Bruno to Albert Park and committed a very serious sin with him. I'm telling you this for two reasons. First of all, it is important that you be careful yourself and do not go anywhere with strangers. Secondly, you are Bruno's friend and must be very kind to him from now on. He has had a very bad time and you must do your best to be nice to him.'

Benson nodded. He was relieved to know that it was not he who was being accused of being a homo. But Dad's words, combined with the cat-calls of 'Homo!' from school, made him certain that he was indeed a homo. It was just that he had not been exposed this time. It was looking at other boys, and Bruno in particular, that made Benson want to make stuff and made him feel sick and well and faint and excited. He had not been caught this time. That was the only difference.

And it was not over; indeed, it was far from over. Either Bruno or Eric could still spill the beans on him. It had not happened yet. But it could. There was still plenty to worry about.

Dad had now started to talk about his garden. Benson decided that he would take the unusual step of getting up at six-fifteen and go to seven o'clock mass. Before it started he would press the Confession bell and make his Confession. He could not go on like this until Saturday.

Mum came in with the supper. There was milky coffee and scones for her and Dad; just scones for Benson.

He announced that he would be getting up for mass in the morning. Dad said very good and Benson basked in the thought that Dad probably thought that he was going to pray for Bruno.

He kissed Mum and Dad and went up to bed.

There he wondered what on earth he would say to the priest in Confession. How would he put it? In the past he had said he had taken wilful pleasure in irregular motions of the flesh and left it at that. But that would not do any more. To conceal a grave sin was a still graver sin and negated the rest of the Confession. All serious sins had to be confessed along with all relevant details. Benson, by the use of tortuous catechetical euphemisms, had managed to cloud the seriousness of his sins.

But tomorrow he would have to add, 'By myself and

with others, Father.' The 'with others' stuck in his throat. The prospect of further delving from the priest filled him with fear. Would the priest shout? Would he lecture?

But whatever happened it was worth going through in order to make his soul white again and remove the weight which was oppressing him. He just had to get out from under that weight. And Confession was the only way out.

He set his alarm clock for six. Before switching off the light, he watched the hen on the face of the clock pecking for grain in time to the passing seconds. Then he switched off the light and lay back on his pillow, seeing the memory of the hunter's moon light bulb filament before him in the dark. As it faded he closed his eyes, but this seemed to activate the shape again. He rubbed his eyes and countless stars appeared. Then he tried to relax, waiting for sleep to come.

But sleep did not come. And Benson found that his hands were below the covers languidly stroking himself. He did not try to stop. He would just have to cross out three and put in four in Confession.

'Forgive me, Father, for I have sinned. It is one week since my last Confession, Father. I have taken wilful pleasure in irregular motions of the flesh by myself and with others four times, Father . . .'

Yes, he thought, that should be enough. If his luck held he might get Canon Preston and he couldn't hear a thing anyway. 'Please, God, let Canon Preston be saying mass tomorrow!'

Benson folded his legs, knees against chest. He crossed his ankles and slowly rocked backwards and forwards. It was nice. It was cosy. But he knew he needed a story. He searched around for one, dismissing a story about Bruno because of the unfortunate circumstances.

In the middle of Albert Park there was a private house and in the house lived an elderly couple, Mr and Mrs Grace. Mr Grace had once pinched Benson and told him that he would like to take a few steaks off his rear and eat them for supper. Mr Grace's no doubt jocular remark had sent a strange sexual shiver through Benson which had resulted in a new direction for his solitary sexual adventures.

Now he rocked and imagined arriving at Mr and Mrs Grace's front door.

'Come in!' boomed Mr Grace. 'It's dinner time.'

Mr Grace took off Benson's clothes and put him on a platter surrounded by roast potatoes. Benson lay on his front while Mr Grace poked around, pinching him and announcing to his wife, 'What a feast he'll make! I can't wait!' Then Benson was scared just for a moment. 'Where's the notice? Where's the notice?' But it was all right. The notice was there, taped to his back:

'EVERY SLICE YOU
TAKE FROM ME
WILL BE INSTANTLY REPLACED!'

With the notice in place everyone could settle down and enjoy themselves. Mr Grace sharpened his carving-knife and took slice after slice off Benson's back, bottom and legs, placing the meat on plates in tidy piles. As he sliced Mr Grace made clucking, sucking noises and Benson in bed rocked faster and faster and the friction on his sex and soft thighs excited him towards a sort of climax, as Mr Grace chomped and slobbered, 'And now for the best part! The best part!' With his carvers Mr Grace turned Benson over . . .

He felt himself jerking down there as if his sex was swallowing. He continued to rock but the story had faded and, indeed, now that he recalled it, he was aware only of how ridiculous it was.

Soon he turned over on to his front and prayed into his pillow, 'O my God, because Thou art so good. I am very sorry that I have sinned against Thee. And by the help of Thy Grace I will not sin again.' And he also prayed not to die in the night.

He knew he was only covered by the leakiest of

insurance. Tomorrow it would be better. All-risk. Fully-comprehensive.

The relief was heavenly.

Father Lynch – Benson's prayer for deaf, old Canon Preston fell on Deaf Ears – gave Benson a short chat on the trouble chastity gave everyone, including himself. He compared it to an insect bite which one should not scratch but which kept on itching. Boys Benson's age, he asserted, were more prone than most to itch and to scratch. Not to worry, he said, and would he serve Mass for him?

Benson had been somewhat taken aback at having been recognised, despite the light tenor he had tried to bring his voice down towards. But the sweet feeling of peace that always came to him after Confession was already drenching him in a lightness and a bliss that sent small worries scurrying away. His feelings were mirrored by the rising light of dawn creeping into the church through its east-facing windows behind the altar.

As he knelt down to say his penance, the sun's light caught the life-size frieze of the crucifixion and made the pewter catch fire. He gazed up at it and the scene was as wonderful and spectacular as the feelings going on inside him. He began to weep tears of joy for the return of innocence, for the Christ smiling down at him, for Mary and for all the saints once more on his side.

'Thank you! Thank you!' he kept repeating. 'From now on I shall be faithful . . . faithful unto death! I swear it! Lord, it will be death rather than sin from now on! I would far rather die in a sea of molten lava than offend You and Your Blessed Mother! Please help me to stay pure!'

He went into the sacristy and quickly changed into the black and white robes of an altar boy. Then he took a lighted taper and went to the altar to light the candles for mass. As he lit them he looked out into the church. There was only a handful of people there. Mr Stone was there of course. He was always there. He seemed hardly ever to go home. The Miss Dooleys were there too; two retired teachers in identical black suits, bent and frail. He did not recognise any of the other people in the congregation but felt his warmth overflowing past the altar rails to the small flock. The Church Militant! Three or four thus arrayed could change the world!

He returned to the sacristy, then a minute later led Father Lynch to the altar. The priest bowed and stood at the foot of the steps, while Benson knelt beside him and responded to the priest's introductory prayers.

'Ad Deum qui laetificat juventutem meam.' He rattled off the responses as fast as he could but it was not fast enough for Father Lynch who always started the next part of the prayer before Benson had quite finished his bit. This had often irritated Benson in the past. He had always felt sure that, were he God, he would be extremely irked by such indecent haste. But this morning nothing could irritate Benson.

He bowed down to say The Confiteor. He bowed down so low that his nose practically scraped the second step leading to the altar. And as he spoke the words his joy almost choked him.

The Consecration arrived. The Host rose white above the priest's head and Benson rang the bell and gazed at the transubstantiating Host for a moment before swooning in adoration. Then the chalice was raised. He rang the bell again and glanced up at the perfect symmetry of the gold chalice, held with such grace by the pale, tapering fingers of Father Lynch. As he bowed down again he could feel a shiver passing up his spine to his neck and fancied that he was feeling there the footprint of Christ as He walked up to the altar to take possession of the bread and wine and enter into it and lose Himself in man's daily food.

And when he received Christ upon his tongue every thought disappeared save for the slight physical sensation of the softening wafer in his mouth and an image of light-rays radiating from it and filling his body and soul with a vast, silent waterfall of grace and peace. Automatically he stood and led Father Lynch down to the altar rails where he held the plate beneath the chins of the other communicants. He found himself longing to be relieved of these duties so that he could commune with The Friend alone and in silence; discuss past problems and disagreements and make a pact with Him to be Best Friends from now on forever and ever.

'O Lord, be merciful to me, a Pharisee,' Benson repeated as the Mass came to an end and he set about clearing the altar.

He spent longer than he should have done alone in the church on his knees. Sin felt like a complete impossibility to him now. The future would be as different from the past as night is different from day. The Rude Club now seemed like a terrible misunderstanding between friends, Benson and Jesus, that could not possibly be repeated. Nothing, absolutely nothing, could make him let his Friend down again. Jesus was all he wanted or would ever want. And when his exile on Earth ended and he cast off the bitter yoke of life's sorrows, he would meet his Friend face to face. The interim would have its share of trouble and sorrows but could be borne now.

He was in Grace.

He was too late for breakfast and too late for the train but he didn't mind. The energy of happiness had taken hold of Benson's rotund frame and he asked Dad for the keys to the shed.

'You're not going on your bike, are you?'

'Yes, I am,' replied Benson.

'Wonders will never cease.'

'How do you mean?' asked Benson, making for the back door.

'Oh, nothing,' said Dad, pleased that his son was taking the bike. A keen cyclist himself, it had disappointed Dad that the heavy, pristine Raleigh which he had bought Benson for Christmas from a retiring policeman had not been used more.

'Got your lunch, dear?' asked Mum.

'Yes, Mum.'

'Bye.'

'Bye.'

The truth of the matter was that Benson did not care to be seen on the big bike because he felt his bottom overflowed the saddle and became an object of mirth and ridicule to drivers behind him. He had tried to solve this problem by wearing his raincoat over the saddle instead of tucking it in underneath him. A nasty mishap had been caused by this attempt at camouflage with the end of the coat getting itself caught in his back wheel, causing it to lock and sending him at speed against the road surface. The bike had not suffered too much because it had landed on Benson. Benson had not suffered too much either, because the heavy raincoat and his own natural padding had cushioned the impact. The raincoat, however, had been a writeoff.

So the bicycle had been sent into ignominious exile in the shed. Dad's plan for turning Benson into a slim and muscular example of Catholic Youth had floundered on his son's fear of being made fun of while en route to that desirable state.

To get to school Benson had to negotiate the docks, which were criss-crossed with railway lines that could easily swallow the wheels of his bicycle. Today, though, he challenged the railway lines to unseat him. He was not careful. What need of care when all is well with the world? He approached each set of rails much more acutely than he had ever done before and not once did the bicycle falter. He was not in the least surprised. Guardian Angel Tom was once more back on his shoulder and was as gay as he was.

He did not change into an easier gear, even when he was negotiating the long hill that led up to St Bede's. Neither did he stop pedalling for an instant. Mr Plunkett passed him on the road through the park. He beeped his horn and Benson waved and remembered that he had forgotten Mr Plunkett's jam-jars. At once, reasoning that to be faithful unto death required that he be faithful in small things too, he stopped his bicycle, reached into his pants pocket and tied a knot in his grubby handkerchief. Then he continued on.

He passed a gang of boys dawdling towards school. Their cries of 'Fall off Wobbles!' fell on deaf ears. Even his overhanging bottom did not worry him. To worry, fast-pedalling Benson decided, was a betrayal of Our Lord. He resolved never to worry again.

It was five minutes before Assembly time when Benson, glowing somewhat from his exertions, took his place in the Hall surrounded by his classmates. He did not talk to anybody but took out his library copy of 'Robinson Crusoe' and pretended to read. His heart was still pounding from his exercise. Benson closed his eyes to shut the hubbub out and prayed.

'Thank you, Lord, for the Grace of forgiveness. Thank you for forgiving me the unforgivable sins of my past life. I am a miserable sinner, Lord, and deserve to be cast down into the pit of everlasting fire for ever and ever. But you, Lord, saw fit to forgive me and not demand the just and reasonable punishment for so wounding Your Sacred Heart and the Blessed Heart of Your Most Holy Mother, Mary. Please help me, Lord, to keep myself pure and sweet to You. Help me to avoid temptation and the company of wicked companions.'

Then Benson turned his attention to his favourite saints to put in a good word for him:

'St Aloysius Gonzaga! You who were so pure at my age and went on to die in the odour of sanctity, pray to Jesus for me so that He, hearing your words and seeing my abject weakness and powerlessness, will see fit to grant me the miracle of a pure and good life, Amen.

'St Dominic Savio, whose motto was "Death rather than sin!", intercede for me with Jesus and his Holy Mother, that I may at all times shun sin as you did throughout your tragically brief sojourn in this, our Vale of Tears. Amen.

'Guardian Angel Tom! You who look just like the faithful soldier in "Faithful Unto Death", only you've got wings where he has got secular armour, guard my unworthy soul in the same way as the faithful soldier guarded Pompeii. Stay with me! Do not look away for a minute! You know what a sinful creature they have given you to guard! I am like the city of Pompeii, Tom! All the time the lava of sin threatens the fragile home of my soul! I implore you, by the wounds of Our Lord and Saviour, Jesus Christ, to be ever-vigilant in keeping my step steady on the path of righteousness. Amen.'

Then Benson opened his eyes to find that Eddie Rudge was sitting on his left side and was staring at him unsmilingly.

Usually, Benson by much toing and froing managed to avoid Eddie Rudge, the most notorious boy in 3B. Eddie Rudge was trouble, even though he had only one lung and false teeth top and bottom. He had once thrown a blackboard compass across the classroom. Like a javelin it had whizzed through the air, missing Benson's head by inches, and lodging in the door of the cupboard where Drury kept a bottle of school milk to see how the passage of time would change it. Eddie Rudge smoked in the toilets as a matter of routine and made dates with the girls from Maria Assumpta Convent in the park. Eddie Rudge had dirty pictures in his wallet and stole from the school tuck-shop, which he ran with his henchman, O'Gorman.

'Deep in thought are we, Wobbles?' asked Eddie Rudge.

'My name isn't Wobbles,' said Benson.

The teachers filed in at that moment and took their places at the back of the stage like some motley Greek chorus. Then a few seconds later the swish of a cassock announced the arrival of Brother Hooper. The whole school froze into silence and the swishing sound made its way down the right aisle of the Hall and then stopped at Benson's row.

The tall, bespectacled Brother pointed, Benson thought, at Benson.

'You!' barked Brother Hooper.

Benson stood up fearfully. 'Me, sir?'

'No. Not you. You! Rudge!'

Eddie Rudge stood up.

'You! Stand out in the aisle.'

Eddie Rudge got up without another word and stood in the aisle to attention.

Something dreadful was about to happen to Eddie Rudge, thought Benson. He was relieved no longer to be sitting next to him but could not help feeling sorry for Eddie all the same.

The swishing sound of Brother Hooper continued to the stage and ascended the steps. Not a sound was heard in the Hall. In the silence Benson could hear the shrill tinkling of milk bottles being stacked in the far corner of the playground. Then, as if the need for silence had communicated itself to them too, even that sound ceased.

Brother Hooper stood behind his lectern and gazed out over the silent boys. His thin, fortyish face communicated a cynical distaste for what he surveyed, rather as if a bad smell was wafting up at him from the body of the Hall. He smiled a thin, dry smile and inhaled breath to say, 'Good Morning, School!' but at that precise moment Eddie Rudge let out a fart, and a giggle like birdsong in a cemetery rose from the section of boys near enough to have heard.

The Headmaster, aware of the giggles but not of what had caused them, stared long and hard at the mid-section of the Hall. Benson fancied that he was looking directly at him. He had not laughed. He did not find that sort of thing in the least bit amusing.

'Good Morning, School!' said Brother Hooper even more coldly than usual.

'Good Morning, sir!' replied the school.

Then, with a greatly magnified gesture, the Head-master crossed himself: 'In the name of the Father and of the Son and of the Holy Ghost . . .'

'Amen,' replied the school.

The Headmaster launched into the Litany of the Blessed Virgin and the school responded, 'Pray for us!' to each recitation of the names of Mary:

'Queen of angels!'

'Pray for us!'

'Queen of Patriarchs!'

'Pray for us!'

'Queen of Prophets!'

'Pray for us!'

'House of Gold!'

'Pray for us!'

But Benson, as he responded prayerfully, head lowered and eyes closed, could hear some of his companions responding, 'Play with it!'

He increased the volume of his own response to try to drown out his companions' blasphemy. At the same time he tried to persuade his Friend, Jesus, and His Holy Mother and all the saints to ignore the wicked responses of the wicked minority. Why, wondered Benson, was he surrounded by wicked boys? How was it possible to remain good and pure in the company of evil, indecent and impure companions?

'Ark of the Covenant!'

'Play with it!'

'Gate of Heaven!'

'Play with it!'

'Morning Star!'

'Play with it!'

'Tower of Ivory!'

'Play with it!'

The Devil, Benson knew, was all around him. The Presence was almost palpable. Tom and the Devil were waging an invisible battle for Benson's soul just above his head among the climbing ropes and the scout flags. 'Pray for us!' and 'Play with it!' were alternating through his brain. He could not think of one without the other. He said the good and thought the bad.

'O Lord! Be merciful to me, a Pharisee!' screamed Benson to himself.

Then, mercifully, the Litany ended and a boy came on to the stage to read the lesson:

'Put you on the armour of God that you may be able to stand against the deceits of the Devil . . .'

'How true!' thought Benson, mentally strapping on a set of burnished armour. He stood guard, portly and determined, holding his spear at the ready to ward off the Devil in all his guises.

'Stand, therefore, having your loins girt about with truth . . .'

Benson could hear Eddie Rudge tutting over 'loins' but shut him out as he tried to imagine his own loins covered in Truth. It was a problem, but once again 'Faithful Unto Death' inspired him and he was able to imagine himself in a brown pleated skirt with 'TRUTH' written on it in beautiful calligraphy.

Then prayers were over and it was time for Brother Hooper either to dismiss the school or talk to it. He settled, his arms folded across the lectern. He was going to talk.

'I have two items to draw to your attention today, school. One is pleasant and one is most decidedly not pleasant. Let us dispose of the latter first. Edmund Rudge!'

Eddie Rudge squirmed where he stood. Benson noticed that his left hand had clenched into a nervous fist and felt sorry for him again.

'Yes, sir,' said Eddie Rudge in a trembling but dark voice.

Benson envied Eddie Rudge that voice, especially when – as now – he was under pressure. His own voice was betwixt and between. For the purposes of everyday intercourse it had descended to the lightest of light tenors, but whenever he was nervous or excited it piped up into a childish soprano. Eddie's never did that. Not even now when pressed to the limits.

'Edmund Rudge!' repeated the Headmaster in his quietest, thinnest tones that boded least good. 'Where did you go after you left school yesterday?'

'Home, sir.'

'Eventually you went home. Where did you go on your way home, Edmund Rudge?'

Silence.

'I'm waiting, Edmund Rudge. The whole school is waiting. Where did you go on your way home?'

'Nowhere, sir!' Eddie's voice wobbled.

' "Nowhere, sir!" Well let me tell you, Edmund Rudge, that you did go somewhere on your way home. You went to St Michael's church. Is that not true?'

'Yes,' replied Eddie in a whisper.

'I did not hear you, Edmund Rudge!'

'Yes, sir!'

'And what did you do in St Michael's church?'

'I said the Rosary, sir.'

The school, including some of the younger members of staff, laughed at the unlikelihood of this. Not one boy, even on the wildest shores of his fantasies, could envisage Eddie Rudge on his knees saying the Rosary at St Michael's on a late February evening.

'Nothing else?'

'No, sir.'

'Well, that is strange indeed. Who else was in St Michael's church with you, Edmund Rudge?'

'Nobody, sir. The church was empty, sir.'

'Ah, there you are wrong, Edmund Rudge. You may have thought the church was empty but in fact it was not empty. The curate, Father Richardson, was in the church at the time.'

Every eye in the Hall was on Eddie Rudge. Benson could see that Eddie's whole body was shaking. What could he have done?

'Father Richardson saw you in St Michael's. Would you like to tell the school what you did at St Michael's, apart from saying the Rosary?'

Eddie Rudge was silent.

'I will tell everyone, so. There is at the back of the church a noticeboard. On the noticeboard there is an advertisement for the Annual Diocesan Pilgrimage to Lourdes. At the bottom of this notice there is a space for parishioners who are interested in going on the holy pilgrimage to write their names or, indeed, the names of their crippled loved ones, who would like to avail themselves of the pilgrimage. Now, would you care to tell us what you did?'

Eddie Rudge hung his head and was silent.

The Headmaster paused and then reached into his pocket, producing a piece of paper which he unfolded and held out in front of the school. Another silence, and then he spoke in a loud voice:

'This is the advertisement for the Annual Diocesan Pilgrimage to Lourdes on which several of the devout parishioners of St Michael's were to have written their names. Indeed several have already done so. However, below the names of these good people, a poison pen has been at work. YOUR poison pen, Edmund Rudge! Am I right or am I not right?'

Eddie Rudge seemed to stumble as he replied in a whisper, 'Yes, sir.'

'I'm afraid I did not hear you, Edmund Rudge! Please repeat so that everyone can hear you!'

'Yes, sir!'

'Ah, I am right. Now let us see what your poison pen has written on the sheet. M. Mouse, D. Duck, Brother Hooper, Alma Cogan, Wobbles Benson . . .'

The whole Hall except for Benson, Brother Hooper and Eddie Rudge, exploded in long gales of laughter.

'Silence!' commanded Brother Hooper. Then, when the laughter had died away, he continued, 'I suppose you contacted these persons prior to inserting their names on the list?'

'No, sir.'

'No, sir. You certainly did not consult me prior to inserting my name on the list. Did you by any chance intend to present the pilgrimage to me as a belated Christmas gift?'

Brother Hooper paused. Slowly but surely laughter spread around the Hall at his joke, as laughter spread when a dotty and unpredictable Roman emperor cracked a joke and senators who wanted to keep their heads thought it best to crack their cheeks.

Benson did not laugh, however. He was deeply resentful at Brother Hooper for including his nasty nickname in the list. Had he been Brother Hooper he would have just said 'Benson', but Benson had long since despaired of anything approaching sensitivity from Brother Hooper. He had received a couple of digs in the back after the reading of the list and felt mortified. He could not help hoping that Eddie would get a severe beating from Brother Hooper.

'Come here, Edmund Rudge!'

Slowly Eddie walked to the front of the Hall and then up the steps on to the stage. He stumbled while climbing the steps and the school laughed. A look from the Headmaster at once returned the Hall to silence.

Brother Hooper reached into his deep pocket and produced from it a leather strap about two feet long. The strap was black and so thick that it was almost rigid. It was of Irish manufacture and was elaborately stitched along its length. The grip was narrower than the rest of it, two bites having been taken out so that the hand fitted snugly.

This was the king of straps and Benson had never seen it close to. But he had heard about it from those who had: how the boy to be punished was ushered into the Headmaster's office; how the Headmaster went over to a chest of drawers below a huge crucifix and removed the strap; how it caused a totally different sensation of pain to all the other straps in use at St Bede's, a feeling that hands had swollen to twice their original size and that within the swollen mass, the bar of an electric fire had been inserted and switched on.

'Hold out your right hand, Edmund Rudge! And do not move it!'

Eddie did so. The Headmaster held the strap out in front of him, measuring the distance between himself and Eddie's outstretched hand, and nudged the hand to the left. Eddie, smaller far than the Headmaster, looked at his hand as if it were something that did not belong to him. Then he gazed up at the strap as it was raised into the air, waggled grotesquely at the zenith of the movement, and descended with a sickening smack upon his fingers, palm and wrist. He yelped and hid the hand under his arm doing a little hopping dance upon the spot. But Brother Hooper gestured with the waggling black strap and Eddie put out his hand again. Again the Headmaster nudged the inflamed hand into position and raised the strap above his head. The strap descended but Eddie withdrew his shaking arm slightly and the blow caught only his fingers and set Brother Hooper off balance and he had to step forward a pace. This angered him and he seized Eddie's hand and hit it again and again. Eddie's hand became the only still part of him, as a chicken's neck at killing time is its only point of stillness. The rest of Eddie squirmed and jerked. He cried out and appealed for clemency but Brother Hooper took no notice of him.

Benson and many of the other boys looked at their hands.

'Other hand!'

'Please, sir!'

'Other hand!'

Eddie retreated three paces from Brother Hooper and said something to him which Benson could not hear.

'Other hand!' shouted Brother Hooper.

Eddie held out his other hand, but only then did he shuffle back towards the Headmaster. This time he held still as the strap descended four times. Then he stood in front of him looking very small and cold. He buried both hands in his armpits and shook.

Brother Hooper put the strap back into his deep pocket. 'You will go to the presbytery of St Michael's this afternoon and you will apologise to Father Richardson. Is that clear?'

'Yes, sir.'

'Now go and sit down!'

Eddie came back down the hall, moving hunched

through the silence, and sat down next to Benson.

'Are you all right, Eddie?' whispered Benson.

'The fucking fucker!' said Eddie Rudge.

Benson asked Jesus to forgive Eddie and give him a chance to change his ways before it was too late. He wanted to tell him not to fill his heart full of hate, but to forgive as he hoped to be forgiven. However, the time was not propitious as the Headmaster had resumed his place behind the lectern.

'And now I want to tell you boys about an altogether more pleasant matter. You may have heard that Brother Kay, the Brothers' Vocations Director, is visiting the school today to talk to those boys who are of an age when the Lord may call you to follow him. A Brother's life is not an easy one to follow, but the Church is crying out for labourers to work in His vineyard, and your country is just as much a missionary area as Africa. When I was a boy about the same age as some of you, I heard the Call. I thought then that I would love to serve the Lord by going out to Africa and teaching the heathen. But, as you see, I was not called upon to venture so far. I pray that some of you will feel the Call to serve God as a Brother and help to bring up good Catholic youth by becoming a teacher. Listen to Brother Kay with an open heart, boys. Listen to the voice inside you, and, if you hear God talking to you, it may well be that He wants you to be a Brother. Now let us pray that nobody who hears the Call will ignore it.'

And Brother Hooper prayed, 'O Lord, You who said: "The man who loves father and mother more than Me is not worthy of Me," grant that from among the group of Your servants here assembled there may be some who will hear Your Call, so that, through their labour in Thy vineyard, they will produce a harvest of souls who will fill the Great Barn of heaven with Thy praise for ever and ever . . .'

'Amen,' responded the school.

'The fucking fucker!' repeated Eddie Rudge.

'Dismiss!'

The school dismissed row by row. Nobody spoke, for

the Headmaster continued to stare down at them. It was not until Benson and his classmates were safely round the corner and into the long corridor that a chattering began, at first tenuous but growing in intensity the farther from the Hall they went.

Just before the end of the corridor the growing hubbub quite suddenly dropped to nothing. The cause of this change was the presence of a small podgy Brother in a black suit who was standing next to Brother McNulty outside 3 Alpha. An overstuffed brown briefcase lay at his feet. He wore thick, rimless spectacles which Benson had always associated with piety. He had often wished he could fail his yearly eyesight examination in order to possess a pair – but he never managed to get enough letters wrong.

This would be Brother Kay. He was chatting with Brother McNulty but was not looking at him. Instead he gazed at the passing line of boys, smiling and nodding to them as they passed.

Benson said, 'Good morning, Brothers!' as he passed, and was rewarded with his very own smile and nod from Brother Kay. It cheered Benson, warmed him up, after the cold half hour in the Hall.

At last he turned the corner and entered 3B's classroom where all the boys except Mellon, Drury and Vincent Latos were gathered around Eddie Rudge who stood by the door, his hands around the hot pipe of a radiator. This was believed to lessen the pain in strapped hands. Benson could hear Eddie uttering further colourful expletives to describe the behaviour of Brother Hooper, but he took no notice of him and went straight to his place at the back of the class. There he shook hands with Vincent, said hello to the two boys in front. Then he sat down, opened his desk and studied the timetable that he had attached to the inside of the lid with drawing pins.

Period 1: P.T. Well that isn't a problem, it's started to rain. That meant the class would have library reading. Period 2: English. I'm ready for that. Then he stared at the next two squares: Double Maths, Double Maths!

He felt glum when he contemplated the one-and-a-half hours of unintelligible shapes and opaque problems with which Brother Wood filled the time. He imagined the young, unsmiling Brother, dark, almost Spanish-looking, with a jaw like Dan Dare and an Irish accent that Benson's ear could often not cut, going round the class to check homework, lashing out whenever he was displeased. But it would not happen. The vocations Brother would save the day!

Benson's thoughts were confirmed by Drury who turned round and said, 'He'll go to Alpha first, then A, then us. That's how it was last year. It looks like he'll definitely be here for Maths – what we've got to do is keep him here with lots of good questions.'

'Yes,' agreed Benson, 'that's what we have to do.' One of his special talents was the ability to ask lots of questions. 'But you'd better tell the rest of the class to have lots of questions prepared.'

Drury and Mellon spread the instruction.

Then Vincent Latos tapped Benson on the shoulder and said, 'Where your lunch? Is in bag on floor. No good. Grime will go inside.'

Benson thanked Vincent. He took his lunch out of his satchel and placed it in the corner of his desk. Then he worried the piles of books into shape, arranged his pencils in order from longest to shortest, and, receiving a smile of approval from Vincent, closed his desk.

A few minutes later, 'Such' Atherton, came into the classroom dressed in his navy-blue tracksuit and grey plimsoles.

'Get out your library books,' Such told the class.

Benson got out his 'Robinson Crusoe' and looked at Such's cauliflower ears. They definitely added to his appearance, Benson thought. If he had cauliflower ears the rough boys from Sir William Grout's would think twice before they barged him and threw his cap into the trees.

Mr Atherton had got his nickname long before Benson had arrived at St Bede's. How he had acquired it was a much-told tale and known to one and all. Apparently, on his first day at the school, young Mr Atherton, fresh out of Training College, had gone into his first class and said, 'My name is Mr Atherton and I wish to be known as such.'

Such played rugby for the county side and had seven children. His wife was called Elizabeth and Benson's mum knew Elizabeth's mum. However, Benson did not feel that Such liked him very much, despite the fact that his mum knew Elizabeth's mum. Such had often teased Benson about his weight – not the best way of winning the boy's affection – and had forced Benson down into the scrum far further than Benson felt he could comfortably go. He had even run on Benson's heels during crosscountry runs, not letting him stop even though he had developed a severe stitch.

So whenever it rained Benson was glad and relieved. Library reading was infinitely preferable to the pain and humiliation that P.T. involved.

As he fiddled to find his place in 'Robinson Crusoe', Benson idly wondered if he should get out his Maths homework and try to have a go at it – just in case. But, as if intuiting what was going on in Benson's mind, Such said, 'Library reading means library reading,' without looking up from his copy of 'Teach Yourself Plumbing'.

Benson felt relief at being thus thwarted. He started reading.

Natives had landed on the island. They had prisoners with them whom they clubbed to death and started cooking. A bolt of peculiar pleasure went through Benson. He fought it. He stopped reading. He could see the scene as clearly as if it were happening in the rain just outside the classroom window. He was none too happy about the natives being killed prior to being eaten. Why did they not have notices pinned to them? But, he reasoned, they probably could not read or write.

His mind wandered. He wished himself alone with his new story.

'Jesus, help me! Mary, refuge of sinners, protect me!'

pleaded Benson. The devils were returning. Temptation had sneaked up on him and he was yielding. The happiness of a mere two hours ago was ebbing out of him. Devils, like molten Pompeii lava, were spreading over the expiring husk of his virtue.

He decided to present a moving target to the tempters. Raising his hand he asked permission to change his library book.

'Finished it, have we?' Such asked.

'Er . . . well . . .' replied Benson.

'What's it about?'

'It's about this man who is shipwrecked on an island and meets Man Friday and they live together on the island for ages.'

'What happens in the end?'

'Er . . .'

'You didn't finish it, did you, son?'

'No, it's – er – too difficult. I can't understand a lot of it. And it's boring, sir!'

Such sighed. 'I used to love "Robinson Crusoe" when I was your age, Benson. Go on, change it if you have to!'

'Thank you, sir.'

And Benson went over to the library cupboard. He knew most of the titles there. Closing his eyes he picked out one at random, but it was a Biggles book and Benson could not abide Biggles. He chose again and found himself holding 'Short Lives of the Saints'. This, he decided, was preordained and he returned to his seat with it.

He had read the first two pages of the tragically brief life of St Philomena when the bell rang.

'Get ready for your next class,' said Such over his shoulder as he made for the door.

But instead of Brother O'Toole, in walked the Vocations Brother, accompanied by Brother McNulty.

'Good morning, boys!' said the Vocations Brother.

'Good morning, sir!' replied the class.

Benson for one was stunned by the premature sight of the Vocations Brother, a full period earlier than expected. It threw everything out. There'd be Double

Maths for sure now and everything that entailed. Devoutly he wished that he had done his homework like a good boy. He could already see Brother Wood shouting and slapping his way towards him, banging boys' heads together and knocking on skulls with his hairy knuckles.

Brother McNulty left the class. Brother Kay, the Vocations Brother, opened up his briefcase and took out of it a thick wad of small cards. These he carried with him to the empty seat next to O'Gorman. He sat on the desk, his feet on the seat, and smiled at the class in general, and then at O'Gorman. O'Gorman, unused to smiles from persons in authority, gazed back at Brother Kay blankly.

Reverently, Brother Kay handed the wad of cards to O'Gorman and asked him to give one each to every boy in the class. O'Gorman did so, muttering under his breath, 'Dirty postcards! Get them here! Rude as anything!'

The card was a holy picture. It showed a handsome young Brother standing in the middle of a half-harvested wheat field. Lots of cheerful boys, newly harvested, were playing in the field and the Brother gestured with his right arm towards the unharvested side of the field as if to say, 'We need help! Come and join us in the harvesting of souls!' With his other hand the Brother pointed past the frolicking boys to the horizon where Jesus and His Mother sat, somewhat precariously, atop a rising sun. Some of the boys in the picture had noticed the vision of Christ and were gazing at it blissfully. One appeared to be wringing his hands. Overprinted down the right side of the picture was a poem.

'I'd like one of you boys to read what you see on the picture in his best reciting voice,' said Brother Kay.

Benson put up his hand. He liked reciting.

'The well-made boy at the back!'

The class turned to look as Benson stood up and began to read:

> 'I found a lump of modelling clay
> And fiddled with it one fine day.

I pulled it out. I crushed it in.
It changed and softened to my whim.
I found it again when days were o'er
But I could change its shape no more.

'I found a lump of living clay
And lovingly moulded it day by day.
I filled it with Truth and Virtue and Art –
A young boy's soft and willing heart –
I returned again when years were gone.
A good Catholic man I looked upon.
The form I had given him he still bore.
And I could not change him any more.'

Benson sat down. He had read the poem without error, and, he felt, not without expression. He glowed as the Vocations Brother said, 'You know, boys, I have heard that poem read many times in the course of my travels, but never have I heard it read with such expression. What is your name, young man?'

'Benson, sir.'

'Thank you, Benson.'

Brother Kay continued to smile seraphically at Benson for a long moment. Then he reached into the pocket of his jacket and produced his glasses-case. He took off the pair he was wearing and put on another pair, these ones with gold rims, which Benson, basking at the back, thought he would almost prefer to the rimless pair. Then the Vocations Brother re-read the poem. He paused and, removing his glasses and gazing mistily out of the classroom window, began:

'You know, boys, our lives are short. Our lives are like the blinking of an eye, or like a clay pot. The clay pot is made by the potter and then sold. It is used for a while but after its useful life is over it is broken and thrown away and returns to the dust from which it was wrought. Our lives are like that, boys, and, like a pot, we often get ourselves into hot water; we often get filled up with all sorts of strange things. Our journey through this

Vale of Tears is fleeting but it is also difficult and complicated. Now you know that I am the Vocations Brother. I have come seeking souls who . . .'

Benson sat, as still as a pot on a shelf, listening to Brother Kay. His attention was diverted from the Brother's words from time to time by the sight of Rudge, now seemingly fully recovered from his ordeal with Brother Hooper, chalking 'Kick me please! I like it!' on the back of Hepher's blazer. But the Vocations Brother's words struck a chord in him, filled him up with enthusiasm. For Brother Kay was describing him. He was not looking for strong souls, he said. No, he was looking for souls who would be easily broken in the world, souls who could not keep themselves from becoming chipped and scratched by temptation. Benson knew that Brother Kay was describing him. Had he not come out freshly glazed from the kiln of Confession that very morning? Were not stains and cracks already appearing? It would only take another meeting with Bruno to completely shatter his brittle virtue! Perhaps God was telling him that the only way to save his soul was to become a Brother!

Benson felt himself rising from his seat with enthusiasm and happiness when Brother Kay went on to describe the life of a Brother:

'When you join the Brothers, you have a family made up of all the other Brothers throughout the world – Brothers all united by a common purpose to save their souls and to make of their lives a living sacrifice to Jesus Christ and His Holy Catholic Church. However, if a wife is what you want – if a wife is what you need – the Brother's life is not for you. But if, on the other hand, you love Jesus and want to serve Him, then today may change your life.'

Brother Kay stopped speaking and closed his eyes. He clenched his hands together, placed them in front of his mouth, and continued.

'Boys! Close your eyes. Think carefully about your lives. Are you good? Are you pure? Are you happy? Listen. See if the Lord has anything to say to you. Only listen!'

Benson listened.

There were two voices at work. One voice said that he ought to be a Brother. The other told him that he had not done his Maths homework. The second voice won and for most of the rest of the time of silence Benson wondered how he would get through Brother Wood's double Maths without abject pain and humiliation.

At the end of five minutes the Vocations Brother lowered his hands from his face and gazed out over the class.

'In a few minutes I will ask any boy who thinks he might have heard the Call to be a Brother to put up his hand. Any boy who does so I will take with me to the Brothers' parlour for a talk about what a Brother's life entails. Do not think that by raising your hand today you will have made an irrevocable decision. No, you will just be saying that a little voice is telling you something. Now will somebody please read the poem again.'

Nobody volunteered, so Brother Kay chose Dexter, whose mother, Benson's mum said, was a snob.

As the poem was being read, totally without expression, Benson thought, by Dexter, he decided that he would put up his hand. It would, no doubt, cause him to be ridiculed later by the rougher elements in 3B, but Jesus too had been ridiculed. Also, by putting up his hand, both voices would be satisfied and he would be spirited off the dissolving cliff that lay between him and the yawning chasm of double Maths.

When the recitation was over, Brother Kay elicited from the class the meaning of the poem. As the bell for the end of the second period rang, he was pointing out to O'Gorman how O'Gorman was living clay – a metaphor the rest of the class had tumbled to some minutes previously.

The Vocations Brother consulted his watch. 'Tempus fugit, boys!' he cried. Then he looked out over 3B as if it represented some grand vista which he again found himself overjoyed to be viewing, after many years away and many times imagining.

'Hands up anyone who wants to be a Brother!'

Benson put up his hand. Heads turned to look at him. Benson made his eyes go out of focus so that the staring boys became a blur.

'So it's the bonny poet at the back! Come with me, son!'

Benson stood up and walked to the front, looking straight ahead.

The Vocations Brother put his arm round his shoulder and led him from 3B.

Two hours later Benson telephoned Mum from the Brothers' parlour.

'Is that you Mum? It's me.'

'I thought it was your dad. What's wrong, son?'

'Nothing's wrong, Mum. You know I told you that the Vocations Brother was visiting the school today? Well he wants to come home with me and have tea and a nice chat with you and Dad. Is that all right?'

'A nice chat. Why does he want a nice chat?'

'I want to be a Brother.'

'Oh, you do, do you?'

'Yes.'

'I thought you wanted to be a T.V. Personality.'

'No.'

'Did the Vocations Brother ask if he could come and see us?'

'Yes.'

'Well, all right, son. But I don't know what your dad is going to say, I really don't.'

'Thanks, Mum! See you later!'

Benson put back the receiver and turned to Brother Kay who was smoking a cigarette in an easy-chair near the fire.

'Mum says it's all right, Brother!'

It was lunchtime by now and Benson cheerfully walked back to 3B, bathed once more in Divine Light and a feeling of relief at having avoided double Maths.

3B was transformed by thermos flasks, lunch wrappings, yawning Oxo tins and about twenty boys all talking with their mouths full. Benson's appearance caused a momentary silence to descend.

Then Eddie Rudge shouted, 'It's Brother Wobbles!' and the class laughed hard. Benson sucked in his stomach and strode, a fine specimen of Christian manhood at bay, to his safe corner beside Vincent. He unpacked his lunch and started eating.

Drury turned round, but, before he could speak, Benson asked him with a gleeful smile, 'Double Maths OK?'

'Didn't have it,' replied Drury. 'Brother Wood had to go to the dentist. We had the whole time free to catch up on our homework.'

Benson felt greatly let down but he did not comment. The time in the Brothers' parlour with Brother Kay had set him on fire and the fire could not be doused by such a small reversal. He was 'called'. He was going to a special Brothers' school in Lancashire to take his 'O' levels and then to a monastery in Wiltshire to become a novice and train to be a Brother. He would take vows and milk cows. He would meditate and cast out the old man of sin. He would put self to death and save souls and die in the odour of sanctity. And he would escape temptation and bad companions and not become a homo.

Just at that moment Bruno's face intruded. Then Bruno's thing shooting stuff. Benson stopped chewing his sandwich.

'Lord, when temptation comes I break like a clay pot! Please put me up on a high shelf out of the reach of searching hands and things!'

After lunch he went out into the still-wet playground. He had threepence to spend but did not fancy approaching Eddie Rudge or his gang in the Tuck Shop, so he sat on the railings outside the gymnasium and watched the boys playing football with a tennis ball. They shouted to one another, cursed and bellowed. He could never understand why they did this. He looked down at his fat thighs ballooning against the bar of the railings he was sitting on and idly compared his wobbly self with the long, thin legs of his schoolmates.

He had been the only one to volunteer to read. He had been the only one who wanted to be a Brother. He was the only one who wanted to make stuff when he saw Bruno's thing. Why?

'I am different from other boys,' Benson told himself. 'I am strange and mysterious.'

But the thought did not fill him with any joy.

By the time Dad came home at seven, Benson and Mum were a little tired of the company of Brother Kay. He had gone on and on about the Brothers and his own vocation and his childhood growing up in Ireland during the Troubles. He had also eaten vast quantities of sandwiches and cake, even wolfing down the only Jap Fancy on the plate, which was Benson's favourite.

The Vocations Brother had wrongly assumed that Mum was Irish and that she would relish all his fireside banter about the Old Country. He talked of his life in England as an old colonial might speak of the peculiar world in the dark beyond the range of his fans and electric light, where drums beat out irritating rhythms and people worshipped idols and would not be told that they had got hold of the wrong end of the cultural stick.

'Sure isn't the Protestant religion a glass of warm water, Mrs Benson?' he said. 'Imagine the Queen of England appointing bishops and the like! And all the mixed marriages there are! To my way of thinking Old Nick is laughing all the way to Hades when he surveys England. Ninety-nine people out of a hundred would rather jitter about to Helen Shapiro records than darken the doors of a Church! Sure, the whole place is going to the dogs!'

He did not seem to notice that Mum was pursing her lips and saying little, but Benson noticed Mum's reaction and that Brother Kay was cutting little ice with her.

It was with a sigh of relief that both of them greeted Dad's return.

The whisky bottle was produced and, while Dad ate his tea, it became clear that he had taken to Brother Kay and that the feeling was reciprocated. Dad did have Irish blood and far more respect for anyone in a clerical collar than Mum.

Then Brother Kay said, quite out of the blue, 'It will be a very noble sacrifice to give your only son to be a Brother.'

'Early days,' said Dad.

'Quite right. But that's what I'm here to talk about. Perhaps I could talk to you both alone for a while.' He turned to Benson. 'I'm sure you've got a lot of work to do for tomorrow.'

'Yes, I have,' admitted Benson, relieved that he was not going to have to participate further.

Mum, Dad, and Brother Kay went off to the lounge, leaving Benson with the dishes.

He put too much Tide into the water and the bubbles were soon in danger of overflowing the bowl. Then he sunk the plates and cutlery beneath the clouds, hoping to bury his own anxieties with them.

Things were progressing at a pace he was not at all sure he approved of. Had not Brother Kay said that he had only to *think* he *might* have a vocation prior to putting up his hand? It was as if the Vocations Brother wanted to wrap up his vocation in a neat parcel and present it to him as a gift prior to his departure. But then he consoled himself with the thought that Mum and Dad would know best and either consent or refuse as was appropriate. Then Benson would merely have to drift along like a leaf blown by the wind of his parents' decision.

And now, despite being in a state of Grace, he felt uneasy. Nobody had mentioned Bruno since the night before, but the matter could not be over and who was to say what shocking revelations were about to come from Bruno's mouth? And Eric! He would deflate like a balloon on the thirteenth day of Christmas before the gentlest interrogation. And interrogations there were sure to be!

'The Devil made me do it but he's gone now,' Benson

saw himself saying to the massed inquisition of Church and Lounge. 'Yes, I confess that I was moved by the sight of Bruno's thing but it is over now. It was just a passing enthusiasm like Hula-Hoops. Now I realise that it was wicked. I am now wedded to Christ and His Holy Catholic and Apostolic Church and have cast off the Old Man of Sin and Depravity.'

But had he? Could he? A scant twenty-four hours had passed since he was last immersed in the cesspool of irregular motions of the flesh and the thought of it excited him even now. Would the temptation ever leave him? He tended to think not. He did not know why he thought not. Other sins had faded and lost their appeal. He no longer drank down whole tins of condensed milk. Neither did he any longer cut up worms or steal pennies from the Bishop Mumby collection box by the telephone. But no sin had ever been as totally compelling as this one. Every pleasurable feeling he had ever felt combined at the sight of Bruno's thing, catapulting him towards it with no possibility of avoidance. He could not conceive of the day arriving when, confronted with Bruno's thing, he would ever be able to pass by and observe, 'That's Bruno's thing,' as if he were saying to Mrs Brown, 'Your monkey is a bit dusty today,' and pass on to something else, unmoved.

As he dried the dishes and stacked them on top of Mum's new twin-tub, he looked at himself in the dark kitchen window.

'I'm fat and I'm a homo,' he told himself.

A Catechism question and answer occurred to him.

Question: 'What sins commonly lead to the breaking of the Sixth and Ninth Commandment?'

Answer: 'The sins that commonly lead to the breaking of the Sixth and Ninth Commandment are: Gluttony; Drunkenness; Intemperance; and the neglect of prayer.'

He knew he wasn't given to drunkenness. He didn't think he was given to intemperance (whatever that was); but a glutton he most definitely was. If he weren't a glutton he wouldn't be fat. And he was idle. And he sought out bad company. There would be no bad company in the monastery, that was for sure. There would be no time for idleness either. There would be fasting. No Mars Bars in the monastery. But the trouble was that he would miss Mars Bars. Mars Bars were nice. Yes, he would most certainly miss Mars Bars. He would also miss fruit gums, sherbet lemons, bubble and squeak, fish and chips, egg and chips, after dinner mints, bacon sandwiches, scotch pancakes with butter on, sherry trifle, Rose's Lime Juice, cream soda, dandelion and burdock . . . all these things he would miss.

But in return Jesus would give him His Friendship. Benson would become Jesus' slim friend, chiselled down through prayer, sacrifice and fasting. He would never be alone. Temptations would come but they would bounce off his spiritual muscles like gamma rays off Flash Gordon. Of course, he knew that there would be times when Jesus might seem to turn away to test his faith, to put him through a Deep Night of the Soul, like St John of the Cross and Gwen Watford were always having. But Benson would know that it was all like a game between friends and would prove to his Friend that he could take it.

He took the clean dishes and put them away in the morning room dresser. Then he looked at the picture of the Sacred Heart on the wall beside the dresser. He approached it, gazing at it intently. The eyes were filled with love for Benson. The lips seemed to be moving – 'Did they move?' – to form the words:

'Follow Me!'

Benson bowed his head, adoringly and unblinkingly, until tears came to his eyes.

'My Lord and My God! Thy Will be done!' prayed Benson. He leaned over the picture and kissed the bearded Face reverently. Then he went into the pantry and wolfed down all the left-over scones.

Shortly afterwards Dad summoned him back to the lounge. There sat Brother Kay in Dad's chair. Mum was seated on the far end of the settee. She looked a little dazed and was using her puffer energetically.

Benson was forced to sit on the armchair next to the television that nobody ever sat in.

'Here's our new Brother!' cried Brother Kay.

'God willing!' agreed Dad.

Mum sipped her sherry and said nothing.

'We've been having a chat about you, young man,' said Brother Kay. He winked at Benson and Benson smiled back at him nervously. 'It's a great blessing when the Lord chooses a boy from a good Catholic family and calls him to His service.'

'But don't you think he's a bit young yet, Brother?' asked Mum helplessly.

Brother Kay answered, 'The younger the better. The Lord places mature thoughts in immature bodies before the Devil can seduce the innocent with his wicked wiles; before the Old Adam rises up and takes charge. Your son is young, that is true. He needs guidance for many years to come. The danger is, that if he remains in the world, he will slowly lose his ideals and get wrapped up in the ways of the world. He'll listen to the radio and dance to Alma Cogan records and forget his Maker. That is the danger. A vocation is given when the Lord chooses. If His Voice is not listened to He does not ask again. He is God after all. He will just go on down the street and call on another family.'

There was no answer to that. Mum sat and contemplated the empty sherry glass.

'It sounds like a tough regime at the monastery,' Dad confided to Benson, a look of no small satisfaction on his face.

'Anyway,' continued Brother Kay, looking at his watch, 'tempus fugit! I fear I have many miles to go before I sleep. There is plenty of time for further discussion and of course there will be medicals and lots of other formalities before your son can be accepted for training. For the moment, let us kneel down and say the Rosary and ask for the guidance of our Most Holy Mother, Mary.'

The light was switched off and the four knelt and started the five Sorrowful Mysteries.

Benson could think of nothing but the invisible people in the room praying for his vocation. The voices droned on in a monotone which Benson knew he would find distasteful, were he God. He had always attempted to put some expression into his prayers.

'I can always say it was a mistake,' Benson told himself.

But then it was his turn to lead the prayers.

'The fourth Sorrowful Mystery of the Holy Rosary: The Carrying of The Cross,' began Benson with expression.

'Do you want to leave us then?' asked Mum.

Brother Kay had gone, waved up the road by the Benson family, until his grey snub-nosed Standard Vanguard disappeared out of sight. Dad had at once retreated to the garden without another word, leaving Mum and Benson to go back inside alone.

Benson went into the lounge, his Maths book at the ready. He knew he would have to attempt to do the work or the morrow might prove unbearable. Mum had joined him there. She tried to help him with the equation problems, but Maths was not her strong point and, at last she left him to it and pretended to read her 'Woman's Own'. But Benson knew she wasn't reading with any concentration, just as he was not working on his Maths homework with any concentration. He had fully expected the question when it came.

'Do you really want to leave us?'

'I don't er . . .' said Benson.

'Your dad seems very taken with the idea. But I'm not, not at all.'

'Why not, Mum?' he asked her, though he thought he knew.

'To be candid, I don't like the Brothers much. Too Irish. Cold fish and too hard on the boys.'

'They're hard so's to make us better boys, Mum!'

'Oh, are they? You've changed your tune since last

week! Wasn't it you who told me that your Maths teacher knocked you about whenever you couldn't do the work? You call that Christian? You call that Brotherly?'

'Yes, but . . .'

But Mum did not hear. 'It's a long jump from complaining about them to wanting to join them. I just don't understand how the change came about so suddenly.'

'I heard a Call,' answered Benson defensively.

'Oh, you did, did you? Well, look, son, I know the Lord works in mysterious ways but this is just a little too mysterious for my liking. Are you sure it isn't *you* telling *yourself* that you want to be a Brother? You know how moody you are and how you get enthusiastic and then cool off. Remember the Scouts?'

Benson preferred not to remember the Scouts. He had pestered Mum and Dad for months to be allowed to join. Then, once he had joined and had wet his sleeping-bag at Easter Camp so that the Scoutmaster had had to send him home in his wife's car, all enthusiasm for the Scouts had disappeared and a barely-used Scout uniform had found its way to the Parish Jumble Sale.

'That was different!'

'No, son, it isn't different. Your dad thought becoming a Scout would make a man of you. Now he thinks becoming a Brother will make a man of you. But you and I both know that you are a long way from being a man. It will come in its own good time but at the moment you've still got this problem with the bedwetting. How would you cope in the monastery if you kept wetting the bed? The Brothers would probably rub your nose in it!'

Benson gave his mother a sideways glance laced with great reproach. Bed-wetting was his one public vice. All the others he had managed, he fancied, to keep to himself.

'Remember Harrogate?' asked Mum.

'Yes.'

He would never forget it. The posh hotel in Yorkshire full for the summer and Benson told to share a room with the son of the owners, a couple who had spent years in Burma. Every night a wet patch on the mattress where his water had leaked over the edge of his rubber sheet. The son, a slim, athletic, blond who spoke like someone on the radio and had cups for running on his mantelpiece and a Scout's Cord and a fierce dog called Reggie only he could control, had told his mother about Benson's accidents and called him 'The Wet Whale'. The boy's mother had told Mum that it was disgraceful that a boy of Benson's age should still be wetting the bed and that something must be wrong with him. Mum had taken offence and insisted that they leave the hotel, even though Dad did not want to leave. They went to a boarding house in Pickering, but Benson had continued to wet the bed. He had ruined everyone's holiday.

'Well,' continued Mum, 'it will be worse than that at the monastery. You just mark my words!'

By the time the weekend came Benson had changed his mind about becoming a Brother. It was Maths the following morning which had partly brought this about. Mum's tears when he returned from school had clinched his decision. He told himself that it would be much better for him to love and serve the Lord in the world.

He had done his Maths homework after a fashion, but had solved the equations in a random fashion while praying fervently to St Jude for inspiration. $x + y - 2y = x + 2xy - x$ wrote Benson randomly. However, St Jude had remained a hopeless case and every sum he did was hopelessly wrong.

Brother Wood had made his way down the aisle like a black-clad reaper through a field. The scythe of his nervous hand flashed and left boys' faces red and smarting. By the time Brother Wood had arrived at Benson's desk, Benson was speechless with fear.

He had corrected Vincent Latos' book first. Big red ticks soon covered the page. 'Good lad!' exclaimed Brother Wood and gave Vincent a rare smile. Then he reached across and took Benson's book. Livid red crosses marched down the page like a cemetery. Brother Wood began to perceive the randomness of Benson's answers and with his left hand he hit the back of Benson's head. He completed his marking and shouted, 'Out to the front, you!'

Benson, dizzy with pain and fear, marched to the front of the class. Brother Wood let him wait by the board as he continued marking around the class. Nobody else was hit, not even Eddie Rudge.

From the back of the class Brother Wood surveyed Benson with distaste. He slowly screwed the cap on to his pen and paced up the aisle, never once taking his eyes off Benson.

He came up very close to him. 'Where's your copybook? Get your copybook, fat boy!' On the word 'get' he slapped Benson's right cheek hard. Benson went to get his book. Vincent was holding it out to him but had averted his eyes.

Benson's eyes were smarting water from the blow as he handed his copybook to Brother Wood.

'Crying are you?' asked Brother Wood, approaching very close to Benson, so near that Benson could smell the Brother's unpleasant breath. Mum said that such breath was caused by not being able to go to the toilet every day.

'No, sir! My eyes were smarting from the smack, sir!'

Brother Wood glared at him, then went over to the board and wrote out one of the problems.

'Show the class how you do this!' And he held out a piece of chalk.

'I can't do it, sir! I don't understand them at all, sir!'

' "I don't understand them at all, sir!" ' mimicked Brother Wood, putting on a fruity English accent. Then he hit Benson on the other cheek.

'Come and see me after school, you!'

Benson sat down.

After school he was set to doing the problems but could manage nothing. After an hour of tense nonachievement, Brother Wood came up to him and said,

'You're a stupid boy, Benson! Stupid and fat! What are you?'

'I'm a stupid boy. Stupid and fat, sir,' said Benson without conviction.

'Get out of my sight!'

And Benson had done so.

Late home and he had had to ask Mum, 'Why are you crying, Mum?'

He had never seen Mum cry before.

'I've been at it all day!'

'Why, Mum?'

'Don't go and be a Brother! I don't want you to be a Brother!'

Benson thought for a moment and then said: 'OK, Mum, I won't go.'

Mum cheered up immediately.

She set about preparing the evening meal and Benson used the time to weave the prongs of a fork through the tablecloth. When he had done this, he withdrew the fork, sprinkled some salt around and tried to place grains of salt into the tiny holes in the cloth. While thus gainfully employed, he asked Mum, 'Am I fat, Mum?'

Mum did not answer for a long moment. Then she turned around and advanced towards him, wiping her hands on her apron. She took him in her arms.

'No, you're not fat, son. You're just well-made,' she said softly.

Although luxuriating in the warmth of Mum's hug and feeling the hurt of the day lessening, Benson did not feel convinced. Mum had told him on several occasions that he was well-made. She had also insisted that he was 'big-boned' and blamed the Irish side for that. But increasingly the evidence of his own eyes and the daily expletives hurled at him at school had gone a long way towards convincing him that he was, indeed, fat.

'No, Mum, I think I'm fat,' insisted Benson.

'It's just a stage, puppy-fat,' said Mum, turning back to her work.

'I am fat,' thought Benson.

Later that evening he was leafing through Mum's copy of 'Woman's Own' when he came upon an advertisement:

RUB AWAY THOSE UNWANTED POUNDS!
GET YOURSELF OUR BALL-MASSAGER!
AN OFFER EXCLUSIVE TO READERS OF WOMAN'S OWN!

There was a picture of a very slim woman rubbing a round pad set with what looked to Benson like tiny marbles.

The Ball Massager seemed to have worked wonderfully well for the woman in the picture. Benson decided that it was just what he needed and took down the address. The nine-and-six-pence including postage would be harder to arrange, but arrange it he would! He'd cash in some of his savings stamps, the ones with Prince Charles on the front, and send off for it. It would make a new man of him.

Eric Jenkins called humbly at the back door. Benson did not invite him in and dismissed him with a few curt phrases. He realised that Bruno had not been given a thought for at least twenty-four hours. So he thought about Bruno and resolved to make a Pastoral Visit to him at some indefinite future date. Benson devoted the remainder of the evening to the refurbishment of the wardrobe altar.

Before he slept he thought of Mum and the promise he had made to her. What could have made him reverse himself like that? In truth he was sick – fat and stupid too. What would Brother Kay say? What would Jesus say? What would Mary say? What would Brother Hooper say? What would St Joseph say? What would Guardian Angel Tom say?

Then he consoled himself with the thought of the massager he would send for. Yes, that is what he would do the following morning. Yes, that is what he'd do . . .

'Does your mum know you're cashing in your savings stamps?' asked the man in the post office.

'Oh, yes, Mr Bolton. She's anxious that I do it, in fact,' replied Benson.

Mr Bolton raised his eyebrows and took Benson's savings book wearily. He pulled out the four half-crown stamps and passed a ten shilling note across the counter.

'Can you give me a postal order for nine-and-six and one twopence-halfpenny stamp please?'

Mr Bolton did so.

'It's a pity you're taking out all that money, sunny Jim. Only two more half-crown ones and you'd have been able to buy a Savings Certificate, you know. Then you'd be earning interest.'

'I expect you're right,' replied Benson, though he had absolutely no interest in interest.

'It's never too early to start thinking of the future, you know,' continued Mr Bolton doggedly.

'Yes, I'm sure that's quite true, Mr Bolton,' sighed Benson, though he felt that without a massager he did not have a future.

'Before you know it you'll be my age and then where will you be?'

'Er . . . yes,' said Benson. He turned and saw Bruno at the other end of the shop, browsing through the paper-back books.

With Mr Bolton forgotten behind his glass, Benson retreated to the writing counter to address his letter to 'Woman's Own'. He kept a weather-eye out for Bruno, realising with some certainty that he did not want to see him ever again.

He wondered as he stuck the envelope down if he would be able to get past Bruno without his seeing. This he attempted by walking past the stationery display, keeping well to the right. He felt he was about to succeed in this daring enterprise, but as he came level Bruno spun round and looked him straight in the eye.

'I saw you down there at the post office. What were you doing?' Bruno asked.

'Something for Mum,' lied Benson.

'I've been reading these books. Have you read "Camp

on Blood Island"? It's about the Japanese during the war. It's all good, but page 42 is really, really good. Have you read it?'

'No, I haven't, Bruno. Is it there?' asked Benson by way of making polite conversation.

'Yes, it is. There it is. Have a look.'

Benson picked up the book and turned to page 42. He read it for a while, then he asked, 'Why does he want to give her chocolate?'

'It tells you! Can't you read?' And Bruno quoted from memory: ' "To make you strong and healthy for me." '

'Why does he want her to be strong and healthy for him?'

'You still don't know anything, do you? So he can do it to her, that's why!'

'Do what?'

Bruno came closer to Benson, and took the book out of his hands. 'Do her, that's what.'

'Do her?' The question was intended to act as an antidote to the powerful aphrodisiac effect that Bruno's presence was having on Benson. 'I should be going home. My mum . . .' he added helplessly.

'Where are you going? I'll come too.' Bruno took Benson's arm and led him from the post office.

'Er . . .' said Benson.

'What?'

'I was just thinking, I mean, I was sorry to hear about what happened to you.'

'Well, least said soonest mended. That's what my dad says anyway.'

'Yes, I suppose so,' agreed Benson. 'Look, I must post this letter . . .'

He ran over to the post-box wondering if he could just wave at Bruno and then go off in the opposite direction. But, he told himself, that would probably not work and anyway he was not sure he really wanted to retreat. He was curious about Bruno. It was amazing how casual he seemed about everything that had happened to him. He had expected to find him a physical and emotional wreck, but such did not appear to be the case.

'Where's your bike?' he asked.

'It's gone. My dad's buying me a new one and he's given my old one to the shop to go towards it. I'll get the new one on Monday night. It's a yellow-and-black Dawes with drop-handle-bars,' announced Bruno proudly.

'Gosh! You lucky thing!'

'Where shall we go?' asked Bruno.

'How do you mean?'

'Well, don't you want to know what happened to me?'

'No. Yes.'

'Well, I can't tell you here, can I? Someone might hear.'

'Where shall we go?' asked Benson.

'Back of the Prom?'

'All right.'

'The back of the Prom' referred to the area behind the promenade, built to protect Benson's town against encroachment by the Irish Sea. The area, to the seaward, bounded by low sandstone cliffs, marked the former coastline.

Between these cliffs and the merchants' houses that hugged the crest of the crocodile-profiled hill lay a half-mile strip of rough, wild ground. Gun emplacements littered the area, remains of the Second World War; steel rabbit warrens among the hawthorn bushes and sand-gullies.

There greying men walked their dogs and gossiped to them about the War and their time in the Home Guard. There courting couples found a private trysting place out of sight of all but the most curious in the affluent houses at the top of the hill.

There that February morning Bruno led Benson.

On the way Bruno took 'Camp on Blood Island' out of his pocket.

'Here, you have it. It's good stuff,' he said, offering it to Benson.

'Did you pinch it, Bruno?'

'Course I did! You want it or don't you?'

'No, thank you. Look, Bruno, maybe I should go home now.'

'We're nearly there.'

They walked under a railway bridge and turned on to the rough land. Bruno seemed to know where he was going and Benson followed meekly.

The two boys went down the steep stairs that led to a corridor under one of the huge canyons which pointed out to sea, a sea from which no enemy was any longer expected. They walked along the corridor until they came to a dead-end.

Then Bruno stopped.

'In "Camp on Blood Island" this Japanese officer falls in love with one of the women prisoners and he does her every night. He gives her chocolate to keep her strong and healthy for him. The other prisoners are not strong and healthy, you see . . .'

'What happened to you, Bruno?' asked Benson, suddenly losing patience.

'In the end the other prisoners kill the girl on page 42.'

'What happened to you, Bruno?'

'One of the prisoners gets his head chopped off! It's dead good!'

Benson screamed at Bruno: 'What happened to you?'

The sound of his voice, amplified by the steel cladding of the chamber, startled both boys. They looked at one another.

'It happened here but don't tell anyone,' whispered Bruno.

'But you said . . .'

'I know what I said,' interrupted Bruno pedantically, 'but what I said and what happened aren't the same thing.'

'You lied to your dad?'

'Yeah.'

'Why?'

Bruno shrugged. Then he said, 'I didn't want to get him into trouble.'

'Who?'

'The man.' He looked around the steel chamber. 'He comes here every night.'

'Who does?'

'The man.'

'So how did your mum and dad find out?'

'I told them.'

'Why?'

Bruno shrugged.

'What did he do to you?'

'I'll show you.'

Benson struggled with Bruno for a while. The dank smell of the place both attracted and repelled him. Bruno was stronger than Benson. He made him get down lower than he had ever had to get down in the scrum. Bruno hurt Benson but the pain abated when he stopped fighting him and accepted his place beneath the bigger boy's weight. Benson closed his eyes tight, and in the stars that formed, and in the echoing grunts from Bruno, he found, in the midst of pain, that all soul-searching and worry had momentarily been cast out.

He ran all the way home then straight upstairs to the bathroom. There he ran himself a bath and while the tub was filling he stared at himself in the mirror.

'I am lost if I stay in the world!' he told his reflection. Then he lay in the bath quite still, looking down at the part that was wrecking him.

He looked a little too long. It stared right back at him, demanding attention. Then, when attention was paid and Benson's mind crowded full of steel walkways, dank odours and faceless men with gaping trousers, it repaid the attention by doing what Bruno had been able to do for quite some time.

He scoured and scoured the bath. He would go to Confession and make everything all right. This time everything would stay all right too! But only if he left the world! He had to leave the world!

He was sulky at lunch and when Mum asked him what

the matter was, he told her that he was upset because he had told her a lie the day before. He did have a vocation after all, he said. He had only said he hadn't to please her.

Mum didn't say anything, just nodded.

Benson flicked through 'The Catholic Herald' and a few minutes later Mum came back to the table and said, 'Your dad will be pleased.'

Benson fidgeted away the afternoon and then went for a walk down to the back of the Prom.

A week later a parcel addressed to Benson dropped on the mat. It was the Ball Massager. Benson took it straight up to his bedroom and slowly, reverently, undid the package.

Opening his wardrobe door he gazed at the plaster statue in the alcove altar. Then he stripped himself naked and commenced rubbing his flesh with the Massager.

He continued until he drew blood.

Part Two
Joachim

'I'm going to be a saint before I'm thirty,' Brother Henry whispered to Benson through a hell of steam and crashing plates.

'But you may still be alive when you're thirty, Brother?' Benson whispered back. He picked up a stack of cereal plates which had been newly released from the ordeal of a dunk in Brother Henry's sink full of impossibly hot water. He dried the top of each plate with a rapid circular motion while tickling the bottom of the stack with a wipe that also supported the stack. Then he shuffled the top plate to the bottom, and, being careful to remember that he would have to go through the procedure eight times in order to come back to the first one again, he wiped the top of the next lucky plate.

While Benson was thus employed, Brother Henry, a devout personal ejaculation, seen but unheard, upon his quivering lips, plunged his hands deep into the scalding water. His mouth opened wide. The blood drained from his taut, stretched, thin lips. His eyes rolled heavenward in anguish, his hands poached as they searched, frantic as any hands at a January sale rummage counter, to retrieve the submerged dishes before his flesh fell off the bone.

'Why don't you add some cold?' asked Benson, though he knew the answer.

Brother Henry replied, his whisper amplified to a strangled shriek by the soundbox of his tumescent mouth, 'I have to mortify my flesh, Brother. If I don't mortify it, it will mortify me.'

Benson nodded but said nothing. There was really nothing to say and, even if there had been, now was not the time to be saying it because it was still only 7 a.m. And the Great Silence did not end until 8 o'clock. But he allowed himself to think; and in his thoughts he chided Brother Henry severely for his ostentatious piety. Had he not a week ago put a piece of holly down his underpants and gone to the washroom with a couple of leaves sticking out? The Novice Master, who always supervised washtime, could not have missed it. Benson had certainly noticed and had decided then that Brother Henry needed to take himself in hand and not let his left hand know what his right hand was doing. But then Benson recalled himself and tried to rein in his own uncharitable thoughts. Who was he, anyway, to judge? Was not he, like Brother Henry, a miserable Son of Adam?

He smiled benignly at his companion as his red hands emerged from the scalding dishwater without any dishes in them. Brother Henry waved his hands about while he screamed a whispered, 'Jesus! Mary! I love you! Save souls!' again and again.

Benson waited patiently.

Once again Brother Henry plunged into the water and fished around frantically for the cooking plates. Once again he emerged red-handed but plateless.

'Please, Brother! I've got my housework to do still! We're already late. You know what Novvy's like. Can't you just add some cold?'

Nodding his head sadly, Brother Henry turned on the cold water. 'You know, Brother Joachim, denying oneself self-denial for the sake of others may also be a short cut to sanctity.'

'Perhaps you're right,' replied Brother Joachim.

'Yes, perhaps I'm right. One can never be sure. The only thing I'm sure of, Brother Joachim, is that it is not easy.'

'What isn't easy, Brother?'

'Sanctity.'

'I know, Brother,' said Brother Joachim. And he did.

Benson was now sixteen and had been away from home for fourteen months. He had spent a year at St Patrick's Juniorate and had then, armed with 'O' Levels, been moved to St Finbar's. Almost three strange years had passed since he had first decided to become a Brother. His slowness in leaving home had been caused largely by his own on-and-off vocation. It had been as if God's Call of 'Follow Me' was constantly being interrupted and fiddled with by a satanic jamming set as it made its ethereal way from heaven to Benson's soul. His urge to serve the Lord was the 'heads' of his desire, the 'tails' being his sexual desires, on the rack of which he had continued to languish as thirteen turned to fourteen.

Mum and Dad had not known what to think. They shook their heads, prayed about it, consulted Canon Preston. Mum had even been seen deserting Frances Parkinson Keyes in the library and making a quick, self-conscious dart to the psychology shelf. There she leafed through book after book, trying to find out if her child had any precedent in the annals of behavioural science. What she found there consoled her somewhat and she was able to go home and respond with confidence when Dad asked what had got into the boy.

'It's puberty.'

'It's what?'

'Puberty. Everything in the lad is changing.'

'I wasn't like that.'

'He's sensitive.'

'Well I'm sensitive too, lady! I like to know where I stand and I don't know where I stand with him. This vocation of his. He's blowing hot and cold and I don't like it.'

Mum decided it was time to drop her bombshell. 'Siblings,' she said, flatly.

'Siblings?' asked Dad.

'Yes, siblings. The lad never had any siblings.'

'What's a sibling, lady?'

'Brothers and sisters.'

'Well why didn't you say so?'

'I thought you'd have known what a sibling was, being a policeman and everything,' Mum replied archly.

Dad had gone all silent, humphing round the kitchen disconsolately in a way which told Mum that he would rather be in the greenhouse. But Mum was not going to let him off the hook that easily.

'I think,' she stated, 'that our son is too much alone and you know what the Bible says.'

'What?'

'The Bible says that it is not good for man to be alone. I think that's his trouble all right. No siblings to keep him on the straight and narrow.'

'It's not my fault he hasn't got any bloody siblings! It was your insides that got jammed, don't forget!'

Mum grimaced and reached for a cigarette. She blew blue smoke between herself and Dad before saying, 'Well I'm for making him wait. If he has got a vocation to be a Brother it'll do him no harm to have to hang about a bit.'

'I suppose you're right but I do want him to get good "O" levels and Brother Kay said that he'd be brought on wonderfully if he went to the Brothers. Individual tuition, he said.'

'Yes, but . . .' continued Mum.

The upshot of the conversation was that Dad and Mum decided to inform Brother Kay that they would give their consent to Benson becoming a Brother, but not until he had spent another year at St Bede's. If he still felt he had a vocation then, he could go away with their blessing. Brother Kay had tried his hardest to protest this decision. He argued that the Call was only made the once and that one could not expect the Lord to hang around on the offchance that an unworthy vessel like Benson might deign to be filled at some future time. The Lord simply did not work like that.

When this line of argument did not cut any ice with Mum and Dad, Brother Kay repeated his pitch about the wonderful results achieved by students at St Patrick's Juniorate. Dad had come close to caving in then, but Mum remained adamant. Brother Kay, seeing at last how the land lay, bowed to the inevitable. Benson's vocation was put on hold.

For Benson his parents' decision ushered in a period of great indecisiveness, a cake he filled and decorated with turpitude. He was becoming more and more convinced that he was abnormal. At times he was of the opinion that this abnormality was a good thing: that he had somehow been blessed, singled out, was in possession of a destiny. But more usually it was his abnormal interest in male bodies, and in particular, male appendages, which, he knew, singled him out for the Mark of Cain.

His schoolmates were obsessed too. Tits and twats had taken them all by storm. Conkers were left to rot into the ground as Benson's contemporaries lusted and longed and told one another what they would do to the girls from Maria Assumpta if only they could get them alone for a minute or two. Benson, as a result of hours of covert study of his school mates' finer features, could judge what the girls would be subjected to – and quaked for them – but he had no sexual siblings in whom he could confide.

Desperately, he tried to excite himself with thoughts of girls – girls he knew – but it did little good. Then he tried the exotic girls from films and television. He cavorted with Deborah Kerr, Gwen Watford, Ann Shelton, Lucille Ball and Rosalie Critchley. But he always remained frustratingly flaccid. While he might start on the normal path he invariably ended his walk through the phosphorescent perfumed garden of nightly fantasy by discovering John Wayne or Man Friday or Long John Silver behind some tree. Sometimes he would be squeezing a woman's softer parts. Enthusiasm flagged and he was only saved from sleep by the entrance of a man who, after a moment of shock, would show Benson how it was *really* done. Then the woman would make an excuse, go out to see if the jelly had set, leaving Benson and the man to squeeze one another. Of all men Desi Arnaz was his favourite and it was usually Lucy who went out to see if the jelly had set. Then, all passion spent, the three of them would sit round the kitchen table and eat the jelly. Maybe Fred and Ethel would drop in and if sleep would not come Fred would say that he had left his hanky in the bedroom and Benson would go in to help him find it . . .

All this convinced Benson that he was a homo without hope. The idea of becoming a Brother always waxed as his virtue fell into the mud. It seemed like the only thing that could possibly save him.

When, a year later, he was called into the lounge by Mum and Dad for a final talk and was asked if he still wanted to go, he said he did. Had they asked him a scant twenty-four hours before he would have answered no. He had managed a full month without a sexual lapse. But that night, in a toilet near the library, a man had shown Benson his large erect penis and played with him until he ejaculated his excitement into the sewers and unbearable excitement was in a trice replaced by unbearable depression, fear and self-loathing.

'Fair enough,' Dad had said.

Benson took Brother Joachim as his religious name. The name appealed because it had an unusual and exotic ring to it. It might have been Indian or Tahitian. All the prospective novices were permitted to write down three choices for names. Whether they got their choices depended on whether there were any other Brothers with that name in the Order. So, for instance, there was little chance for anyone who wanted to be John or Peter. There was a good chance for someone who wanted Henry, Dunstan, Ninian or Egbert. Neither was Joachim in great demand, so he put the name down as his first choice.

St Joachim, apart from sporting an exotic name, also

enjoyed the undoubted benefit of being the grandfather of God – on His Mother's side. He had been the husband of St Anne, the mother of Mary. Not mentioned at all in any of the Gospels, he did have a Gospel all his own which, however, had not been accepted as Holy Writ. This bothered Benson a little, but only a little. After all Mary had to have had a father and it was inconceivable that the father of our Blessed Mother would not be holy. And it was also obvious that, as father of Mary and grandfather of Jesus, St Joachim would have a great deal of 'pull' with the Family, more than enough to pull Benson out of the abyss. Anyway, thought Benson, St Joachim would be grateful to him for having taken his name and thereby in some small way having spread it among men.

Some disappointment had followed for Brother Joachim on the day when the Superior General of the Order came to the monastery to bestow the habit and religious names on to the ten novices. Benson had always assumed that Joachim was pronounced Joachim. But, as he approached the altar in his long black cassock, the reverse collar biting into his throat, the Superior General was heard to say, 'I welcome you, Brother Joachim to the Order. May you endure unto death.' Benson had gulped at the name. If the Director General had said it like that it would surely stick. But it did not sound right somehow. It offended his sense of aesthetics. Had he thought that the name could be so manipulated he would have chosen something else. Joel had been a possibility. Raymond had also appealed.

He tried to see the bending of his new name as a heaven-sent opportunity to puncture his petty vanity. But it did not come easily. For sure, the road to sanctity was going to be tough.

Brother Joachim left Brother Henry rinsing the sink and yelping like a pinioned St Sebastian. He made his way along the corridor which led from the kitchen area to the main building of St Finbar's. He kept carefully to the left, eyes cast down, and worked his hands up the sleeves of his cassock to ward off the cold. As he walked he passed other Brothers but no greetings were exchanged.

The area Brother Joachim was leaving was a recent addition to the building, which had until the late forties been the family home of an aristocratic English family, the forefathers of whom had played a part in the martyrdom of St Thomas Becket. Built of Bath stone, the building was a nineteenth-century Gothic structure, and aped a medieval monastery. A central garden was surrounded by a cloister with flagged floors, separated from the garden on all four sides by peculiarly secular stained glass which seemed to depict the life of Jane Austen. The rooms of the manor house on the ground floor all gave on to this cloister and were matched on the first floor by similar rooms, now divided by curtains and plasterboard into bedrooms and bathrooms for the Brothers. Atop the building, facing east, was a high, square tower into the side of which was set a statue of Henry the Eighth.

The ruins of the original manor house lay some hundred yards from the new one, to the south-west. It had been destroyed by fire but its wild, picturesque walls and arches had been cleverly incorporated into the new layout of the place to form a folly on the far edge of the gardens. And the gardens were the real crowning glory of St Finbar's.

Brother Joachim walked half way round the cloister, passing the second seven Stations of the Cross. He allowed himself to look at the white stone plaques depicting the passion of Christ. They had been donated to the monastery by a devout local Catholic and hung around three sides of the cloister. It had been said that the donor had had his own features carved on Simon of Cyrene and that of his mother on St Veronica. Brother Joachim was not sure if that had been a good idea or not. However, it did seem to him to be a small price to pay for a complete set of Stations of the Cross.

It was his 'charge' to keep the Brothers' Feast Day

Parlour clean and polished. He also had to sweep the side of the cloister off which the Parlour and the Novices' Room were located. The cloister took little time. The darkness hid dust and did not reveal cleanliness. The Feast Day Parlour was another matter entirely, however. It was acknowledged by all the novices at St Finbar's to be the most demanding and frustrating household charge given to the novices.

He opened the heavy door of the Feast Day Parlour and sighed. The smell of polish fumed up at him and he could take no delight, as he had at first done, in the spectacular views over the Italianate gardens to the artificial lake on the far side of the carved balustrade. Nor did the elaborate stucco work of the room please him. The Greek Keys and cherubs, once objects of awe to him, were now dust traps which he had to tickle each week with a feather duster borrowed from Brother Cuthbert, the kitchen supervisor. This he would lash to a long piece of garden cane and offer up to the stucco, like a soldier offering comfort on the point of his spear.

He shivered. Though only late October, the weather had turned cold and the wind was blowing frigid air into the stone of St Finbar's, where it whistled and sighed and settled in for the winter. He wished himself back in the hot and humid kitchen trying to be decent to Brother Henry. Then he changed his mind and wished himself at home in front of the fire with Mum watching 'Take Your Pick'. But he pushed the last temptation away. 'You will not give up! This is your only chance!' he told himself. He set about collecting his cleaning materials together.

The trouble with the Feast Day Parlour was that it never repaid the labour spent on it by smiling a clean smile. Like a spoilt princess it had been polished and primed and fussed over so much that it took all further ministrations dourly and pouted. For example, the floors had been so frequently waxed for so many years by so many Brothers, all out for jewels in spiritual crowns, that the polish polished polish. Once finished the floor only deigned to shine if not walked on. Every step left telltale footprints which would only disappear when given another fix of polish.

Brother Joachim had come to dread Feast Days because then the Brothers would tread all over the floor leaving it ravaged with sticky ground-in dust which was nearly impossible to get off.

He set about his work with a will, however. He must not expect satisfaction in this life, he told himself. Those who did would get little in the life to come. He offered up his frustrations for the Holy Souls and the heathens.

When the bell went for the end of the Great Silence, he was putting away the cleaning equipment. Straight away he set off for the Novices' Room for the first session of the day with Brother Edward, the Novice Master, known to all the Brothers as Novvy.

All the ten novices were seated when Brother Edward entered.

'All for Jesus!' said Brother Edward.

'Now and Forever!' responded the novices.

'Now before we get down to business, I have a couple of matters to draw to the attention of certain of the Brothers.'

Brother Joachim stiffened at once. He could have been back in the Hall at St Bede's with Brother Hooper about to deal a blow to some erring unfortunate. But then he looked up at Novvy sitting at his table facing the novices, and his apprehension disappeared. In his two months as a novice he had grown to like and respect the tiny bespectacled Brother who had sole charge of the novices during the year of the Canonical Novitiate. He could be hard but he was always fair and the twinkle in his eyes, amplified by a pair of half-moon, National Health glasses, was never absent. Brother Joachim's initial fear was just a knee-jerk reaction. He would get over it with effort.

'Brother Henry,' continued Novvy.

Brother Henry stood up. He sat in the front of the room in the row next to the window, just in front of Brother Egbert who was very brainy.

'Brother Henry, would you like to tell your fellow novices what you are wearing?'

Brother Ninian, seated immediately behind Brother Joachim giggled. All turned to smile at him. Brother Ninian was permitted giggles which in other novices would have received reprimands, because he had been nominated as the novice with the childlike heart, was headed in future life straight towards the kitchens rather than the classroom, and was thereby judged by different criteria.

'Thank you, Brother Ninian. Now I thought I had asked you to try and deal with that levity to which you are prey,' smiled Novvy.

'Yes, I'm sorry, Brother Edward. I keep forgetting.'

Novvy turned his attention to Brother Henry. 'What are you wearing, Brother?'

Brother Henry looked down and around himself to see if there was something wrong. Then he looked back at Novvy but said nothing.

Novvy asked him again.

'Er, I'm wearing a cassock, black shoes and socks, a stock, a collar, a belt . . .'

'And what are you wearing under that?'

Brother Henry reddened. He stammered, 'Vest. Underpants.' He ran out of items, and was then inspired. 'A crucifix on a cord.'

'And that is all?'

'I think so,' replied Brother Henry, hanging his head and reddening again.

'Well, the little bird must have been wrong then. The little bird told me you were wearing something else. But if you aren't, you may be seated, Brother.'

Brother Henry sat down slowly, but only for a moment. After a couple of seconds he bounced up again and shouted, 'I confess!'

Novvy regarded the flushed novice with a mixture of sorrow and disbelief. 'Oh, I see. You *are* wearing something else. Perhaps you would like to tell us what else you are wearing.'

Brother Henry closed his eyes, raised his head high as if standing before a firing squad waiting for the bang. After a long moment his contorted mouth spat out the words, 'A chain, Brother.'

Novvy did not seem distressed at the news. 'Where is this chain, Brother Henry?'

'Around my waist,' replied Brother Henry, Brother Joachim thought, at his theatrical best.

'Why?'

'I thought it would help me.'

'How did you think it would help you?'

'To mortify my flesh. If I don't mortify my flesh it will mortify me.'

'Well I suppose you've got a point there, Brother. But isn't the chain rather tight?'

'Yes, Brother.'

'And doesn't it hurt?'

'Yes.'

Novvy said in a rather tired voice, 'Go and take it off and bring it to me please, Brother.'

Brother Henry left the room abjectly. He returned carrying a heavy piece of chain which he gave to Novvy.

'It's still warm,' observed Novvy, gesturing Brother Henry to sit down. 'Now, Brothers, there you have an example of extremism,' said Novvy, 'and extremism is a great enemy to the Spiritual Life. I do realise that all you novices are of an impressionable age and get strange ideas about things. I know exactly where Brother Henry got his hairbrained idea for the chain. It was Matt Talbot, wasn't it, Brother?'

Brother Henry nodded. Brother Joachim remembered Matt Talbot. He was a Liverpool docker who had died in the odour of sanctity and had performed many penances on himself. He had tied a chain round his waist too. The only difference between Matt Talbot's chain and Brother Henry's was that Matt Talbot's had been revealed only after death and had been found to have buried itself beneath his flesh, so tightly did it contain his passions.

Novvy continued, 'All of you novices are starting out on a long spiritual journey. The journey is not full of drama and events of the kind you read about in the Lives of the Saints. You make a grievous error if you think it is. In the world people go to the pictures and have their heads filled with false ideas about life. They see Robert Mitchum driving round in a big car and they want one too. That is the way of the world. Envy abounds out there. But here in the monastery we must face other dangers, different, but no less damaging. The Devil is a subtle creature, perhaps the best wrought of all the Lord's creations. If he can't reach your soul in one way he'll reach it in another. Chains and whips and freezing showers, I believe, are the Devil's tools. You want to make the grand, dramatic gesture when a simple one will do.'

Novvy then turned his attention back to Brother Henry. 'For example, at breakfast today, Brother Henry, I could not help but notice how thickly you were spreading butter on your bread and then you added insult to injury by piling heaps of jam on top. In my view, you would have been better off cutting down on that. Better than any chain. Am I not right, Brother?'

'Yes, Brother,' replied Brother Henry.

'Good. Remember that chains are for locking doors. Make sure you're on the right side of that door, Brother.'

The novices laughed then.

'Open your Rule Books,' commanded Novvy. The laughter ceased.

Each novice kissed his green copy of the Brothers' Rule Book and opened it at the appropriate page.

Novvy read, 'Particular friendships between the Brothers are to be discouraged because they tend to erode the spirit of Universal Brotherly Love which should prevail in all the communities of the Order.'

Then, as always, each novice read the Rule in turn.

'To be honest with you, Brothers,' Novvy began, 'I never like dealing with this item in the Rule.' He looked out over the group. The Novices looked everywhere but back at Novvy because they knew exactly what he meant.

'Brother Joachim, what's a P. F.?'

Brother Joachim flushed crimson with guilt at once. 'A Particular Friend, Brother.'

'Have you got a particular friend, Brother?'

The class laughed. It was well known to all that Brother Joachim and Brother Ninian were inseparable.

'I, er, well I . . .' replied Brother Joachim tentatively.

Novvy smiled and looked down at the Rule while the rest of the Novices continued to giggle. Then he looked up and asked, 'Brother Ninian, do you have a P. F.?'

'Yes, Brother.'

'May I ask you who it is?'

'Brother Joachim, Brother.'

'I see.' Novvy turned his attention back to Brother Joachim: 'Did you hear that, Brother? Would you like to tell us if Brother Ninian's feelings are reciprocated?'

Brother Joachim at that moment felt that Brother Ninian was very far from being his P. F. But he could imagine Ninian's open face smiling without guile behind him. And that face, and the simple, decent fellow who inhabited it, melted him at once.

'Yes, Brother.'

'Good. Well done! Honesty puts the Devil to flight.'

Novvy looked down at the Rule and read it yet again. Then he asked all the other novices about their particular friendships.

It emerged that Brother Xavier's P. F. was Brother Anselm and vice versa; Brother Alban, a gangling lad from Newcastle, liked Brother Ralph best. Brother Ralph, however, insisted that he did not have a P. F., to the great discomfiture of Brother Alban. Brother Aiden's was Brother Bosco and Brother Bosco, who stuttered, stuttered that Brother Aiden was his. Brother Egbert denied repeatedly that he had a P. F. and was repeatedly believed.

Only Brother Henry remained. He thought for a long moment, then answered, 'My Lord and Saviour, Jesus Christ!'

'Very creditable, Brother,' said Novvy quietly but with a steely edge in his voice. 'That is what you are here for, to make Jesus your special friend. But I don't believe the Rule is concerned with your particular friendship with Jesus. No special favourites among the novices?'

'No, Brother.'

'You are sure?'

'Well maybe Brother Joachim, Brother.'

'Goodness gracious me!' exclaimed Novvy. 'Things are getting complicated!'

Brother Ninian dug Brother Joachim in the back but he did not respond.

'Well perhaps we have an example here of what the Rule is about. Although our Order is a mere four hundred years old, we have inherited the Rule from the Fathers of the Church, from Benedict, Dominic, Francis and Ignatius. There is much tried and tested wisdom in it, Brothers. Now it is natural that you should like some people more than others, but if that liking is too strong, it takes away from the love you owe all your Brothers and may interfere with your quest, which is and must always be, to become one with Christ. I think that is what the Rule is talking about.'

Novvy strode over to the window, where he stood looking out over the garden and the lake. 'Well, Brothers, it's cold out there, but it isn't raining. I think you should walk around the grounds for a while and meditate on the Rule we've looked at today. When I ring the bell come back here. All for Jesus!'

'Now and Forever!' responded the novices. They got up and filed out.

'Oh, gosh!' meditated Brother Joachim. 'What did Henry have to go and say that for?'

He was walking up and down in front of the east door of St Finbar's. He glanced up to look at Henry the Eighth glaring down from the tower. It did not seem right that the licentious monarch who caused England to lapse from the True Faith should be allowed to occupy such an exalted place in the monastery. Had not God shown what He had thought of Henry the Eighth by making his dead body leak out of the coffin? Brother O'Toole had said that they had to keep putting new coffins around the body until the dead king was encased in one of lead. But even then, Brother O'Toole had asserted, a terrible stench of putrefaction had pervaded the air – the very opposite of the odour of sanctity. God was telling all the benighted English Protestants what *He* thought of the Reformation! But they, being the ancestors of the Black and Tans, took not a blind bit of notice!

Indeed, there were moves afoot to have the statue torn down and one of Our Lady of Lourdes put up there instead. Expense was holding back this pious plan, however. Henry was in a difficult position. Hard to get at without cranes, scaffolding and much labour.

On each side of the Gothic Arch over the main entrance door, gargoyles had been carved. The left one showed a knight in a Norman helmet, a sword in his hand crossed by part of a right arm over his face and ready to strike out at the other gargoyle. This had been carved into a hapless Thomas Becket who cowered away from the stroke which was endlessly on the point of being administered.

Brother Joachim, who habitually chose this place for his meditations, often wanted to take an axe to the gargoyles. It did not seem fair to show Thomas Becket shrinking away from the blow of martyrdom. Martyrs did not shrink. They stood up straight like the soldier in 'Faithful Unto Death', and rolled their eyes heavenwards.

He pulled his mind back to the matter in hand. 'What am I doing with two P. F.s? Brother Henry only said that to get me into trouble and slander my name before men. No he didn't. Forgive me, Lord. I am unworthy.' He switched his attention to thoughts of Brother Ninian.

Their friendship had begun the year previously in the boarding school atmosphere of the Juniorate. There the emphasis had been not so much on spiritual matters as on getting everyone through 'O' level examinations and physically fit through daily doses of rugby and cross-country running.

Both Ninian and Benson had bed-wetting in common and had come together because the housekeeping Brother had made them wash out their sheets after breakfast each morning.

Had it not been for Ninian, Joachim did not think he would have made it through the first year away from home. He had been desperately unhappy at first.

The fat had quickly dropped off him under pressure from the daily sessions of hard physical effort. That was fine. But the struggle to conquer lapses against Holy Purity met with little success and he often found himself in the morning line for Confession waiting to stammer out his sin of the night before to a Franciscan priest who came in to say mass each morning. The priest had told him more than once that if he could not control his sexual urges then a life of chastity in the monastery was, perhaps, not for him. Maybe the Lord was telling him that a married life was what He wanted from him.

But if those sins did indeed convey any heavenly hints they did not nudge Benson towards matrimony but rather to deserted places where men in macks devoured his virtue and where hope died. Surely that could not be the fate to which the Lord was calling him? It was too horrible to contemplate.

Of course, he could never bring himself to tell the priest that. Each time he left the confessional he resolved to reform, but each time he fell and was back, shamefaced, in the line before too many mornings had passed.

But Brother Joachim, a year later, was happier than he had been for some time. He had passed five subjects at 'O' level; he had lost his fat and could run for miles without tiring; and, best of all, since starting at St Finbar's, he had not given way to one single sin against Holy Purity.

It had not required any effort on his part. Purity had

just happened. From his first hour in the building, feelings of awe at the surroundings and of the great step he would shortly be taking, managed what endless rounds of prayer and worry had been unable to do.

As the Novitiate year got under way, so concerned were all the novices to banish the tiniest imperfection from their spiritual lives that the idea of serious sin became almost unthinkable. The new worries were sins against charity, minor greeds, laziness and worldliness. Brother Joachim was still prone to all these things but the great trees of impure vice which had hidden the view had been felled – or, at any rate, cut back.

He pulled his mind back from the gargoyles to the matter in hand. Two P. F.s! No, that was not right. He had only one. Brother Henry was not his P. F. No, definitely not. He loved Brother Henry, of course. That was required. But not especially. Not particularly.

But was his relationship with Ninian getting between him and the full flowering of his spiritual life? Worse still, was it sexual? The thought chilled him. Then his mind wandered again and he did not recall it until the bell rang.

'So what have you decided?' Novvy looked round the room for a long moment before pointing to Brother Ninian.

'We're just good friends, me and Brother Joachim, Brother!'

'I see. Good friends but not particular friends, is that it?'

'Yes, Brother,' replied Brother Ninian.

'And you, Brother Henry,' said Novvy. 'Where do you stand now?'

'I have decided to root out my particular friendship for Brother Joachim and cast it from me.'

'And what does Brother Joachim think of all this?'

Joachim did not reply straight away. He was a trifle hurt. A mere half hour ago he had two novices vying for his special friendship. Now he had none. 'I don't really know,' he replied. 'To tell you the truth, I was very pleased that Ninian said he was my special friend. I like him very much and honestly don't think that our friendship gets in the way of our quest for Christ's love. Perhaps it helps us with the quest.'

Novvy nodded as if he agreed, but then he asked, 'But what about Brother Henry? You haven't mentioned him.'

'No, Brother.'

'Why not?'

'Well I'm fond of Brother Henry but he isn't a special friend.'

'And how do you think Brother Henry feels about this?'

'Er . . .'

'You see,' continued Novvy, 'we have some confusion here. Ninian and Joachim are just good friends. Brother Henry wants to be a special friend of Brother Joachim but can't. Well, you've just heard that he is going to try and root out this feeling, but that is going to take him a great deal of effort. Special human relationships, their development and their demise, take a great deal of effort. What the Rule is saying, I think, is that all your effort must go towards loving Jesus. You have no time for anything else. Do you understand?'

He turned his attention to the other novices in turn and pointed out the error of their ways. When he had finished, the group were silent and not a little uncomfortable.

Novvy smiled. 'OK. Manual work time. All for Jesus!'

'Now and Forever!' replied the depressed group of Novices.

'Come on, no long faces!' shouted Novvy as the group filed out.

Joachim tried to smile serenely as he made his way to the stables on the north side of the main building. There he changed out of his cassock, put on a pair of boots and collected garden tools which he piled into a wheelbarrow.

It had been his responsibility to look after the flower garden that had been set up against the south-facing wall of the balustrade. It grew mainly dahlias and gladioli to supply the altar of St Finbar's chapel. The garden stretched along the whole south-facing wall of the balustrade and was fenced off from the pastureland that led down to the stream and fed the artificial lake. In the field cattle grazed.

He set about weeding the garden, trying to clear his mind by repeating a psalm.

Then Brother Michael's old face appeared over the balustrade.

'Good morning, Brother!' he said.

Joachim murmured a greeting back, feeling guilty and anxious again.

Novices were only allowed to speak to other novices and the Novice Master. It was absolutely forbidden for any novices to speak to anyone else at all.

There were about fifteen other Brothers in training at St Finbar's, Brothers who had completed their novitiate and taken vows of Poverty, Chastity, Obedience, and Free Missionary Work with Youth. All these Brothers were out of bounds to the Novices, though some of them often tried to make contact and had to be repulsed politely but firmly. More troublesome were some of the older Brothers on the staff at St Finbar's. These seemed to be Brothers who had retired from teaching in the Brothers' schools or were at St Finbar's for reasons that were unclear.

Brother Michael was the worst offender at leading Novices astray. He was a thin, white-haired Irishman of about seventy and never let a Novice pass him without a smile. Joachim liked him for that but was terrified that Novvy would find out that he talked to him.

'How are you, Brother Joachim?' asked Brother Michael, leaning over the balustrade.

'Very well, Brother, thank you,' replied Joachim, keeping his eyes on his work and hoping that this would serve to discourage the other Brother. It did not have the desired effect, however.

'Look at me, Brother!' cried Brother Michael.

Joachim did so.

'Yes, you're the one all right!' said Brother Michael triumphantly.

'How do you mean, Brother?' asked Joachim, looking round for witnesses.

'The blue eyes. You're the one.'

'Am I?'

'There's no mistaking it. You're the talk of St Finbar's. Blue eyes to lead a saint astray!'

Joachim stuck his hoe into a dahlia tuber. He pulled it off and stuck it back into the ground, heeling it in and hoping it would not be ruined. Then he looked up at Brother Michael and said, 'Brother, I really shouldn't be talking to you. It's the Rule.'

'The Rule! The Rule! What is the Rule compared to those blue eyes!'

'Yes, but . . .'

'See those bulls?' asked Brother Michael, changing the subject as he often did.

'Yes?'

'Bulls serve cows.'

'How do you mean?'

'To get calves.'

Joachim said nothing. He felt embarrassment reddening his face.

'They can't manage it themselves very well. That's where Brother Luke comes in.'

'Is it?'

'Yes. Brother Luke has to take the bull's big thingy and aim it at the cow's hole. Brother Luke can look and do the necessary and it isn't a sin.'

Now it seemed to be Brother Michael's turn to become agitated. Leaning further and further over the balustrade, he looked to left and right before continuing, 'If you or I watched that sort of thing it would be a mortal sin. Even poor dumb beasts have a right to privacy, don't you know? And what is more, such a sight could inflame the passions. But Brother Luke's job it is to do that sort of thing so it's all right. Do you get my meaning?'

'Yes, Brother,' replied Joachim abjectly.

'Come closer, Brother,' commanded Brother Michael.

Joachim edged towards the balustrade a couple of paces while Brother Michael leaned still further over.

'Fiddling!' whispered Brother Michael.

Joachim's morale fell at his feet and was buried by the hoe.

'Brother Michael, I . . .'

'Don't try and tell me you haven't! Don't tell me that! With those eyes! You're the undoing of many a pious Brother in this monastery, Brother Joachim. It's the truth I am telling you. There's many a soul in this place wracked by the sight of your blue eyes! Don't tell me you didn't know!'

Grumpily Joachim prodded the soil and said nothing. He felt extremely depressed at that moment.

'You shouldn't be saying these things to me, Brother!' he managed.

'You shouldn't be saying these things to me, Brother!' mimicked Brother Michael unkindly. 'Sure, don't I know that! What are you going to do about it Brother Blue Eyes?'

Joachim lifted the hoe and shook it in the direction of Brother Michael. 'Stop it! Stop it! You're evil! Evil!'

'Evil am I?' gasped Brother Michael in a strangled whisper. 'Well let me tell you, Brother, that when you have been here as long as I have you can be forgiven a little bit of plain-speaking even if it is forbidden by the Rule!'

'So why do you stay here, Brother? Perhaps you belong back in the world!' countered Joachim boldly.

'No, Brother Blue Eyes. I'm in the right place! It's you who belong back in the world! There are people waiting out there for you. They've got their tongues hanging out waiting for a taste of you, so they have!'

He didn't say any more. His face disappeared from over the balustrade. Joachim looked up and saw only sky.

He returned to his work, upset and anxious again, only to hear Novvy's voice above him.

'There's a lot of weeding to be done, Brother. Still not to worry. With winter coming, it'll get easier.'

Joachim looked up and smiled. He hoped that the agitation he felt did not show.

'I see Brother Michael was giving you some advice about the flower beds. Don't take anything he says too seriously. He's no expert.'

Then Novvy too was gone.

Lunch was taken in silence in the novices' refectory.

Novvy sat at a table by himself and faced the long novices' table that stretched the length of the room. At the far end a wooden crucifix, almost life size, hung on the high Bath stone wall. On the table bowls of vegetables and boiled potatoes in their jackets steamed like incense.

Behind the lectern to Novvy's right, Brother Alban was reading the day's meditation. He would read throughout the meal and, only when everyone had finished, would he be free to eat his own meal. Each novice read at mealtimes for a week. He read:

'SEVENTH MEDITATION: HELL'

'PREPARATION
'One. Place yourself in the presence of God and humbly ask His help.

'Two. Imagine yourself in a city of gloom, a city of burning pitch and brimstone, a city whose inhabitants can never escape.

'CONSIDERATIONS

'One. Like those in this city, the damned are in the depths of hell, suffering unspeakable torments in every sense and member; having used their life to sin they suffer pain befitting their sin; eyes which looked on evil things will endure the awful vision of devils and of hell;

125

ears which delighted to hear evil conversations will listen forever to wailings and lamentations and cries of despair.'

Joachim nudged the potato on his plate with a fork, listening hard, thinking of Brother Michael. Brother Alban's reading, amplified by the high ceilings of the refectory, bombarded his ears. It confirmed his own worst fears. He tried to shut out the sound, to concentrate on his food. He cut the potato in half. The potato opened like a chocolate Easter egg but, inside, he found himself staring at black rotten flesh. Joachim dropped his knife on to his plate with a clatter that turned heads and caused Brother Alban to stumble in his reading. Joachim looked down at his dinner, and listened.

'Three. Consider that what makes hell intolerable is the fact that our suffering can never have an end. If a little tickle in your ear or a slight fever makes the night seem endless, how terrible that eternal night when afflicted with so many sufferings! An eternal night which gives birth to eternal despair and frenzied blasphemies without end.'

Joachim was still staring at the plate. Brother Alban's echoing voice had become a drum beat and he saw himself marching in time down a wide road which led straight into the hottest part of hell. Then the rotten potato blurred as the tears began to fall. He became immediately embarrassed and quickly started to eat the potato, forcing it down as a penance, as a purge.

'So ends the reading from "Introduction to the Devout Life" by St Francis De Sales.' Brother Alban closed the book and opened another: 'Period Piece' by Gwen Raverat. He read on, describing cosy lives in turn-of-the-century Cambridge, but Brother Joachim could not banish hell from his head so easily.

He felt that his new feeling of safety in the monastery was an illusion. Satan could penetrate even here and, in the form of a leering old man's face, turn him back towards a seemingly inevitable fall. For what Brother

Michael had hissed at him that morning had thrilled him in the same way that long-buried memories of gun emplacements at home could thrill him. For sure Brother Michael was Satan's tool.

The thought alarmed him almost to the point of panic. Satan had found him, even here among the Bath stone and the beautiful gardens. He looked over towards Novvy, who sat contentedly chewing alone at his table, listening to Gwen Raverat's words and obviously enjoying them. Joachim wanted to get up and run to Novvy and bury himself in his arms. Instead, he stayed where he was and wondered about Brother Michael.

Perhaps he was Joachim in fifty years' time. Perhaps he would be like Brother Michael then! He would be the one hanging round the boys' toilets at some school in the hope of corrupting some child with blue eyes. Between Joachim now and Joachim then lay merely fifty years of failure to conquer passion and sin.

Truly he and Brother Michael were at different ends of the same boat plying its way inexorably towards the abyss. He had no reason to feel self-righteous and superior to the older Brother. He was no innocent. He could not say that he had been corrupted by the men he had played with. In some ways his need had been greater than theirs. No, Satan was everywhere: in himself, in Brother Michael, in Ninian's pretty face, in the whole of Creation. Everyone and everything teetered on the brink of a chasm. The ocean of Time eroded the ground on which they stood. Hell would get them in the end.

He shook.

'Is anything wrong, Brother?' asked Novvy.

Brother Joachim, sitting rigid behind a stewed pear bathed in custard, replied, 'No, Brother. I'm fine.'

'Are you ill?' continued Novvy. 'You haven't finished your pudding. That isn't like you.'

'I er . . .' said Brother Joachim.

Novvy led Brother Joachim along the cloister and into the Novices' Room.

'You can help me get the music ready for this evening,'
he said as they walked.

The other novices were busy cleaning up after lunch.
Then they would go to the chapel to read 'Self-
Abandonment to Divine Providence', a text which gener-
ally led to self-abandonment to a post-prandial snooze.

Novvy took a key from the pocket of his cassock and
unlocked the cupboard under the window that held a
large collection of L.P. records. He crouched down and
peered along the stack of records. At last he selected a
boxed set and pulled it out.

'I think this will do for tonight.'

Brother Joachim read WAR REQUIEM on the front
of the box in large white letters on a deeply black
background. The letters seemed to dance in their
whiteness.

'It's by Benjamin Britten!' exclaimed Joachim.

'Yes, you liked the last one by him we listened to,
didn't you?'

'Yes, I did.' The piece had been 'Noye's Fludde'. All
the novices had enjoyed it. 'It was full of good tunes. I
especially liked the mice and Mrs Noye.'

In fact he often found himself singing and whistling the
tunes from it during the day. Occasionally he wished
himself alone in the front room with the mirror. There he
would have really been able to give full expression to the
music. Still, in the circumstances, whistling was almost
enough.

Novvy started polishing each of the two records of
'War Requiem' in turn.

He handled the shining records as reverently as the
priest handled the host.

'This one will make you weep, Brother,' said Novvy.

'Will it, Brother?'

Novvy nodded. 'It made me weep, Brother. I heard the
first performance on the wireless a few years ago.
Brother Michael and I were in the Brothers' Parlour.
We were both weeping like a couple of girls. It's a very
sad and wonderful piece of music, Brother.'

The idea of Novvy and Brother Michael howling by a wireless struck Joachim as funny.

'You're laughing! You can't imagine an old man like me crying!'

'Yes. No,' replied Joachim.

'Do you cry easily, Brother?'

'Well I . . . I try not to.'

'Why were you so upset at lunch?'

Joachim looked at the cover of the records. 'War Requiem' danced in the darkness.

'Did the reading about hell upset you?'

'Yes, a bit,' confessed Joachim.

Novvy sighed. 'I sometimes think we take you novices too early away from your families.' He replaced the records carefully in their transparent plastic covers. 'All that talk of hell! St Francis De Sales is not one of my favourites I tell you, Brother. Enough to put anyone off their food. Did it scare you, Brother?'

'Yes.'

'Well a bit of fear is no bad thing. It can nudge us in the Lord's direction. But too much fear is a great enemy to the spiritual life. Above all things, Brother, you must seek to love Jesus as a Friend. He knows your weaknesses. If you fail sometimes – and who doesn't? – you will not fall into hell. You wouldn't send a friend to hell. Jesus won't sent His Friends to hell either. You do believe me, don't you, Brother?'

Joachim did not know whether or not he believed Novvy. He had started to cry again as Novvy spoke. More than anything else, he wanted to be held tightly by Novvy and to tell him everything that was on his mind and hold nothing back.

He was slowly edging over towards Novvy when Novvy asked, 'Is there anything you want to tell me?'

Joachim wept on for a long moment, trying desperately to think what to answer. Had Novvy at that moment touched him, he would have been released. The touch would have been like the dove coming to Noye's ark. It would have been the signal that released all the fearsome creatures that lurked in his brain, fowling it, crowding it – into the full light of a New Day. He saw the animals bounding free away from Ararat, dispersed, harmless, leaving him alone in the heights to sing 'Hosanna'.

But Novvy did not touch him and Joachim saw Novvy seated with Brother Michael by the wireless in the Brothers' Parlour, weeping to 'War Requiem'. He could not tell him. He just could not. It was impossible. And, as he made the decision, he knew that he would surely live to regret it.

'No, Brother. Thank you.'

'Right you are. You'd better go and join the other novices in the chapel. It will be time for cross-country soon. You've got "War Requiem" to look forward to. Try to be cheerful, Brother. All for Jesus!'

'Now and Forever!' replied Brother Joachim.

In the chapel the novices were bent low over their copies of 'Self Abandonment to Divine Providence'. Quietly and carefully, he manoeuvred himself past Brother Ninian who was slobbering on to his book as he slept. He hardly stirred at the disturbance.

Joachim opened the book at his place, marked by a picture of St Thérèse. He read for a while but could not concentrate. The book had no good bits at all – no martyrdoms; no miracles; nothing at all to get excited about.

He closed the book and gazed up at the tabernacles on the altar, seen between the lolling heads of Brother Bosco and Brother Aiden. Behind the red curtains, he knew, dwelt God. There could be no doubt of it. Behind the locked door, cradled quietly in the dark and the silence, dwelling in the white bread of the Host, was the Body, Blood, Soul and Divinity of Jesus, his Best Friend and Only Hope.

He stared at the tabernacle unblinkingly. He repeated, 'Help me!' until Novvy came into the chapel quietly and told the novices that it was time for cross-country running.

*   *   *

And it was wonderful to run and not to tire. Then it was wonderful to tire but not to have to stop running.

The dying autumn leaves crackled beneath his feet as he ran down the footpaths. The trees in a canopy above his head seemed to race past him, dissolving into fantastic shapes as they disappeared behind him into memory. Behind them the sky was as blue as Mary's mantle. Late birds fled from the path as Joachim sped towards them.

He was alone now. Other novices ran ahead and others behind. He had carved out a place between the groups. In no time at all his mood had lifted. He felt cheerful and well, just a running body, aware of who he was, but only in a general, unworrying way. He looked at himself from afar and was happily unable to focus on the details which might startle him.

After twenty minutes he came to the hollow tree, an elm, and stopped running. He took up his station in the tree, like a soldier on guard. There, hidden, he let the other novices pass and waited for Ninian.

He had to wait over five minutes and was beginning to get cold. The sun had dropped in the sky and a premonition of how cold it would become once it had set came over him, making him shiver in anticipation.

Then Ninian came straight to his hiding place. 'I thought you might not be here!' he said.

'Why? I always wait here, don't I?'

Ninian smiled. 'Yes, you do. It was silly of me to worry but you were upset today, weren't you? I thought that maybe you wouldn't want to stop today.'

Joachim punched Ninian in the arm. 'You know I'd never leave you to run back by yourself.'

Ninian rubbed the spot where he'd been punched as if he were buffing a campaign medal. 'Yes, but with all this talk of P.F.s and you getting upset at lunch, I thought you'd be angry with me. You aren't, are you?'

'No, I'm not angry with you.'

'Well, that's good.'

They headed off through the wood along a path they knew, a short cut which would bring them out close to St

Finbar's. They would be way behind everyone else, but not so far as if they had taken the full route, and close enough that no questions would be asked.

Ninian took Joachim's hand and they walked on for a while in silence, synchronising their paces. Then Ninian asked, 'Joachim, do you understand that "Self Abandonment to Divine Providence"?'

'Some of it, yes.'

'I can't understand a word.'

'That's because you fall asleep.'

'Yes, that's true.'

'Make an act of contrition.'

Ninian did so.

'O my God, because Thou art so good, I am very sorry that I have sinned against Thee; and, by the help of Thy Grace, I will not sin again.'

'Good.'

Ninian squeezed Joachim's hand hard and was startled when Joachim pulled it away.

'What's the matter?'

'You shouldn't do that!'

'I was only playing. We're like David and Jonathan, aren't we?'

'Yes, I know, I'm sorry, Ninian.' But he did not take the other boy's hand again. They walked along the footpath keeping a space between them.

At last Ninian asked, 'So tell me, what's been happening? I've been worried about you. And when you've told me your news I'll tell you mine.'

'No, you tell me yours first,' said Joachim sulkily.

'All right. But first you must promise that if I tell you mine you will tell me yours straight afterwards.'

Joachim took a deep breath and then sighed, 'Oh all right . . .'

'Well, Brother Ralph was talking to me during washup.'

'He shouldn't have been.'

'Well he was . . . anyway, he says that one of the novices is leaving!'

'No! Who?'

'He wouldn't say, but I think it might be Henry.'

Joachim made a face. 'Henry! He's the last one who would leave. What would become of his sanctity then? No, you're wrong.'

Ninian pursed his lips and kicked at a pile of dead leaves in the path. Then he brightened and said: 'Well, that's my news. How about yours?'

Then it was Joachim's turn to kick dead leaves: 'I don't think I can tell you.'

'But you promised!'

'Well ... you know I told you about my Great Temptation . . .'

'Yes, and I told you it was just a stage.'

'Well temptation has penetrated the monastery. The Devil has found me even here.'

'The Devil's good at that. But how do you mean?'

'Brother Michael's been talking to me.'

'Only talking! He pinches me whenever he gets near me!'

Joachim stared at Ninian. 'He does what?'

'He pinches me and strokes my hair too if I let him.'

'And do you let him?'

'Well I don't stop him. He calls me "My little angel with the brown eyes and the blond hair". He says I've been sent to the monastery to give light to his declining years.'

'He doesn't!'

'He does!' replied Ninian matter-of-factly.

'And what do you do?'

'Nothing.'

'You don't!'

'Well, what am I supposed to do?'

Joachim did not know what to reply. Instead he got down on to his knees on the path and motioned Ninian to do likewise. After some hesitation Ninian joined him.

Joachim gazed upwards through the autumnal canopy of trees to the sky, and past the sky to heaven. There in his imagination sat Christ and His Mother on their thrones looking depressed at what was taking place on the footpath near St Finbar's. Behind them Benson saw a bearded St Joachim whispering conciliatory words into Mary's ear. But Mary had a sad face, probably due to the fact that Her blessed heart had a dagger right through it. Joachim knew that it was the sins of the world that had placed that dagger there and that now he and Ninian had given it a cruel three hundred and sixty degree twist.

After making sure that Ninian's head was bowed, Joachim bowed his own.

'O blessed St Joachim, please ask your Holy Daughter, our Blessed Mother, Mary, to intercede for us with your Grandson, her Blessed Immaculately Conceived Son, Jesus, who, for our sins, suffered an excruciating death on Calvary for our sakes, to please look down with pity upon Ninian and I, two erring sheep who totter on the brink of the everlasting bonfire, and grant us the strength to resist manfully the wiles of our great enemy, Satan, for we know that without your help, we will inexorably be lost and consigned to the depths of hell for all eternity. Amen,' prayed Brother Joachim.

'St Ninian, pray for us!' added Ninian, somewhat more succinctly.

For a long moment Joachim stayed where he was, eyes cast down, hands joined devoutly in front of him.

Ninian broke the spell. 'You're getting as bad as Henry,' he said.

Joachim chose to ignore the remark. 'Come on, let's run. We're going to be late.'

Ninian stood watching Joachim running away along the footpath. The tower of St Finbar's could be seen in the distance through the trees. But Brother Ninian did not attempt to follow him. Instead he shouted, 'You don't really love Jesus, Brother Joachim! For you He's just another bully! You're scared stiff of Him! You can't be His friend if you're scared! You can't be anybody's friend if you're scared!'

But, if Joachim heard his friend's shout, he did not let on. His thoughts were still fixed on the depressed trinity behind the sky.

*　　　*　　　*

The novices showered after cross-country, wearing for modesty's sake voluminous black bathing costumes kept in a bin near the showers for that purpose and used communally. Then they said the rosary outside, walking round and round the building, through the gardens, with Novvy leading the prayers and striding out in his aged, shining black boots.

There then followed a Bible Study class which led to a bread-and-butter tea. When the tea things had been washed up, a twenty-minute recreation period was allowed.

Joachim walked into the Novices' Room. He saw that Ninian was sitting at his desk chatting to Brother Aiden. He did not want to talk to Ninian and looked around for other company. Brother Egbert was by himself, writing in a note-book, Brother Egbert was usually by himself.

It occurred to Joachim that he could kill two birds with one stone by going over to talk with Brother Egbert: he could do a good deed by talking to the novice whom everyone found to be heavy going; and he could show Ninian that he was not pleased with him.

However, any satisfaction he may have felt soon paled when confronted by the actuality of twenty minutes of Brother Egbert's conversation.

After five minutes of agony, listening to Brother Egbert expounding on the merits of the Douai Translation of the Bible over the King James Version, Joachim made an excuse and left.

He fled back to Ninian, made friends with him and spent the rest of the time swopping Holy Pictures. The time flew by.

It was ten p.m. The novices sat in a semi-circle around Novvy who presided over the Black Box stereo player. It was an unheard-of time for them to be still up. Not since the day trip to Walsingham had the novices been up so late.

Novvy read from the libretto the conclusion of 'Strange Meeting'.

135

He did not say anything else. He knew his audience and knew that the music was moving, teaching some of them; felt that he had sown a seed for music that would last for life. He had given short introductions to each section of 'War Requiem' and then left the music to work its magic.

He looked from face to face of the group of novices in front of him. They were just children, he thought. It would be his tenth group, and over the years he had been saddened that so few of the youngsters who thought they had a vocation to be a Brother had managed to continue as far as Final Vows. The vast majority would leave long before they took those last binding vows. Then what would happen to them?

Side four of the work began. The orchestra, chorus and Soprano started the 'Libera Me' and the room shook with the sound. Novvy wondered for a moment what the rest of the Brothers trying to sleep upstairs would make of the loud music coming from the Novices' Room. But he decided they would just have to offer it up. A novice, the first from this group, was leaving tomorrow; a novice for whom he had been unable to feel much affection and one whom he knew would quickly fall away. Still, he would leave him with a few memories to hold on to. This 'War Requiem' would be one of those memories. What would become of the kid once back in the world? If what he heard from the Brothers was anything to go by, for a few months he would stand out and be conspicuous for his piety. Then, slowly but surely, the world would take its toll. A reaction would set in. The detailed knowledge of the Church he had gained in the Novitiate would be used to argue against that Church. He would need to gain popularity with his sceptical schoolmates. He might even lapse from the Faith completely. Now most of them did not know who they were or what they were. Trying to keep them sober and moderate, to banish their youthful tendencies towards extremes, was an uphill, no, an impossible, task. He had done his job as well as he could because he had vowed to obey.

The tenor had begun to sing 'Strange Meeting'. Novvy looked over at Joachim. The tears were rolling down his cheeks. He had attempted to cover them at first but now was weeping unashamedly. The lad needed to weep, Novvy thought. It was a pity that his mother was not there to be wept upon. He knew that something was eating into the kid which he could not understand or deal with. He wished he could. Whatever it was that was consuming him would just have to consume him. Perhaps he could come out on the other side cleansed.

The music was coming towards its conclusion. He prayed that the lads in front of him, no matter where they ended up, would continue to search. One or two of them, he knew, were on the right path already, had chosen right first time. But the rest? They would have to unpack and repack many times before their quest was through. Some would not have the strength and would settle for the path of least resistance.

The music faded away and left a silence hanging in the air of the Novices' Room which seemed to spread through the fabric of the building in waves and out towards the world beyond its gates.

'Let us sleep now . . . All for Jesus!'

'Now and Forever!' replied the novices and they left in silence.

The Great Silence had taken effect for another night at St Finbar's.

Joachim lay down to sleep on the narrow bed in his cell. He crossed his arms over his breast and prayed the prayers of his childhood. He blessed everyone he could think of; wished eternal rest to all the dead who came to mind and finally made an Act of Contrition, examining his conscience scrupulously.

Then, as instructed by Novvy, he set himself to thinking of the Four Last Things: Death; Judgement; Heaven; Hell.

He saw himself dying with weeping Brothers all around him. His eyes were wide open and he pointed towards the ceiling. The Brothers followed his gaze. Then he fell back in a swoon. Everyone in the room was moved to tears. An odour of roses pervaded the room and the snow-white dove of Joachim's soul flew up, straight as a stick, from his remains and through the ceiling. The Brothers were impressed and placed a cross between his whitening hands. The cross was seen to glow.

Then he saw himself laid out in a glass sarcophagus. His body was refusing to decay like other bodies. A blissful smile which moved all who saw it played about his dead lips. Brother Ninian stood by the sarcophagus saying, 'Surely he is in heaven with the Lord! I was the P. F. of a saint!' All the other Brothers nodded their heads.

Next Joachim switched his attention to Judgement. He saw himself on his knees in front of Jesus, His Holy Mother and St Joachim. St Joachim was saying, 'Sure, 'tis true he was a little bit on the impure side when he was a youth, but forget that! Rather think of all those years of work in the missions! Did he not convert the Shona tribe to Christianity? Have we not been besieged by the prayers of those poor ex-heathens! Daughter, as your father, I command you to appeal to your Son to have mercy on Brother Joachim and let him into heaven immediately.' Mary whispered something into Jesus' ear. Jesus nodded and it was all fixed. Joachim got up from his knees, the great doors of heaven swung open and Joachim walked in to be greeted by Grannie, Mum, Dad, and all the other people he had loved and prayed for and saved from perdition by his prayers and good works.

Thus did Joachim dispose of Death and Judgement.

Heaven came next. Heaven was wonderful. Mars Bars hung from the trees. You could pick as many as you liked and pay nothing and no one would say, 'Haven't you had enough?' Rivers flowed down gentle green hills, but instead of water there flowed Dandelion and Burdock. Great white clouds scudded across the blue sky but never obscured the sun. And on these clouds sat

Happy Souls singing, 'How Beautiful are the Feet' and 'Strange Meeting' and 'Dies Irae'. They could control the clouds in the same way that the Mekon could control his vehicle. They laughed and called their congratulations to Joachim who at once found a cloud for himself and joined them in playing in the ether. It was wonderful. He could swoop down on one of the Dandelion and Burdock streams and siphon up the Ambrosia without moving. He drifted over idyllic pastures and saw Fluffy A, Fluffy B, Fluffy C and Hilda, the three rabbits and a cat he had buried in early childhood, gambolling over the fields and smiling up at him. So they had been saved after all! The prayers he had said while Dad shovelled the sod on top of them had not been in vain! It was heaven! In the evening, Jesus and Mary took a walk around heaven to see how everyone was getting along. They had a word for everyone and never left anyone out. They asked questions about relatives still on Earth and seemed interested in the answers. They nodded and waved like the Queen and the Duke of Edinburgh – but were ten times more sincere. St Joachim would often come for a ride on Joachim's cloud. It was a tight fit when he did because, of course, Guardian Angel Tom was there too. It was wonderful. Wonderful.

Joachim had to pull himself out of heaven and into hell. This was prompted by a question from St Joachim: 'Whatever happened to that big lad, Bruno?' The question forced Joachim out of heaven straight away. Yes, what had happened to Bruno?

He approached the great black door that led to hell. He took hold of the latch. It was searingly hot to the touch. Joachim tugged and the door slowly opened. It was like standing too close to the fire in the lounge but, worse than the heat, were the cries emanating from the wrecked, wretched, souls at the bottom of the steps.

A devil with horns, a snake's tongue, a dragon's tail and a fork in his hand, asked him what he wanted. Joachim said, 'I am saved. You can't touch me. My soul is without spot. I call your attention to the notice on my back which says SAINT, in case you cannot read. I've just come here for a look around.' The devil raised his arms high and shook. He cowered back from Joachim's washday-white soul and retreated into the sulphurous murk. Joachim, his courage repaired after the pleasing confrontation with the creature of Satan, started to walk down the hot steps into Hell. A blast of cool, green-sward air surrounded him. He passed lost souls by the hundred, all going through the most dreadful tortures being administered by a willing staff of devilish tor-turers. He spotted Diana Dors. 'Novvy said you would end up here for exciting men's passions!' Joachim told her. She screamed at him but Joachim was moved to compassion and breathed cool air on her. 'God bless you!' exclaimed Diana Dors. He passed Alma Cogan too. She said nothing but Joachim gave her some of his cool air as well. 'I wish I hadn't sung all those immoral songs!' she told him. 'I bet you do!' replied Joachim. And he moved on.

'You don't happen to have someone here called Bruno Tencer, do you?' Joachim asked a devil.

'Bruno Tencer! We certainly do! Come and behold!'

The devil led Joachim along miles of subterranean passages. They passed Nikita Khrushchev drinking molten steel from a ladle. He was saying that he did what he did for the People but his torturer just said, 'Yes. Yes. Drink!' At last they came to a place that was almost too hot for Joachim's Air Conditioning to deal with. And there was Bruno. A devil kept applying a red hot branding iron to Bruno's private parts and Bruno screamed.

'I'm sorry!' said Joachim to Bruno.

'You're sorry!' answered Bruno. 'It's all your fault!'

'Now that's not strictly true, Bruno. You did have free will! You didn't have to continue along the path to perdition. You don't get sent here by accident, you know!'

'Yes, but it was you got me started! I was never the same after The Rude Club. I became a slave to my passions and couldn't stop. I didn't have your advantages!'

That seemed reasonable enough. 'That's true,' opined Joachim. 'Still, it was not easy for me to conquer my passions, you know. If I, a weak vessel if ever there was one, can do it, then you could have done it too.'

'Well, I didn't,' replied Bruno, rubbing himself where the devil had been branding him. 'But look, you couldn't put in a word for me with God, could you?'

'I'm afraid not. You know that hell is final. If you were in purgatory I could, perhaps, do something for you. I could earn a Plenary Indulgence for you and you'd be OK. But now you're in hell and hell is for all eternity. For ever and ever and ever and ever.'

'How do you mean?'

Joachim recalled how he had explained eternity to the Shona tribe. 'Well, let me put it this way: imagine a desert place. It is as flat as a pancake. To this desert place, once every one hundred billion years, a bird brings a tiny grain of sand. In the time it takes for that bird to bring enough grains of sand to build a billion billion mount Everests . . . that is one second of eternity. Do you get my drift?'

Bruno's chin began to quiver. 'But that's a dreadfully long time!'

He started to cry. Bruno's devil said to Joachim, 'Well I think it is a bit much myself.'

'How dare you!' exclaimed Joachim.

'I dare because I have nothing to lose. If you ask me it seems unreasonable to condemn a fellow to hell forever. I mean, God is Infinite Justice, I'll grant you that. What I want to know is: where does His Infinite Justice end and His Infinite Love begin? Bruno here isn't a bad sort of chap and yet here he is condemned to torture for ever and ever and ever. Just doesn't seem fair. I mean he wasn't a Hitler or anything. He just liked to play about with blokes from time to time. He was married and had kids, did you know that? Was a wonderful father by all accounts. Yet here he is. Doesn't seem right.'

Joachim decided to ignore the devil. He turned his

attention back to Bruno. 'Look, Bruno, nobody could be more sorry than I that you have ended up in the everlasting bonfire. If there was anything I could do to alleviate your sufferings, believe me, I would do it. But . . .'

'I don't believe you!' shouted Bruno. 'Tell that to Eric! He's having a worse time than me!'

Joachim was startled. 'Eric! He isn't here too, is he?'

'Yes, he is!'

'Why?'

'Eric,' spat back Bruno, 'was worse than I ever was! At least I got married and had children! Eric started wearing ladies' dresses and using Max Factor. He was the first Methodist to have a sex change. He married a Russian wrestler and died in a toilet!'

'No!' exclaimed Joachim. 'Say it isn't true!'

'It's as true as I'm standing here. His sister, Rosemary, told me. Yes, she's here too. She got killed while riding her bicycle without lights.'

'Well that doesn't surprise me. But Eric! I must see him.'

'I'm sure he'll enjoy that!' scoffed Bruno.

Joachim left Bruno. He had been about to say: 'I'll pray for you,' but didn't. There seemed little point.

Down endless festering passages Joachim walked with his accompanying devil. They passed Hitler being dismembered and put together again and dismembered again.

'Well, what can you expect?' Joachim told him.

At last, around a corner, quite suddenly, Joachim found himself face to face with Eric.

He was as small as he had always been and he was whimpering like a baby as his devil hammered nails into his ears, into his skull, into his legs, into his chest.

'Stop it!' cried Joachim.

'All right. But just for a while,' said the devil.

Eric continued to whimper.

'Is that you, Eric? It's me, Joachim.'

'Get them to stop! Please get them to stop!' pleaded Eric.

142

'I can't get them to stop, Eric. You are in hell, Eric. You must realise what that means?'

'I do! Oh, I do! But please! Enough is enough! Make them stop! It wasn't my fault! I couldn't help it! After The Rude Club I was never the same. I tried to be good I really did. But it was too strong for me to resist. I started listening to Alma Cogan records and watching Robert Mitchum films. I got excited by John Wayne in "The Quiet Man". The bit where his shirt gets all wet in the rain. I just couldn't get it out of my mind! I wanted to be Maureen O'Hara so much! I got dressed up in the winter curtains in summer and the summer curtains in winter and paraded myself in front of the mirror. I didn't know it would lead here. I didn't know. The Minister never told me it was like this. I thought I'd be given a ticking off and that would be that. Please, go back to heaven and tell them I didn't know!'

Joachim sighed. 'Well you know I would if I could but, as you see, the Catholic Church was right all along and you Methodists were wrong all along. Of course, being as I am, a Saint, I do feel compassion for you, Eric. I always knew you were a weak vessel. I never dreamed you would end up here! Believe me, if it was in my power to help, there is nothing I would rather do. You do believe me, don't you?'

Eric became angry. 'No, I don't believe you! You Catholics are all the same! You don't care what happens to us poor Protestants.'

Joachim shrugged and said to his devil: 'I do not think there is anything further to be gained. I will return to heaven now, thank you.'

He walked back along the endless passages of hell with Eric's screams echoing in his head. But what could he do? That was how it was.

That was enough of the four Last Things, Joachim told himself.

His cell consisted of a curtained off section of a large room. He shared it with three other novices: Henry,

Aiden and Egbert. Joachim's cell had a window set into the foot-thick walls of the monastery. The window was slim and tall, ending in a Gothic Arch. He looked through the window and tried to count the stars outside in the moonless sky. He failed in his attempt and remained as wide awake as before.

From Brother Aiden's cell he heard the sound of scratching. Poor Brother Aiden was a martyr to eczema and nightly scratched it in his sleep. At first Joachim had thought that Aiden was giving way to taking pleasure in the irregular motions of the flesh. He had been greatly relieved to learn that such was not the case and that Aiden was simply an eczema sufferer.

But what about Bruno and Eric? Devoutly Joachim prayed that his meditation had not been prophetic. He decided that his meditation had been a sign. He got up out of bed and knelt down next to it on the hard wooden floor. He raised his arms, cruciform, level with his shoulders and began to pray at the piece of heaven visible through the window of his cell.

Then, with an ache spreading through his arms, he stayed mute, looking at the stars. He remained thus until he could stand the pain no longer. Stiffly, he got up and went back to bed.

But still sleep would not come and he did not know what to do. After some time he heard footsteps coming towards the room along the long corridor. They were Novvy's footsteps. Perhaps he was checking that everyone was asleep. Joachim turned over.

The footsteps got louder. Novvy came into the room and pulled aside the curtain of Brother Aiden's cell. Joachim heard, 'Wake up! It's time to go!' Then the footsteps retreated and all he could hear were the sounds of Brother Aiden moving about. These went on for a long time and then he heard Aiden's footsteps disappearing down the corridor.

Silence returned and Joachim wondered what it could all mean. He did not get up to find out. At last he fell asleep. He dreamed of Bruno at the back of the Prom and woke up sticky and ashamed.

Brother Aiden's cell was stripped bare. His statue of The Little Flower was gone, the bedclothes had been piled up on top of the bed. Brother Aiden had left the Novitiate!

'Many are called but few are chosen!' whispered Brother Henry as he wiped the dishes that Joachim washed.

'Yes, but I never expected Brother Aiden would go.'

'Didn't you?' asked Henry knowingly.

'No, I didn't. He's the last one I would have expected. Look at his devotion to The Little Flower.'

'Well, if you ask me, he was a little too devoted to The Little Flower. Don't forget, Brother Joachim! Our God is a jealous God,' replied Henry.

Joachim was not convinced but decided not to continue the conversation, which was, anyway, strictly against the Rule.

That morning Novvy, sensing the unease at the unexpected departure of Brother Aiden, did not conduct a class. Instead the novices were treated to a recording of the 'Fantasia on a Theme by Thomas Tallis'. The music worked its magic on Joachim. It emptied his brain of distracting thought as nothing else could and transported him back to his heavenly cloud, swooping and passing streams of wonderful ice-cold Dandelion and Burdock. He knew that this would be the music of heaven. He would sit on his cloud with a Black Box playing 'Fantasia on a Theme by Thomas Tallis' at full volume. Who could want for anything more?

When the music had finished, Novvy sat down at his desk and said, 'You will have noticed that Brother Aiden is no longer with us. He has decided that he does not have a vocation to be a Brother. Now many of you may feel that it is sad that he must leave us without our saying "Farewell and God speed" to him. But that is how it must be. That is what is required by the Rules of the Canonical Novitiate. I myself wish it were not so. But there you are. You can best express your feelings for Brother Aiden by praying for him. He may have lost his vocation to be a Brother but this does not mean that he has lost his vocation to be a good Catholic. So, Brothers, pray that Aiden may find happiness and the love of the Lord out in the World. Now get changed for Manual. All for Jesus!'

'Now and Forever!' answered the nine novices.

Brother Michael had been watching from his office window for the approach of Joachim. His work on St Finbar's accounts was a trial to him and he looked for any form of diversion. Joachim would do. Would do nicely.

He scowled down at the bread bill and wondered how the novices could manage to eat so much. 'We'll be in the Poor House if this goes on,' he told himself. 'Still, that's not my worry.'

Brother Luke passed the window and gave Michael a cheery wave but he was gone before Michael could return it. He was left looking at the hand he had been about to wave, now poised in front of his eyes. What had happened to that hand? It was blotchy and gnarled, the blue veins mushy and meandering all over it. He could even see veins on his fingers and count the weak pulse on his wrist.

With the hand he tried to wave away the thought. So he was old. Wasn't that what the Brothers prayed for? To grow old in Grace and to die and start on Real Life. Life here below was a cruel exile from all that was wonderful, was it not? He had entered the monastery over fifty years ago believing that. Why then did he feel so let down?

The young novices moved him in a way he did not understand. In scary ways, in ways that made him want to weep. He was moved by them as he was moved by the sight of Brother Luke's bullocks being taken off to the slaughter house in the wagon. The novices, like them, were trusting and young and . . . and . . .

He pushed the last thought away with his old hand. It was a sin to entertain such a thought. Worse, the thought made nonsense of his whole life. He pushed the thought out of his brain again and straight away it was back and articulated: they, like he had been, were about to start living a lie. There was no God. He knew it as sure as he knew that the livestock would end up as bleeding carcasses in the Butcher's shop.

So why had he become a Brother? It was expected. He had been a younger son. The farm went to the eldest. Big sister, Maureen, had gone off like a lamb to the Carmelites and had only ever been seen through a grille mouthing clichés which always began 'Please God' or 'Thank God'.

His brother, Liam, had gone off to be a priest. It was not thought that he had had the ability for that. The Brothers were the logical alternative.

He had been proud to go away. His parents had been as pleased as punch! Three children given to God. It was cast-iron insurance for them. Heaven was theirs for their sacrifice. And much admiration while they lived from the other villagers.

He looked out of the window and saw Joachim wheeling his barrow towards the Chapel garden. He knew nothing about the lad but knew that, if that lad were going to follow him down the desert track of his life, he would at least do it with his eyes open.

Brother Michael slammed the accounts ledger shut and left the office in search of converts.

Joachim was not surprised when Brother Michael appeared above him on the balustrade. He had been expecting him and had worked out what he would say. But Michael spoilt his plans by saying, 'Now before you get all hoity-toity, Brother Joachim, let me tell you that I have your best interests at heart.'

Joachim did not know what to say. Michael jumped into the gap.

'I was once your age,' he said. He looked to right and left, then continued. 'I was once a lad like you with my whole life before me. Look at me now, Brother. Look at me now!'

Joachim looked. In truth, Brother Michael was not a pretty sight with his wispy white hair blown awry by the wind and his nervous face twitching above a slack neck just like Mrs Brown's.

But, Joachim thought, it was uncharitable to go on appearances. He said, 'There's nothing wrong with you, Brother.'

'There is a lot wrong with me, Brother. A lot wrong. You don't know the half.'

'How do you mean?'

But Michael was growing agitated. 'I'm coming down into the garden. I can't stand here. Someone might see.'

He disappeared as Joachim was about to shout, 'No, don't! The Rule!'

In the time it took Brother Michael to climb down to the garden, Joachim had set about weeding and had come to the conclusion that he must just ignore Brother Michael when he arrived.

'Well, here I am. If anybody comes I'm giving you advice on the garden. Is that clear?'

Joachim said nothing.

'Is that clear?' Michael repeated, hissing.

'Yes,' Joachim replied between clenched teeth.

'You can go on with your work while I talk to you. You don't have to say anything either. Just listen. It's no sin to listen.'

Joachim felt he could have started an argument about that but he did as he was told and started turning over the soil with his mattock.

Brother Michael began speaking, and, as he spoke, he mimed giving directions to Joachim about how the garden should look. His arm repeatedly pointed out the flower beds and mimed the correct way to wield a

148

mattock. It even described the growth of dahlias. And all the time, his words belied his actions. 'Brother, in the Catholic Church, when they want to make somebody a saint, they choose a man to argue against making that person a saint. He's called the Devil's Advocate. Well, that is my role at St Finbar's. It is my job to question the novices about their vocations. So: I think you should leave St Finbar's and go back to the world. You have the whole of your young life ahead of you and it would be a crying shame to waste it. There is no God, Brother. There is nobody up there in the sky counting up your good deeds and your bad deeds. There is no hell and there is no heaven. So, you see, young fellow me lad, there is absolutely no point in your staying on here. Take it from one who knows, it will wreck you. Better lads than you have been drowned while trying to dive down deep for the Pearl which may or may not lie inside the encrusted shell of Catholicism! Brother Joachim, there is no God. There is no Mary. There is no Little Flower.'

Joachim had stopped his work half way through Michael's speech. He now gazed blankly at the old Brother, wondering if he could possibly be really hearing what he thought he was hearing.

'Don't!' he screamed.

'The only Little Flower is down there, Brother,' and Michael grabbed Joachim between the legs and held him tightly.

Joachim tried to pull Michael's arm away but the old Brother held on.

'That's the only Little Flower there is, Brother! Let's see if we can get it to grow!'

Joachim stopped struggling then and attempted to reason with Brother Michael. 'Mortal sin. This is a mortal sin!' he told him.

But the claw hand did not stop squeezing him. The contorted white face kept repeating, 'It's growing, Brother! Sure isn't it a Big Flower now!'

Brother Michael suddenly let go of Joachim but

continued to gaze down. 'Sure it's a strong young bull you are!' he exclaimed. 'I can tell you I'd like to fiddle with your strong young stem, my Little Flower. It didn't take long to make you grow, did it, my friend? But don't worry. I'll see you all right. I'll see you satisfied.' He looked round fearfully. 'Meet me at the rubbish dump during your cross-country. You can easily run off the course and come to me there. There's nothing wrong. I'll see you all right.'

'Never!' exclaimed Joachim, though he did not believe himself. The smell of the gun emplacements at the back of the Prom filled his head. He wanted more than anything to go with Brother Michael. His lust rose from him in waves and made him feel he was about to pass out.

Brother Michael smiled. 'Never is a long time. You'd better be getting on with your work now. I'll see you this afternoon. Goodbye, Brother.'

'You won't see me!' Joachim shouted to the retreating form of Brother Michael, who perhaps did not hear. He just gave Joachim a wave and was gone.

If sin were a feeling, Joachim felt he was already deeply mired. Once again God had turned away. The white sheet of his soul was black and filled with crawling maggots. Were he to die he would join the devils of his dreams. How they would laugh! How they would torture him!

'I am lost,' he told himself as he turned back to mattocking the ground. To chide him further, his erection refused to go away. 'I am lost,' he repeated.

As if by some divine intervention the weather turned nasty that day.

During lunch the rain battered against the windows and Novvy said, 'It looks like it's library reading for you lot today.'

And that was how it turned out.

Joachim leaned forward on his desk reading a biography of Saint Philip Neri. He rested his elbows on the desk and blocked his ears with his thumbs.

Was he in mortal sin? Would he have gone to the rubbish dump to meet Brother Michael? He felt that he probably would have. When the rain started he had felt badly cheated.

But what about Brother Michael? What did he mean? He said he was playing Devil's Advocate. Did that mean he was not serious when he said, 'There is no God.' How could he? Is that really what he thought?

He made an Act of Contrition. That would be all right until he got to Confession. He would have to go to Confession about this. But what would he say? But he would have to go. He couldn't go to bed in this state. He might be taken in the night and then where would he be?

Joachim read page after page of his book without taking in a word. At last he dozed off and did not wake up until the bell went for the Rosary.

After supper Joachim went to Novvy and asked if he could go and call on Father O'Callaghan. Novvy said he could as long as he was back in time for night prayers. Joachim trotted out into the dusk and up the path to the lodge where Father O'Callaghan, a retired missionary and chaplain at St Finbar's, lived with his housekeeper, Miss Harper.

It was Miss Harper who answered the door. She was a kind woman who encouraged the novices to visit by always providing tea and cake.

'You'd like to see Father?' she asked.

'Yes, please, Miss Harper.'

'Go on in. He's watching the television. He'll be glad to see you, Brother.'

Joachim went to the sitting-room door and knocked on it.

'Come in!'

Father O'Callaghan sat on the floor of the sitting-room on pillows made from pieces of Oriental rugs. The room was full of Indian carved tables, inlaid boxes and ebony elephants, mementoes of his time as a missionary in Afghanistan.

'It's Brother Joachim, is it? Have a seat.'

Joachim sat down across the low table from the priest. 'What can I do for you?'

'I want you to hear my Confession, Father, if that's all right.'

'Yes, of course. Can we just wait until the end of this programme?'

Father O'Callaghan was watching 'Criss Cross Quiz'. Joachim watched the screen mesmerised. He had not seen television for a long time and was amazed at how strange it looked. The images, blue-toned, danced in front of his eyes and made him feel giddy. He found he was able to answer some of the questions but did not speak them out loud, as he would have done if Mum had been there. Father O'Callaghan showed no reluctance, however. He knew all the answers.

At last the programme finished. Father O'Callaghan reached over and turned off the television. Then Miss Harper brought in a tray with tea and cake. This she laid down on the table and left.

'Well, let's get the business over with and then take our pleasure,' said Father O'Callaghan.

Joachim knelt in front of the priest and told him everything that had happened that day, though he did not mention Brother Michael by name.

'And did you want to do anything with the man?' asked the priest.

'Yes. No. I don't know.'

'Well that's usually how it is in matters of impurity. You want to. Then you don't want to and then before you know it there you are and Bob's your uncle it's all over and you feel dreadful.'

'Yes, Father. That's it.'

'And you've come haring up here when you could be having a well-earned chat with the other novices because you think you've committed a mortal sin, is that it?'

'Yes, Father.'

'You novices and your scruples will be the death of

me!' sighed Father O'Callaghan. 'Let me tell you, son, that a mortal sin is terribly difficult to commit. You've really got to get up early to commit one. You can't do it when you're all hot and bothered and it sounds to me like you were very hot and bothered this morning. So don't worry about that. You just happened to be in the wrong place at the wrong time. Sure, it's easily done. I've spent my whole life in the wrong place at the wrong time. You see before you a missionary who never converted a soul to the True Faith. Imagine that! But that's not the point. You haven't mentioned the name of the Brother who did this thing . . .' Father O'Callaghan left the question hanging.

'No, Father.'

'Well, that's fine. I can probably guess who it was and anyway as sure as eggs is eggs he'll be along to me before much time has passed, the silly old fool.'

'Yes, I suppose so.'

'Well for your penance say ten Hail Marys. No, on second thoughts, don't say ten Hail Marys. You must be fed up to the back teeth with Hail Marys. Instead, say a prayer of your own for me and Miss Harper and, for good measure, you can say one for all my friends in Afghanistan. Who knows, the prayers of a young novice faraway may do more to convert them from the wretched heresy of Mohammedism than a lifetime of my waffling.'

'Is it true you didn't convert anyone?' asked Joachim.

Father O'Callaghan frowned but his eyes twinkled almost merrily. 'Yes, it's quite true. But don't go telling the whole place. It might get back to the relations at home. They think they came flocking in to be baptised in their thousands. Well they came flocking in all right, but only for the antibiotics and the milk powder. The trouble with the Afghan is that he is as certain about his religion as we are about ours. It's the very devil to shift them.'

'They sound a silly people!' exclaimed Joachim.

'Maybe. Anyway, that's by the way. Now make an Act

of Contrition and we'll eat some of Miss Harper's seed cake.'

Father O'Callaghan recited the words of absolution over Joachim while the boy made an Act of Contrition. As always happened, he felt a huge weight being lifted from him and a feeling of light elation taking its place.

Joachim ate three slices of seed cake and washed it down with two cups of tea. Then it was time to go and, feeling as light as air, he thanked Father O'Callaghan; said goodnight to Miss Harper, and skipped back to St Finbar's a different person.

The stars smiled down at him and Joachim smiled back at them, his heart full of love, his stomach full of seed cake.

Time passed. Sometimes it passed fast like a car on a straight road determined to make its destination by nightfall. At other times it dawdled along like a cyclist on holiday with nothing better to do than enjoy the passing scenery.

And, as autumn turned to winter, Joachim found that he had been able to resist the blandishments of Brother Michael. He treated him as a joke. Instead of protesting to him shrilly about hell fire, he used his newly acquired agility to dodge away from his grasping fingers, called him a 'silly old man' and made fun of his protestations. All this was done with the help and connivance of Father O'Callaghan who listened to Joachim's weekly reports and advised him on tactics. The priest also kept telling him that he was only passing through 'a queer stage' and would soon come out of it and be afflicted by the usual lustful temptations of everyman. Devoutly Joachim hoped so.

At last Brother Michael gave up visiting Joachim during manual work. Perhaps he turned his attention to another novice. Anyway, it got Joachim off the hook.

But, as one temptation faded, another one took its

place. Joachim had fallen hopelessly in love with a visiting African Brother.

Brother de Porres arrived at St Finbar's with the first snow of winter. This occurred on Boxing Day and was to presage the hardest winter in living memory. But, for Joachim, the black Brother's arrival brought spring into his heart.

He had been sweeping the dull floor of the cloister when Brother de Porres arrived. Accompanied by the Provincial of the Brothers, he had swept past him carrying a suitcase and a large parcel wrapped in newspaper. Novvy had moved back a pace. The Provincial nodded to him. Brother de Porres smiled ebony and stars and said, 'Good morning, Brother!' in a voice of deepest song, a wave breaking on warm pebbles. Joachim held tightly on to his brush, opened his mouth to reply, forgetting the Great Silence, but could only manage a gasp.

Thus he had his first sight of a black man in the flesh. He had seen Nat King Cole and Paul Robeson on television. The former sang songs which Mum liked and sang at the sink; the latter sang songs which Dad liked and sang in the greenhouse.

Paul Robeson was also Joachim's preference and he had been known to stand abjectly in front of the mirror in the lounge and belt out 'No More Auction Block For Me' and 'Oh, Lord! What a Morning!' But Brother de Porres was not at all like either of these men.

Joachim watched him retreating down the cloister, dressed in a cassock very similar to his, yet seeming to glide along on castors, so tall he was. He towered above the Provincial who was quite tall himself. He came up level with the Stations of the Cross he was passing. He could have dusted them easily without standing on a chair.

The apparition disappeared round the corner, leaving Joachim clutching his brush rather in the manner of St Martin de Porres, after whom the black Brother was named, and who was always seen in statuary holding a brush, while a dog and a cat played around his feet.

He returned to his work wondering who he could be. Nothing had been said about him. He was obviously not a novice. Joachim wondered if anyone could tell him more. It struck him that probably Brother Michael would know something.

Novvy said nothing during morning classes and Joachim could hardly wait for the start of manual work. He dawdled as he passed Brother Michael's window, something he never did.

In no time at all Brother Michael appeared above him over the balustrade, beaming down, as Joachim cleared snow from the path that ran next to the garden.

'And how's my young friend this fine crisp morning?'

'Well, Brother,' replied Joachim, 'I'm curious, though. Have you seen the new black Brother?'

'Sure, wouldn't you have to be dead or daft to miss him?' exclaimed Brother Michael, 'I'll tell you why he's been sent to St Finbar's: He's come to eat up all you young novices while your flesh is still tender and firm.'

Joachim frowned. 'Be serious, Brother! Who is he?'

'Why do you want to know?'

'I just do. I saw him this morning when he arrived. He seemed nice. He said "Good Morning" to me.'

Brother Michael frowned belligerently. 'Oh, he did, did he? I see I've got some competition on me hands. I'd watch meself if I were you, Brother Joachim. You know what they say about negroes.'

Brother Joachim didn't. 'What?' he asked and at once he started to dread the answer as Brother Michael looked anxiously to right and left, always a sign that there would follow an indiscreet revelation. 'They're built like stallions and they just can't get enough. That's why they have to dance all the time. Sure, 'tis either that or go completely berserk.'

'How do you mean?' asked Joachim.

'What I say.'

'I don't believe you! Where's he from in Africa?'

But Brother Michael had withdrawn cooperation. He

looked out over the white fields of frozen Wiltshire and said, 'My niece, Moira, was a nun in the Congo. She's got a little brown baby to prove it.'

'But if she's a nun . . .'

'She was a nun. Now she's a mum in Westport, County Mayo, with a brown baby as a souvenir.'

'But if she was a nun . . .'

'She was a nun until the soldiers came to Leopoldsville. Raped.'

'No!'

'Yes!'

Joachim shook his head hard in an attempt to erase Brother Michael's words. He only half succeeded but managed at last to say, 'Brother! Can't you just tell me who the black Brother is?'

'Oh, very well. He's Brother de Porres and he's from Uganda. He's the first African Brother and he's been studying in Rome. Now he's on a tour of the English Province to encourage Brothers to volunteer for Africa. But I wouldn't volunteer if I were you, Brother. You might get raped like my poor cousin Moira, or sold into slavery. It all happens down there, Brother. It all happens there.'

Joachim pulled a face at Brother Michael and decided to give him a piece of Holy Admonition. 'Well I think Brother de Porres looks extremely saintly.'

'Ha!' commented Brother Michael. Then, after another look to right and left, he whispered, 'Sure sanctity I wouldn't be knowing about but I bet he's got a big one, Brother Joachim.'

'Don't be so silly, Brother Michael.'

'Oh, I'm silly now am I?' cried Brother Michael, sensing the hunt. 'Well let me tell you that if it weren't so treacherous underfoot, I'd get these legs of mine down there to where you are and show you a good piece of Irish beef. The Irish are a bit like negroes in that respect. However, we have the benefits of a thousand years of Christianity. It has given us the ability to keep a tight rein on our passions.'

'You need to roll in the snow like St Francis,' shot back Joachim, who, thanks to the detailed tactical lectures from Father O'Callaghan, felt not the least fear of Brother Michael.

'You haven't decided to return to the world before it's too late, I suppose?' asked Brother Michael.

'No, I haven't, Brother. I feel that my vocation is as strong as ever, thanks be to God.'

'There is no God, Brother,' whispered Brother Michael. There was always a hint of sadness in his voice and defeat in his stance when he said these words, as he did each time he met Joachim.

'There is a God, Brother!' replied Joachim joyfully. 'Look at the snow! Look at that tree!' And he pointed to the old willow by the artificial lake, bent by the weight of fresh snow.

'Accident. Pure accident.'

'I am praying for you, Brother.'

'So you're praying for me, are you? Thanks a lot. I'd far rather you'd come to the rubbish dump with me.'

'We've been through this before. I won't,' replied Joachim paternally.

Brother Michael pouted like a prune. 'Other novices have, I can tell you that, Brother. And they've never regretted it.'

'I don't believe you!'

Again the look to right and left. 'Your P. F. for instance. Brother Ninian and I have had a good time together where nobody can see.'

'You're lying!' shouted Joachim.

Brother Michael looked startled, looked about him and disappeared from the balustrade, but he could be heard saying, 'I'm lying, am I?' as he retreated, leaving Joachim to clear the snow and pray for him and Brother Ninian.

'Grant that the scales of sin and unbelief may fall from Brother Michael's eyes before it is too late! Grant that Brother Ninian has been able to keep his chastity . . .'

Then he added, 'Grant Brother de Porres a happy visit to St Finbar's.'

That day at lunch Joachim noticed that Brother Henry's chair was empty. Novvy said nothing, either because he had not noticed, or because he knew the reason.

Knowing looks were exchanged during wash-up.

'He must have gone too far,' stated Brother Egbert.

'How do you mean?' asked Joachim.

'One too many shows of extravagant piety I would say. You know what Novvy thinks about that sort of thing. It wouldn't surprise me if he'd been sent away.'

'Yes, but . . .' But Joachim did not complete the sentence. He had been going to point out to Egbert that Egbert was not very far behind Henry with regards conspicuous displays of piety. He caught himself just in time. The matter was still unresolved when the novices met in their room to see what Novvy had in store for them in the afternoon. Games of any sort would be out of the question because the snow was now lying deep, and heavy cobalt clouds hung low all round. Joachim was hoping for library reading, as he had decided to find out about Martin de Porres in the Lives of the Saints and flesh out his knowledge of the black Brother's namesake.

Then Novvy came in looking severe. 'I had been going to start you off on calligraphy today, Brothers, but Brother Henry is nowhere to be found. He has not been seen since this morning when he went out to do his manual work. Does anyone know where he is?'

None of the novices put their hands up. Brother Henry had been assigned to tidy up the barns and was alone in his work.

'I see,' sighed Novvy. 'Well, knowing Brother Henry, he's probably to be found rolling in the snow somewhere, the better to mortify his flesh.' The novices laughed, but Novvy frowned them to silence. 'However, the weather is not too good at all. Just in case something has happened to Brother Henry I'm getting all of you to go out and search for him. You will go in groups of two. I will assign areas for you to search.'

Ninian gave Joachim a dig in the back, a sign that he wanted to be his companion in the search. Together they went up to Novvy and were assigned to look through the orchards and all the old greenhouses. These lay on the far side of the artificial lake, to the east of St Finbar's. Joachim had not been there since the day he had been received into the Order. Then the plums were in full fruit. He had gone there in his new habit and, indulging an old habit, gorged.

Now he hardly recognised the orchards. The trees still stretched in long straight lines but the endless pattern of branches and twigs were like scribblings in black crayon on the sky. Looking through the avenues of trees made him go giddy if he looked too hard.

'We'd better take it a row at a time and walk up and down till we've finished,' said Ninian.

'He won't be here. Nobody ever comes here. And didn't you notice, there were no tracks in the snow?' sighed Joachim, cold and dispirited.

'Maybe Henry doesn't make footprints these days, Brother.'

'Don't be silly, Ninian. Everyone makes footprints,' replied Joachim, giving Ninian a punch on the arm.

Ninian rubbed the place. 'Wenceslas didn't.'

'Wenceslas did! Don't you know anything? "Heat was in the very sod that the saint had printed." – That proves it.'

'Have your own way. Anyway, we'd better search thoroughly so we can say he's definitely not here. But –' And Ninian stopped, looking suddenly anxious. 'You don't think anything terrible has happened to Henry, do you?'

'No. Do you?'

'No. At least I . . .'

They turned and walked down the next row of trees. 'Go on, what were you going to say?' asked Joachim.

'Nothing, Brother.'

160

Joachim shrugged.

They walked on in silence for a few minutes while Joachim thought about what Brother Michael had said that morning. He desperately wanted to know if it was true but did not know how to ask.

Then Ninian, just for a lark, tripped Joachim up as they were walking. Joachim fell down in the snow as Ninian skipped away laughing.

Joachim caught up with Ninian and asked him, 'Do you ever go to the rubbish dump?'

'Well I . . .'

'Do you?'

Ninian looked sheepish.

'Do you?'

'Yes.'

'Why?'

Ninian shook his head and started running off down the line of trees. Joachim ran after him, caught up and at once got Ninian into a head lock.

'Let me go, you!' shouted Ninian.

Joachim started to walk down the line of trees with Ninian's head caught under his arm.

'With her head tucked underneath her arm, She walks the Bloody Tower. With her head tucked underneath her arm At the midnight hour,' sang Joachim.

'You bugger!' shouted the head.

Joachim stopped but did not release Ninian. 'You go to the rubbish dump with Brother Michael, don't you!' he shouted.

'No!'

Joachim started to run with Ninian struggling, his head still pinioned.

'Let me go!'

'Tell me and I'll let you go.'

'All right, but let me go!'

Released, Ninian stood panting and untidy before Joachim. He took a long time to say anything.

'I'm waiting.'

'All right. I have been to the rubbish dump with

Brother Michael. That's what you wanted to know, isn't it?'

'What did you do?'

'Why do you want to know? It's none of your business!'

'It is my business!' shot back Joachim. 'Your eternal salvation is my business! You're my best friend, Ninian. I am my brother's keeper. You know that as well as I do.'

Ninian, somewhat mollified, replied, 'Well nothing much happened, honestly. He fiddled about a bit.'

'And you let him?'

'Yes.'

Joachim looked up at the clouds which seemed to be gathering ever-tighter above them to listen to the proceedings. Snow had started to fall again. Unless a wind got up to blow away those clouds it would be a deep fall.

'Did you confess it?' Joachim asked.

'No, why should I?'

'Because it's a serious sin, that's why. You are thick sometimes, Ninian. You really are.'

'Nothing happened! He only pinched my bum. That's not serious. Not like what you used to do in that garage.'

Joachim pouted. 'I thought that subject was closed. That happened a long time ago, Ninian, before I embarked on the Religious Life.'

'Yes, but it happened. I've never done anything like that.'

'Look, we're supposed to be looking for Brother Henry,' said Joachim, changing the subject.

But Ninian was not ready for the change. 'There's no harm in Brother Michael. He just likes to talk and fiddle a bit. There's no harm in it.'

Joachim sighed deeply. 'I will say this once and then we shall drop this whole distasteful subject: In six months' time you and I will stand in front of the Superior General and before God and we shall make four vows: Poverty, Chastity, Obedience, Free Missionary Work For Youth. On that day we must be ready to take those vows for they are vows which cannot be broken. I want you there with me on that day with your soul as white as snow. Is that clear?'

Joachim turned to walk down the next line of trees. Ninian followed and pulled faces at the back of Joachim's head.

'Yes, Brother,' he said.

Eventually the two novices finished searching through the orchard. They had turned their search towards the lines of wrecked greenhouses nearby when the bell of St Finbar's tolled.

'They must have found Henry!' shouted Ninian.

Together but in silence they made their way back to St Finbar's in the gathering gloom. The tolling of the bell seemed to reverberate in the darkening clouds above their heads.

Every Brother at St Finbar's was in the chapel. Hardly a place remained. They were all seated and Joachim and Ninian cut the palpable silence as they made their way, crimson with embarrassment, to their places near the front. Henry's pew was empty. No one seemed to be doing anything. There were no books being read, no public prayers being said. Everyone simply sat and watched the altar.

Joachim could not pray. He stared at the sanctuary lamp, the flame floating on a glass of golden oil. The flame flickered. The flames in every sanctuary lamp everywhere flickered like that. A nun had once told him that the flickering was the way the flame used to say over and over again 'Jesus is here. Jesus is here.' The flicker in the flame was a sign of its fear before the Godhead, imprisoned in its locked, gold box. A flame would never rise arrogantly erect in such a place. It knew its place and so should he.

That day the flame lulled him into reverie. He forgot where he was and instead dreamed his way back to early days at the convent school. The nuns seemed to have loved him. They made a fuss of him. Sister Anne, the dinner nun, had always given him extra chips. He could see her striding across the playground carrying huge pans of food from the kitchens to the gym room and smiling at everyone, but especially at him.

Sister Anne had never taught him, yet of all the nuns he remembered her best. She was small and fat and had round, thick-lensed glasses. He would pass her on her knees polishing the wooden floors. She would look up and smile and say what a wonderful boy he was and make an island of her duster for him to hop across the polish so as not to mark the floor with his pumps.

Joachim heard the door of the chapel open and someone taking his place in one of the stalls at the back.

'The novices will return to their rooms and read in silence. The other Brothers will continue with their work. All for Jesus!'

'Now and Forever!' replied the assembled Brothers.

Joachim sat hunched over a book about St Martin de Porres, unable to concentrate on what he was reading. The novices had been left unsupervised, but nobody had so much as looked around. Everyone seemed intent on their books. This was unusual enough but it struck Joachim as peculiar in the extreme in the light of the questions which he desperately wanted to ask.

Time passed and Joachim looked up from the haze of print before him and then looked around him. His look was met by others who then looked away. He tried again a few minutes later and saw that a silent restlessness had gripped the novices. He wanted to ask what had happened to Henry but could not summon up the courage. Then Ninian whispered, 'Well, what's happened to Henry?'

Brother Ralph looked round nervously. 'Don't you know?' he asked.

'No, we don't,' said Joachim.

But Brother Ralph had turned round again and was pretending to be engrossed in his book.

'Tell us!' insisted Ninian.

164

Brother Bosco turned round and stuttered, 'Brother Henry cut off his thingy with a scythe.'

There was a long silence. Then Joachim, his voice high-pitched after some years in a lower register, asked, 'How do you mean?'

But reply came there none. Bosco's stuttered sentence hung on the air, then buzzed around Joachim's ear like a fly. 'Brother Henry cut off his thingy with a scythe.' He had not needed to ask what that meant. He knew what that meant and he knew why Henry had done it, though he still could not really believe that he had done it. He looked around at the other novices but they were all concentrating on their books. He looked down at his own. 'Saint Rose of Lima, the patron saint of South America, said to Martin de Porres one day: We shall build of this continent, this New World, a flower garden for the praise and glory of the Lord.' He read the sentence again and then again but could make no sense of it. If Henry had cut off his thingy with a scythe he knew why. 'If thy right hand scandalise thee cut it off and cast it from thee. For it is better for one member to die than that the whole body be consumed in the everlasting fire.' How often he had thought of those words as he had held his own recalcitrant member out in front of him! These were the words of Jesus, yet nobody took them literally. He had often wondered why not. Other precepts were taken terribly literally, why not that one, then? It must fall into the category of the one about a man asking you for your coat, and you giving him your shirt as well. Nobody ever did that either. The tramps who came to the back door of St Finbar's were given soup and bread but they never took Brother Cuthbert's habit away or the rug from the hallway. Perhaps it was because they never asked.

But, if Henry had really cut off his thingy, and surely he had not, then why? Henry did not seem to be prey to the lewd temptations that had afflicted him.

'. . . Blessed Martin, ever the humble servant of the Lord, said to the wolf: "Be gone! Thou must know that thou workest out thy lusts in the Lord's flower garden. I bid thee be gone!" ' Joachim too had a flower garden. Brother Michael came to tempt him there. Could it be that Brother Henry had been tempted by Brother Michael?

'Brother Bosco, where did this happen?' asked Joachim to the bowed head nearby.

Bosco turned round: 'B . . . by the rubbish dump,' he replied.

Novvy came in at that moment. He looked smaller, tighter, than Joachim remembered. His mouth was fixed in a downpulled semicircle of gloom. His shoulders were hunched, as if tied round with elastic bands that cramped his torso, cut off the circulation and turned his head and neck florid.

He had seen Brother Bosco speaking but did not remark on it. He sat down heavily in his chair and looked out over the novices.

'Well, Brothers, I've been in touch with the hospital. It seems that Brother Henry will be all right. He will never be the same, but he will be all right.'

There were no expressions of relief, just that ear-splitting silence, for which, Joachim felt, this day would be remembered.

'Because it was Brother Egbert and Brother Bosco who found him at the rubbish dump, there is no point in my attempting to conceal from you the dreadfulness of what has happened. I am shocked. I never thought that any of the novices would be so woefully foolish, ignorant and . . .' Novvy stumbled for words but none would come. He stood up and strode to the window, looking out at the dark and the falling snow. The novices followed him with their eyes. Joachim could see the group reflected in the glass of the windows as Novvy spoke to them, his back still to them.

'. . . Never thought such . . . such wrong-headedness could creep into St Finbar's. God knows, I knew that Brother Henry had a tendency towards extremism, an extremism you well know I tried to bring to his attention.

But to . . . to mutilate himself in this manner betokens a type of madness and a failure to understand our Faith. Brothers, it could well turn out that we may not see Brother Henry again. I tell you that now so that, should it happen, you will be prepared for it.'

Novvy turned from the window and walked slowly back to his chair. He now made no attempt to hide the tears that were rolling down his cheeks. Joachim was shocked by what had been said and completely defeated by the sight of Novvy's tears. He began to weep too. Yet as he wept he felt he knew something which Novvy did not know. Novvy probably reasoned that Henry had done what he had done because of a problem with self-abuse or impure thoughts. Joachim felt he knew better.

But the tears dried up and anxiety gripped him when Novvy next spoke.

'The Provincial has ordered a full enquiry into what happened today and I must warn you that some of you may well be asked to give evidence.'

That night Joachim wet the bed.

One morning a week later Novvy told Joachim to be especially diligent in the cleaning of the Brothers' Feast Day Parlour because the enquiry into Brother Henry's 'accident' was to begin there that day.

Joachim removed all the chairs from the room and commenced brushing and rebrushing the floor prior to applying another layer of polish. He dusted everywhere, applied the polish generously then used a heavy polisher to remove it and bring up the shine. He had borrowed the polisher from Brother Cuthbert and it lifted his spirits a little to see how he was able to obtain a deep shine on the floor by swinging the heavy polisher along the length of it. He tried walking on the shine and found that miraculously he did not leave footprints on it.

But curing the floor of its polish build-up problem gave him little consolation that day. He felt sure he would be called to give testimony by the enquiry. Brother Michael had been nowhere to be seen in the last week. He had waited for him down by the snow-covered flower garden but he had not put in an appearance. He was sure that Brother Michael would be in trouble and would know it.

As he was dusting the window ledges and gazing from the window at the grey, frozen snow outside, Novvy came in with a water pitcher, glasses and notepads. He went up to the table, placed three chairs on one side of the table and one on the other. Then he put glasses and notepads in front of the three chairs.

'Will you get me a cushion from the chapel for this chair, Brother. Father O'Callaghan gets uncomfortable on wooden chairs.'

'Yes, Brother.' And he fetched one of the embroidered cushions from the back stalls in the chapel, thinking that he was well and truly doomed if Father O'Callaghan was on the enquiry. For he had told Father O'Callaghan everything and he had told him not always under the protection of the confessional. He was sure to be in trouble.

The novices filed into morning classes and Novvy told them that he would not be teaching them that day.

'By way of a nice change, Brother de Porres has consented to come and speak to you about the Missions in Africa. I hope you will be attentive. Who knows, some of you may be called to give service out there one of these days.'

With that he left the room and Joachim knew that the three behind the table would be Novvy, the Provincial and Father O'Callaghan. He saw himself sitting alone while the august trio fired searching questions at him. What would he say? How would he survive it? His stomach was knotted with anxiety. His bowels rumbled.

Then Brother de Porres came into the room, smiled and sat down without a word.

The turmoil of the last week had driven Brother de Porres from Joachim's mind but now, here, there he was.

'My name is Brother de Porres,' in a baritone voice which set the hair on Joachim's neck trembling. 'I am not an Irish Brother ...' He paused, perhaps expecting

168

laughter, but no laughter came. The novices were too much in awe to see any funny sides. 'No, I am an African Brother. I come from a small village in Uganda, a country in the heart of the continent. It is a beautiful country, as green as England in parts with many mountain ranges and vast lakes.'

Brother de Porres continued to describe his country. Joachim listened but did not hear. He was too busy marvelling at the Brother's face and the colour of it. Before he had thought it was the deepest black, but in this, he now realised, he had been mistaken. His skin was dark brown. It had a matt patina upon it which made it seem like some sheer velvet. His ears were very small and hugged his head. Joachim felt his own. They seemed odd in comparison and stuck out too far. If he had a choice, he thought, those were the ears he would choose. The Brother's hair, which he had thought was just a dense cap of black, was in fact, from this perspective, a soft halo. He wondered if he touched it how it would feel. Then, when Brother de Porres turned, he saw his face in profile. The nose, quite flat and wide when viewed full-face, in profile was sculpted and honed, a perfect concave arc from the bridge to the tip. At that angle he looked much younger – almost like a child.

And from Brother de Porres' full mouth came the sound which mesmerised him and made him shiver. So deeply affected was he by the tone of the voice that he could not concentrate on the meaning of his words. To him the voice had all the quality of the music he was growing to love. 'The War Requiem' voices moved him for their sound and not for their content.

'I want to tell you about a wicked king we once had in Uganda,' continued Brother de Porres, looking directly at Joachim who came out of his reverie and tried to listen. 'This king refused to accept the true Faith. He was disgusting in his morals, indulging in lustful practices with both women and men. Now it happened that this king had several page boys, many of whom had become Catholics and their Faith meant everything to

169

them. They were all most devout. However, this devotion displeased the king and he decided to force them to commit great sins against Holy Purity. The Catholic pages refused to bow before the lusts of the king and, in a great rage, he sentenced them all to death. He had a great fire built and rush mats were brought to the edge of the fire. Each of the page boys was stripped and forced to lie on the mats which were then rolled up and tied tightly. Then the boys were placed on the edge of the great fire so that, in the course of many hours, they were roasted. But, it is said that all through their agony the page boys sang hymns and prayed for the wicked king who was so abusing them. They all died and their souls went up to live with Jesus and His most Blessed Mother. We call these page boys the Uganda Martyrs. It will not be long before our Holy Father in Rome canonises them.'

Brother de Porres stopped. His tale had been a fairly standard one as tales of martyrs went. Every day the novices listened to brief lives of saints and martyrs who had expired after putting up with the most fearful torment. The Roman martyrs were usually best and had had to put up with the most. But, because it was Brother de Porres who was telling the story, it was invested with a freshness and fascination for Joachim and the other novices.

'Any questions?' asked Brother de Porres.

'Yes, I have!' exclaimed Brother Ninian, standing up clumsily as he spoke.

Brother de Porres nodded and Ninian asked, 'Is your hair easy to comb?'

By way of answer, the black Brother delved into the pocket of his cassock and produced a comb. He inserted it into his hair and pulled it upwards. With a sound of rubbing corduroy the comb passed through the hair, though it left it much as it had been before. 'Does that answer your question, Brother?'

'Yes, thank you.'

Brother de Porres looked around, smiling.

Brother Egbert put up his hand and was called on. 'Do

the Uganda martyrs have individual names? When they are canonised, they're not just going to be called the Uganda Martyrs are they?' he asked.

Brother de Porres stroked his chin. 'That's a good question, Brother. One of the problems is that we don't know their names. They will be saints but they will be anonymous saints – their names known only to Jesus.'

He looked around for further questions. Joachim was thinking what a shame it was that the Uganda Martyrs should have had to go through such a dreadful martyrdom, but end up not being known by their full names. Almost desperately he wanted to ask a question but he did not dare. Had he dared he would have asked if he could touch Brother de Porres' hair.

Brother Ninian was not so bashful, however. 'Why are your hands black on the outside but white on the inside?'

'We have many stories at home about that. Some say it is because when the good God was painting us he forgot that bit. He also forgot another bit, the soles of our feet. They're a little on the pale side too.'

'But the rest of you is black?' continued the unstoppable Ninian.

'Yes, I think so.'

Then Novvy came in. He excused himself to Brother de Porres and turned to address the class of novices:

'Brother Ninian, would you come with me please?' Then he looked at Joachim. 'When Brother Ninian comes back, I'd like you to come to the Brothers' Feast Day Parlour, Brother Joachim.'

He led Ninian from the room.

Brother de Porres continued to talk about Uganda and about the Brothers' work there but Joachim was not listening. The voice no longer had any power to charm. He could only wait fearfully for Ninian's return and the imminent start of his inquisition.

Ninian returned and sat down without looking at Joachim. He made his way to the front and tried to smile at Brother de Porres. His feeble attempts were rewarded by a wide, white beam from the Black Brother. For a moment Joachim felt lifted, but, as he made his way along the cloister, he was overcome with fear and could hardly bring himself to knock at the door of the Parlour.

When he did he heard the Provincial's booming voice telling him to enter. He was gestured by Novvy to the empty seat in front of the table, where he sat wondering what to do with his hands.

'Well, Brother Joachim, we just want to ask you a few questions. It is important that we find out as much as we can about what happened to Brother Henry.' The Provincial sat back in his chair and Novvy leaned forward to speak.

'Brother, have you ever spoken to Brother Michael?'

'Yes. No. Yes. . . . Yes,' stumbled Joachim.

'What did you talk about?'

There was no escape. They had made straight for the heart of the matter. Joachim told them everything.

'But you never went to the rubbish dump with Brother Michael?' asked Father O'Callaghan.

'No, Father, I didn't.'

'Did you know that any of the other novices had been to the rubbish dump with Brother Michael?'

Joachim did not answer for a long moment. He desperately wanted to lie and say 'No' but knew that the lie might be immediately exposed as such. What had Ninian said?

'Yes, Brother.'

'Who?' asked Novvy speaking from between clenched teeth.

'Er, Brother Ninian, Brother, er Father.'

'Brother Ninian said he never went there,' said the Provincial.

'Is that what he said?'

The Provincial nodded.

'Well, maybe he was just showing off, but he said he had.'

Novvy looked hard at Joachim. 'Why didn't you come to me, Brother? Why didn't you say what was going on?'

Joachim shrugged: 'I don't know. It didn't seem so bad usually. I mentioned it to Father O'Callaghan.'

The priest nodded and gave Joachim a smile.

'You realise of course that Brother Henry went to the rubbish dump with Brother Michael and that was the cause of the terrible thing he did to himself?' Novvy continued stonily.

'No, I didn't. When it happened I thought that might have been the reason. I mean that came into my mind. I hoped it wasn't true.'

'But you are sure you are telling the truth about not having committed any acts of impurity with Brother Michael?'

'Yes, Brother.'

'You're absolutely sure about that? I ask you again because Brother Michael says that you went with him to that place. And he says that you tempted him to unchastity rather than the other way round. What do you say to that?'

'No! I didn't. That is a lie!' answered Joachim pale with fear and anger.

Novvy sighed. 'Right, we'll leave that aside for the time being. However, it does occur to me that you seem very well versed in what might have been happening at the rubbish dump. A little too knowing for one so young. Have you ever indulged in such goings on with other boys or men?'

Now they had him, he thought. The devils of the garage had found their way into his hiding place. He had thought that in leaving home he would be able to banish the satanic hound that chased him and waited to pounce on his soul and drag it screaming into torment. But that, he saw now, had been a vain hope. The few miles that separated home from Wiltshire would be no obstacle for those devils. They had found him, taken up their abode in Brother Michael and bided their time.

He did not answer. He wrung his hands. Consciously,

he tried to inspire the inquisition's pity by the intensity of his abject postures.

'We're waiting, Brother Joachim,' said Novvy.

Joachim looked up at the man he had thought of as a father but saw only the face of the headmaster at St Bede's, Brother Hooper. No longer was he the man who had kindled in him a love for music, an eye for wild flowers, a taste for poetry. He was now just another man in a cassock inspiring fear of homework undone, caps unworn, P. T. kit unwashed, soul unclean. Faced by this spectre, Joachim answered.

'No, I haven't. I have always been pure.'

His inquisitors looked down at their desks, embarrassed by the pathetic transparency of his lie.

Still looking down at the table, Novvy said, 'What about those occurrences in the garage?'

Ninian must have told them. There was no other explanation for he had told no one else. His best friend had told on him. So that was how things were. 'Your sin will find you out.' One always got what one deserved. There was now no point in further denial.

He sat, looking at the floor. The floor he had cleaned so thoroughly a couple of hours ago was now scuffed and marked by the shoeprints of the other Brothers who had sat where he now sat. Perhaps that one there was Brother Michael's and the ones at his feet Brother Ninian's. He sat and watched the marks and wept. The three opposite him said nothing.

Then, at that moment, from the novices' room, came the sound of children's voices singing 'Kyrie Eleison' to the accompaniment of an insistent and exciting drum beat. Joachim had never heard such a sound before. It must be music that Brother de Porres had brought with him. Perhaps music from Uganda. The music was much too loud for the inquisitors and Novvy went out of the room to have it turned down.

The remaining people in the parlour sat on in silence listening. The sound lessened. Joachim could see the scene next door. Brother de Porres would have apologised to Novvy and then gone over to turn down the volume. But the sound was still there. The children sang at the upper limit of the human voice and asked forgiveness so merrily. A dark male voice intruded asking for mercy too, but so gay it was that it belied the pleas it was making.

Novvy returned but somehow the mood of doom had dissipated, been dispersed, by the happy sound from next door. Joachim sat on and the tears continued, but he felt cheered somehow. When Novvy repeated his question, he answered that, yes, he had been unchaste before he came to St Finbar's but that he had not done anything bad since entering the monastery.

He did not know if he was believed. Part of him did not care. He wanted only to get out of the parlour and back to Brother de Porres to listen to that music.

'Very well, Brother Joachim, you may go,' said Novvy without looking at him. 'However, we may want to talk to you again.'

Joachim got up and fled back towards the music.

He went straight to his seat. Brother de Porres nodded to him and smiled. The record turned and the male voice sang the 'Credo'. At first he was conscious of Ninian behind him, but then he forgot about him as a long drum solo announced the words 'Crucifixus etiam pro nobis sub Pontio Pilato passus et sepultus est'. Then a different drummer took over and beat out a wild celebration, followed by the words 'Et resurrexit tertia die secundum scripturas' sung by the exultant voices of the children. Despite everything, he could not help smiling.

When the music had finished the novices clapped. Brother de Porres took the record off the player and returned to the front of the class.

' "Missa Luba" . . . the voice of African Christians,' he said. He looked over at Brother Joachim. 'I'm very sorry you missed my introduction to it. This is a mass from the Congo, Brother. I could see from your face while it was playing that you like it. I am happy about that. Whenever

I am homesick for my mum and dad I play it and I am back home.'

Joachim smiled at Brother de Porres, his heart full of love for the man and relief to be near him and away from the inquisition next door.

For one mad moment he wished himself older, preferably black and, above all, the best friend of the black Brother. They would go away together and convert the heathen during the day. Then each night they would return to their hut to eat, pray, and listen to 'Missa Luba'.

'The Congo is having its problems at the moment, Brother. The Belgians have left its people in a very bad state.' Joachim thought of what Brother Michael had told him about his sister, the nun, but dismissed it from his mind. Then Brother de Porres gave expression to what he was thinking. 'Still, a country that can produce such a sound must have some hope for a brighter future.'

Novvy returned and Brother de Porres bade the novices good morning and was gone.

For the remainder of that day and the day that followed, Brother Ninian seemed to be avoiding Joachim. Novvy too behaved very distantly, as did the other novices. When, on the third morning after the inquisition, Ninian was absent at breakfast, Joachim knew that he had been sent away and he was torn between regret, relief and anger that he had not at least been allowed to say goodbye.

He knew too that the matter was not closed and that he too might well be sent away from St Finbar's. The idea of leaving did not strike horror into him. It was only the thought of having to return to St Bede's as a failure that gave him pause. It was obvious to him that the monastery was no place of escape. If he was a homo he would have to fight it here or there. Changing the geography would not change the problem. He would carry around his nature from place to place as a snail carries its shell.

So, when, a week later, he was called back to the Brothers' Feast Day Parlour and sat down next to Brother Michael, he was not afraid.

When Novvy asked Brother Michael to repeat his accusation, he was not shocked when Brother Michael said it had been Joachim who had led him into sin at the rubbish dump. He rather almost felt that the old Brother was telling the truth.

Then, when Novvy asked him, 'Is that true? Did you lead Brother Michael astray?' Joachim thought of Bruno, Eric and the man he had stared at in the toilet and answered, looking at Brother Michael:

'Yes, it is true. I am responsible. I tempted Brother Michael and he reluctantly gave in.'

Brother Michael gazed at Joachim. He inhaled suddenly, startled, as if the inhalation might be his last. Joachim, looking at Brother Michael's old, tired face could imagine how the face would look on a pillow breathing its last breath. His mouth opened and closed like a goldfish in a bowl of water starved of oxygen.

But Brother Michael did not say a word.

After that it was merely a matter of time. Novvy took Joachim aside and told him to say nothing to any of the other novices. He would contact his parents and make arrangements for them to collect him. He would not tell them the real reason for his departure from the monastery. He would tell them simply that Joachim no longer felt he had a vocation.

Novvy was hard and strange as he said, 'You will leave your habit on your bed, together with your crucifix, Rule Book and Office Prayer Book.'

On the morning of his departure, Benson was dressed and ready when he heard Novvy's footsteps coming towards his cell.

He had made his bed and folded the sheets and blankets, placing them over the stains his bed-wetting had made on the mattress. Next to them he placed his cassock, stock, collar, belt, and books. On top of these he put the crucifix.

Novvy nodded at the pile and told him to make his way to the eastern door of St Finbar's, where his father was waiting. Curtly, he shook Benson's hand and wished him luck.

In the cold dark Benson walked along the corridor, hoping against hope that Novvy would not lift the pile of blankets and discover the stained mattress. He walked down the stairs and along the corridor to the cloister. Numbly he walked the length of the cloister. As he turned towards the next section of the cloister, there, under the Station of the Cross showing St Veronica wiping Christ's Face he saw a tall figure.

At first Benson did not know who it was, and, thinking it might be the Provincial, was about to veer to the left, to pass on the other side, ashamed. But then he saw that the shape was Brother de Porres.

Benson looked at the Brother and tried to smile. Brother de Porres grinned at him and pushed a square parcel wrapped in newspaper under the arm that carried the suitcase.

'Go with God! Be happy!' whispered Brother de Porres.

Benson opened the heavy door and, through his tears, saw his father standing by the car.

Part Three
Moses

'Go on, Bob! Read it again. It's a real hoot!' shouted Brother Wood across the crowded staffroom at St Bede's.

Bob Stone held Benson's exercise book out in front of him and, pushing his glasses higher up his prominent nose, opened his mouth wide to start reading. But then he stopped and shook his head. 'No, Brother, I've already read it once. That's enough.'

Brother Wood poured water over his coffee powder and weaved his way towards the easy chair that Bob Stone invariably found for himself in the staffroom. He sat on the arm and reached for the exercise book, 'Give us a look.'

The Brother's hairy hand – Bob Stone did not think he had ever seen a more hairy hand – seized the book. He started to turn the pages slowly, smiling, then guffawing.

'Be Jesus! He puts "Ad Majorem Dei Gloriam" at the top of all his compositions. Isn't he the pious one? Are they all like the one you read us, Bob?'

'More or less.'

'The idjut!'

'That Benson's a religious maniac, that's what he is,' said Brother Fitzgerald, who was sitting at the staffroom table marking Maths books angrily. He went back to scrawling huge red crosses on an exercise book and added: 'It's not natural.'

Brother Wood smirked. 'Sure, there isn't much that's natural in that Benson. He's as queer as a four-leaf shamrock. That's why the Brothers wouldn't keep him.'

Bob Stone took the exercise book back from Brother Wood, 'Well, I wouldn't know about that but I do know that he doesn't stand a chance of getting "A" Level English if this work is anything to go by.'

The bell rang for the end of the break. Bob Stone sighed and pulled himself out of the armchair.

'What that lad needs is a good boot up the backside,' said Brother Fitzgerald with conviction.

'It's worth trying, I suppose,' replied Bob Stone, steeling himself for a double lesson with the Lower Sixth.

Benson had spent the lunch-hour alone in a corner of the playground. He had been reading the short aphorisms of the Spanish founder of Opus Dei, a group of secular religious who, while living in the world, practised the religious life and took vows. The book was small and red. It fitted his pocket easily and had cost him two weeks' pocket money. It had, he reckoned, been worth every penny, for it gave him lots of advice to guide him through the adversity he was encountering back at St Bede's.

Nearly all the boys in the Lower Sixth were a year younger than Benson. Those of his contemporaries from 3B who had managed to struggle through their 'O' level examinations had now attained the heady heights of the Upper Sixth. Vincent Latos was now deputy Head Boy. It was rumoured that he was going to win a scholarship to Oxford. Always polite to Benson, he was, however, monosyllabic and had not shown any signs of becoming his friend again.

Mercifully, Eddie Rudge and O'Gorman had disappeared from St Bede's, following ignominious failure in 'O' levels. Hepher, the one contemporary of Benson's to be in his class – having taken an extra year to pass the required number of subjects – said that Eddie was being detained 'to give Her Majesty pleasure'. He had held up a post office with a water-pistol that leaked. O'Gorman had fulfilled all Brother Hooper's predictions on the destiny of boys in 3B by becoming a trainee-manager at British Home Stores.

Now Benson sat alone at the back of the class. His copy of 'Hamlet' lay open on the desk at the appropriate page. Next to it, an exercise book was ready for note-taking. He had unscrewed his Osmiroid and placed it in the pen-holder at the top of the desk. He sat watching his classmates. Their behaviour did not edify him. Hepher was holding Scott's flask out of the window and threatening to let go. Scott was saying, 'Ar ay Heph! Don't be daft.'

The flask had a map of the world around it.

'Who's gonna stop me, ay?' sneered Hepher, a bully and the best rugby player in the school.

Scott just said, 'Ar ay!'

Nobody dared take on Hepher, Hepher could do what he liked. Even the teachers overlooked it when he made one of his snide comments. He was invulnerable.

'I'll let you off this time,' conceded Hepher. He threw the flask at Scott, who fumbled it. It dropped to the floor with a dead plop.

'Ar ay, Heph! Now I'll have to get me mum to buy me a new inside,' whined Scott, trying desperately to keep an edge of sweetness in his voice to mask his anger.

' 'Snot my fault you dropped your fucking flask.'

Hepher's henchmen laughed and bayed as they invariably did.

Benson found this sort of behaviour extremely distasteful. He knew he should stand up and protest. But then he had done that once and his back still ached from the push Hepher had given him. Instead he crouched down in his desk and tried not to attract attention.

Mr Stone came in carrying the class's compositions. The class settled down in their desks while the teacher sorted through the exercise books. Benson noted with alarm that Mr Stone was holding his. He knew because its cover was the same as the wallpaper in the lounge at home, where he now wished he was.

'Right, then,' began Mr Stone, still looking down at

Benson's exercise book, 'I've marked your compositions. Now, for your edification and instruction, I'd like some of you to read out their efforts to the class. Benson first, I think.'

He threw Benson's exercise book across the room. It turned in mid-air, pages akimbo, and the cover fell off and fluttered to the ground. The exercise book continued on through the air.

Hepher reached up and caught it neatly, his arms above his head. Without turning he threw the exercise book over his head, saying, 'Catch, Moses!'

Benson fumbled for the book but missed it. It fell to the floor next to him. With a heavy heart he picked it up. Brogan handed him the cover.

'Come on, Benson. We're impatient for your insights!'

Benson stood up and read:

'*Compare the characters of Hamlet and Laertes*

'This question is easily answered. In short: Hamlet has a bad character and Laertes has a good one. Now why do I say this? I say this because Hamlet's behaviour throughout the play falls far short of the sort of behaviour one has a right to expect from a Christian Prince . . .'

The class had started to snigger. Hepher was imitating Benson's voice as he invariably did. Benson tried to ignore it.

'. . . In the first Act of the play his father's ghost tells Hamlet to seek revenge for his death. In my opinion it is unlikely that a soul in purgatory would be so silly as to demand revenge. That soul is in purgatory to atone for the actual sin committed on Earth. It is not likely that such a soul would be full of vengeance. That Hamlet does not see this, does not appreciate that the Ghost is probably a temptation of the Devil, says much for his woeful ignorance of the tenets of the Catholic Church.'

Somebody farted.

'Er . . . We can only stand by horror-struck as Hamlet breaks the Fourth Commandment (Honour thy Father and thy Mother) at every turn. He is invariably rude and

184

callous to his stepfather, Claudius, and, in the bedroom scene, treats his mother despicably in language more fit for the tavern than the classical theatre. On top of this he kills Polonius, the great and good father of Laertes, while he is acting as a Guardian Angel to Gertrude behind her arras. He leads Ophelia from the path of rectitude and must be at least partly culpable for her unfortunate suicide. Suicides, we all know, and Hamlet must have known, go straight to hell. Hamlet's melodramatic display of mock affection in her grave is the most hypocritical behaviour I have ever had the misfortune to read. Rosencrantz and Guildenstern are also treated very badly and get killed off stage.

'When Hamlet finally gets killed he has managed to kill two whole families, his own and the family of Laertes, along with other unfortunates. To say that, given this, Hamlet's death is in any way "tragic", is enough to make one laugh. If ever there was a case for damnation, Hamlet is it.'

The class was merry now. Benson had to interrupt his thesis constantly to allow the laughter to fade. He was helped in this by the fact that nobody in the class wanted to miss Benson's next pearl so that they could break up into further laughter. The reading of his essay became like a Rosary in which Benson supplied the first half of the prayers while the class responded. Mr Stone stood at his desk wearing a slight smile on the lower half of his face, while the upper half frowned knowingly. Benson's voice quavered as he went on to analyse Laertes.

'Laertes is everything that Hamlet isn't. He respects his parents. However, one wonders who could not be moved to respect by the advice given to him by Polonius, his father. It would be a poor son indeed who failed to be moved by such sound advice. This advice could well be framed and hung on the wall of every good Catholic household. (I'm sorry I cannot quote it. I have forgotten my book. Sorry.)

'In his turn, Laertes advises his sister, Ophelia, well. He tells her to stay away from bad company. If she had heeded her brother's advice she would still be with us at the end of the play. (Assuming, of course, that Hamlet had not found some other way of disposing of her!!) The one bad thing about Laertes is that he gives way to his passions and seeks revenge on Hamlet. However, I would defend him because he was tried by Hamlet past enduring.

'So, to come to a conclusion, there is little to compare in Hamlet and Laertes. Hamlet is bad through and through. Laertes is vice versa.'

Benson sat down feeling faint, but relieved that he had at least managed to stumble through his essay.

'Well done, Moses!' shouted Hepher.

'That's enough of that,' countered Mr Stone. Then he turned his attention to Benson. 'That just won't do, Benson.'

Benson said nothing. He had heard it all before.

'How old are you, Benson?'

'Seventeen, sir,' replied Benson, wondering what that had to do with anything.

'Seventeen! I wish I were seventeen. But, look, Benson, you must learn that the Joint Matriculation Board are just not interested in a Catholic commentary on "Hamlet". They want something a little more universal.'

Benson shot back from a sitting position, 'The word Catholic means universal, sir!'

At once he regretted his answer. Mr Stone exploded, 'Will you leave all this Catholic talk for the Religion lesson, Benson? God I'm tired of you and tired of marking your sanctimonious essays! Let me tell you, young man, that until you learn to separate your faith from your studies, until you stop rendering to God the things that are Caesar's and to Caesar the things that are God's, you'll be in trouble and silly fools like Hepher will laugh at you.'

Hepher, who had indeed been laughing, stopped then and looked sullenly at Mr Stone.

'I did not notice a composition from you in the pile, Hepher,' said Mr Stone.

'No, sir.'

'Why not?'

'I didn't feel like it, sir.'

'You didn't feel like it. Well at least Benson did his work. Yet you were able to muster nothing but ignorant mirth. If you had half Benson's ability I wouldn't mind. But you're thick, Hepher. You're thick and will get nowhere.'

'I'm going into my dad's business, sir,' Hepher responded.

Mr Stone sighed, 'Well I wish you'd go into it now instead of wasting our time.' He motioned Hepher to sit down and called on another boy to read.

Benson kept his head down and wondered what to do. He could not go on like this for two years. That was certain. He was trying to succeed at his studies. He worked for three hours every night, refusing to respond to the blandishments of the new seventeen-inch television next door. But, when faced with his English compositions, nothing came. He had no idea how to write things that would please. What he did write he wrote because that was how he saw things. At least that was how he was trying to see things.

It was now eight months since he had left St Finbar's. Because he had left in March he had not been able to go back to St Bede's until the follow September. He had filled in the time pleasantly enough, following a programme of reading to get him ready for the Sixth Form. As summer came he spent great swathes of time walking and reading in the open air.

Quite often, hurrying past the back of the Prom – now much changed, the gun emplacement having been removed in his absence and the whole area landscaped into dull, undulating greensward – he would find himself on the seashore. There, where the estuary curved round into the Irish Sea, he walked and meditated on the wonders of creation.

When the tide was out he walked for miles towards

the faraway sea. His footsteps took him directly away from his town and across the sandbanks. The sea like a mirage could be discerned in the distance, but he was never able to reach it. It always seemed enticingly close and on some days when the south-west wind blew up breakers and dark dragon-shaped clouds scudded in from the Irish Sea in hot pursuit of some long-gone Saint George, he would gaze at it and imagine that he could see a white town hovering where the sandbanks ended. Then he would turn back to look at his own town, set on its sandstone outcrop, and it too was insubstantial. Turning and turning on the sand, he could not make up his mind after a while which town was real, which imaginary.

And, like the two towns he saw from the solitary vantage point of the sandbank, he had trouble discerning which part of his life was the real one and which the mirage. Memories of the Novitiate were stronger than his day to day present life at home. The circumstances which had caused him to leave preyed on his mind. He knew that he had not done anything to deserve his ignominious dismissal from the Order, but knew just as certainly that he had perversely engineered it. A part of him felt that he deserved what had happened and deserved to return a failure to St Bede's. Between March and September his main dread, apart from the great fear of falling into his old ways, had been returning to school. For in school the Brothers would surely know everything.

The sandbanks provided him with a private, silent place where he could go to calm himself and try to think. He would sit or lie looking out to sea and engage in one-sided conversations with God. These centred mainly on what he should do with his life, how he should serve Him. Sometimes the monastic life still beckoned, but a kind of religious life which did not lead towards the classroom. Rather, in these moods, Benson imagined himself a silent Trappist tending a garden for the greater glory of the Lord. The Great Silence would last his whole life long; and from this silence would spring a new Benson, a Benson detached from the things of this world and ready only for union with the Eternal Bridegroom in the next life.

He had stumbled on the poetry of St John of the Cross and thought that that would do nicely. Gerard Manley Hopkins too, though not the easiest poet to understand, seemed to point the way to him. He tried to see Christ as the Ideal Man, as 'Dearest Him', and he tended to see Him as swarthy and profoundly masculine.

He now heartily disapproved of the Holy Picture Christs with their long, lank hair and soft faces. Benson's Christ was a different kind of man altogether, a man who was tender but always strong; who would enfold Benson in his arms and carry him off to paradise. The Christ's muscles bulged as He expelled the money traders from the temple. His strong features, a cross between President Nasser and Brother de Porres, were exotic and breathtaking in their maleness.

He had not forgotten Brother de Porres. As the pain and humiliation of his leaving of St Finbar's slowly blurred, the memory of the last kindness by the black Brother remained strong. He played the Brother's gift, a recording of 'Missa Luba', every day on the new Dansette record player he had bullied Mum to bully Dad to buy. Mum liked 'Missa Luba' but Dad didn't.

Dad saw it as the start of the rot. 'That music is the start of the rot. You mark my words,' he said whenever he heard it.

That was blasphemy to Benson who doted on the music both for its associations with Brother de Porres and its beckoning promise of a life of giving in a hot country far away.

For when Benson was not thinking of a life of Silence in some isolated monastery, he was imagining himself, in some role yet to be revealed, ministering to the sick in the company of men like Brother de Porres. The problem was that he could not see how he was to serve. That he wanted to serve was definite. But his calls for help from the Strong Man in the sky had not been answered. Ahead lay two years of study for his 'A' levels, surrounded by fellow-pupils who thought him a Holy Joe and called him Moses. And, after that, a sandbank with an indefinite vision.

'President Kennedy's been shot,' Mum told Benson when he came in that evening.

'How do you mean?'

'It was on the news. He was in a car with his wife and someone shot him.' Mum bent down to take the cottage pie from the oven. Benson could see the studs and bumps on the heavy corset she wore underneath her polka-dot dress.

'He isn't dead, is he?'

'I don't think so but it looks bad.'

Benson went into the back room and turned on the television. It was time for the news but it seemed to take an age to warm up. The newscaster said that President Kennedy was dead. Benson said an 'Eternal Rest' for him. Then he watched, frowning, as Harold Macmillan said how sad he was and how the President's death was a great loss.

'It's because he was a Catholic,' said Mum as she spooned cottage pie on to Benson's plate.

'Those guns will be the death of the Yanks,' said Dad. He started to eat.

'Excuse me, but haven't we forgotten something?' asked Benson.

'Oh, yes. Sorry son,' said Dad.

Benson bowed his head. 'Bless us, O Lord, and these Thy gifts which we are about to receive from Thy bounty through Christ, Our Lord. Amen.'

'And Eternal Rest for President Kennedy,' added Mum.

They started to eat. 'I always had a soft spot for President Kennedy,' observed Mum sadly.

Dad said nothing because he was busy blowing on a forkful of cottage pie. Benson stepped into the breach.

'He was a good Catholic and they struck him down!' he announced, his voice suggesting the onset of tears. 'He could have converted the whole of America had he been given time.'

'He saved us from Cuba,' said Mum, remembering the tense evening she had spent in the company of Richard Dimbleby during the Cuban Missile Crisis.

'How do you mean?' Benson asked. He had been in the monastery at the time, somewhat starved of news.

'Well,' continued Mum, 'the Russians had moved all their rockets into Cuba and President Kennedy said "Take them away or else!" '

'And did they?'

'Well, it was touch and go for a while but they did. It was a worrying time but Richard Dimbleby was marvellous.'

'He'll be missed. We need people like him,' stated Benson.

'It's his wife I feel sorry for,' said Mum.

Then Dad said, 'He was a bit daft over the Bay of Pigs, though.'

Mum demurred, 'But he was a lovely man. Such a shame.'

At half past six Benson settled down to his homework. He could allow himself no break in his routine just because President Kennedy was dead. Indeed, the death of a great Catholic encouraged him to greater efforts. Others must be ready to take up the cross so sadly laid down.

He commenced his reading of the critics. He had found an edition of 'Hamlet' at the library which had a range of criticism of the play drawn from all kinds of sources, old and new. Without much enthusiasm, he read what these people had to say about the play and made notes in his exercise book.

He looked out of the window and saw Eric, now grown tall, leaving his house and striding purposefully up the road. Mum had told Benson that Eric had a steady

Methodist girlfriend. Mrs Jenkins, she said, was worried about him because she thought his work was suffering.

Benson, embarrassed, had studiously avoided Eric since his return home. He only had to see him to recall the awful goings-on in the garage four years before. He had been greatly relieved that Eric was going out with girls. Perhaps it meant that their impure activities had not had any damaging effect on him. Benson greatly hoped that this was the case.

It was not the case with Benson, however. He knew where he stood and what, when he stood, made him stand. Quite often he would be sitting in class or at the dining table in the evening when pictures of debauchery would come to him and send his studious thoughts away. Sometimes, he would sit on, erect, trying to see what was happening to him as a joyous thing, a way of testing his faith and his love. But at the time it was usually harder to see things in that light. Up he would slink to his bedroom. There behind closed doors, sometimes still fighting sometimes not, he would give way to telling himself a tale where he was hero-victim, tied to a stake of longing by a man of impossible strength and dimensions who would have his way with him in a manner, which, he knew, cried to heaven for vengeance. Then the inevitable return of passion-spent common-sense and wonderings about when he could get himself off to Confession.

Already he knew that for him there was no relief. This was to be his cross and would last his whole life long. This was what would damn him or lift him, through a lifetime of daily pain and impossible self-denial, towards sanctity.

He had asked the priests for help. The priests had either pronounced themselves ignorant or advised more prayer. He wished that he had Father O'Callaghan to turn to. He had seemed to understand something of what was going on. But, when caught in a kindly thought for the man, that too would evaporate when he remembered his last days at St Finbar's and the way in which the priest had failed to intervene on his behalf. Knowing what he knew, having been his confidant for quite some time, he felt cheated somehow, though he did not know quite why he felt like that.

He grew bored with reading the pronouncements of the critics. He pulled tongues at the book and slammed it shut, hard. He mooned about the room, surveying himself in the mirror for a while. The weight he had thrown off while away from home seemed to be coming back. Ah, problems! 'To be or not to be. That is a question!' he said to his frowning young face in the mirror.

He went through to the lounge and told Mum he was going to the library.

'Don't be too long,' said Mum. 'And wrap up warm.'

'I won't. I will,' he told her.

He walked up the road in the dark. He did not want to go to the library. He wanted to visit a friend but he could not think of any friend he could visit. He could not think of any friend at all offhand.

The library was a ten-minute walk from Benson's house. It was built on the edge of a park which also incorporated a large cemetery.

Benson's grannie was buried on the Catholic side of the hedge which divided the cemetery along its length. The Catholic and the non-Catholic areas of the cemetery were not equal halves, however. The non-Catholics took up more room. They occupied at least two-thirds of the allotted space.

Asphalt paths dissected the cemetery at severe ninety degree angles, dividing it into rectangular blocks. However, despite the best organisational skills of the Victorians, the graves themselves had refused to keep to the rules of neatness laid down in the grand scheme of things. The headstones did not seem to face in any particular direction.

Benson walked up one of these paths to get to the library. It was dark and the new amber lighting from the nearby road did little more than distinguish between the path and the grass. The crosses and lozenge-shaped graves were barely discernible. An occasional angel atop a grave stood sadly silhouetted against the sky.

He kept up a brisk pace as he walked along the path, all the time repeating 'Eternal Rests' for the dead people he was passing. When he crossed the hedge into the Catholic side he felt better and redoubled his efforts. After all there would be more souls up here in purgatory and fewer in hell. Prayers would have more efficacy on this side.

Momentarily he saw himself in the dark walking a straight path, like a cartoon sower. When his prayer reached the graves, souls in white nighties sprouted from the ground, smiled a quick 'Thank you' to their benefactor before taking off like rockets towards heaven.

But then he recalled that he was walking through a cemetery in the dark and gazed straight ahead for signs of the main road and the comforting lights of the library. He quickened his pace and kept a look out to right and left.

That he had taken this route to the library was understandable, to Benson at least. The route that kept to the road also led inevitably past a public toilet and he did not want to pass it. It had been in that toilet that his last fall had taken place.

Though more than two years had passed since the wicked deed, he still regarded it with perverted fascination. He could remember every detail of the place: the track that led off to it from the road; the three Victorian urinals; the stink of disinfectant. He had even dreamed about it. It had become a visible symbol for the invisible rottenness within him.

Normal sexual acts took place in pink bedrooms with veils around the bed and a crucifix on the wall. Perhaps, if Maureen O'Hara was any guide, they took place in storms on hillsides too, or on the balmy summer days amid green corn punctuated by poppies. That was where normal decent people expressed their love for one another. Benson, on the other hand, was attracted to a stinking toilet, where, scared, attracted, repelled, he grew, throbbed, came and went away miserable and damned. What would Maureen O'Hara think? Benson could not conceive of going to bed with Maureen O'Hara and doing her. He liked her far too much for that. Fancy doing someone you liked, someone you loved!

That day Benson had gone into the toilet hoping to see a man's penis. He had succeeded in that and more. He had left the place running; indeed, had run all the way home and straight into the bathroom. When he went downstairs to face Mum and Dad he was convinced that his rottenness must be visible.

But the feeling of excitement he had felt on the way into that place had been ineffable. A heady mixture of sickness and wellness, giddiness and heightened awareness had suffused him. Did other people feel this? Or was it only him? After kissing John Wayne during the storm in 'The Quiet Man', did storms make Maureen O'Hara go all funny? Surely not? Then why him?

Benson therefore avoided the toilet because it was, for him, an occasion of sin and a trigger that released his safety catch, cocked him and made him lethal to others and himself.

Once inside the library he was still not free of temptation. He made straight for the Literature shelf and sought out a book that would throw some less divine light on to the subject of Hamlet and his works and pomps. But he could not concentrate. His feet itched, tugging him away from the safety of English Literature towards the evil blandishments of Travel and Anthropology.

Resolutely he resisted and for a few minutes browsed through a brightly coloured paperback called 'What happens in Hamlet' by a man with an exotic name, Salvador De Madariaga. Probably a Spanish Catholic, thought Benson. But within the promising pages he did not find anything that diverted his thoughts from the Travel and Anthropology section. He put the book away and started towards the shelf.

But Divine Intervention prevented Benson from reaching it. He remembered that the Classical World shelf could be quite interesting too and that there, when he gazed at the pictures of nude men, he could convince himself that he was trying to foster an interest in classical art. But he only fooled half himself. The other half knew what he was about. The hugely muscled, swarthy Christ was already turning his bare back towards Benson.

He did not seek out picture books because he thought that all the other customers at the library would at once suspect the purity of his motives if they saw him leafing through 'A Pictorial Guide to Greek and Roman Statuary'. Rather he made for books which had lots of print. By looking at the side of the closed book it was easy enough to see whether there were any pictures inside.

The first two or three books he sampled were a disappointment to him. Just heads and ruins on hillsides. But then he picked one called 'Greek Athletics' and found, along with boring pictures of wrecked Olympic stadiums, several pictures of very beautiful men who hid nothing.

Not that most of them had very much to hide. The Greek ideals were remarkably like Benson in the pubic region. Positively prepubescent, he felt. They, like him, would be giggled at in the showers for not being well developed, for not being able to satisfy a girl. Hepher, standing towelling himself after a shower, his penis hanging like a cucumber, his slack scrotum, two new potatoes in a bag, supporting its base like a pillow, had said as much to McCarthy. McCarthy, as far as Benson could judge, resembled Benson in dimensions. Unlike Benson, however, McCarthy went into the showers in the nude, something, which, in the circumstances, Benson could just not understand. It was not really modesty which stopped Benson from baring himself to the other boys, merely a sense of shame and inferiority, a feeling that he did not match up. Had they been able to see him in the nude standing by the Classical World shelf searching through the learned, Benson-titillating books, he felt he too would be proud before his school-mates. But then they would just laugh at his erection and debate its cause. And, of course, their cruellest conclusions would be correct.

He tired of the cold illustrations of white statuary and wanted to be at the Travel and Anthropology shelf. He could see it nearby, just to the right of the 'Today's Returns' trolley. He was excited now and would not be put off by scruples. He had already fallen but had not hit hard ground. He was in that in-between stage where he was reconciled to falling from grace but had not yet taken full pleasure in the act and so was not at that precise moment a victim to the inevitable guilt that his fallen flesh was heir to. No, rather he was at that point that Adam must have come to, the point where he was criticising Eve for having eaten the apple but knew that he too would eat it. But those first male lips had not yet touched sin's smooth intoxicating flesh, discovering as they did so, the maggot lurking beneath.

Adam was not very well built either. At home there was a big leather-covered Bible full of old masters. There was a picture of Michelangelo's Creation of Adam from the Sistine Chapel ceiling. It covered two pages just before the start of Genesis. Adam had nothing to speak of. But perhaps Adam was like Benson in that respect and only flowered when giddy.

Impatient to be elsewhere, Benson placed 'Greek Athletics' back on the shelf and sidled over to Travel and Anthropology.

A middle-aged woman in a large blue hat reached the shelf at precisely the same time as he did. She started browsing at the top of the shelf, around Europe. Benson made straight for the bottom, South America, and soon found his favourite book, 'Vanishing Tribes of the Amazon Basin'. Lots of writing it had, but also a great centre section crammed full of pictures. He had seen them before but not for some time and was thrilled by the sight of the stockily built Indians standing with families and staring at the camera, or aiming blow pipes at the trees, or bathing in the Amazon. They were beautiful and dark and would have made Hepher shut up for a while.

Benson ran his hand over one of the plates. Just then the woman nearby asked him to reach up and get a book on Corsica for her. This he did, and in doing so, noticed a section he had missed on previous trips to the library: Africa.

Back went 'Vanishing Tribes of the Amazon Basin'. Benson gazed upwards at the Africa shelf, above his head but within his grasp.

He did not know where to begin. He read titles: 'Tribes of the Southern Sudan', 'Teaching English in Timbuktu', 'The Karamoja People', 'Ashanti Renaissance', 'I was a Mau Mau Rebel'. The woman had moved away and Benson reached up and took down 'Tribes of the southern Sudan'. He noted with pleasure that there were plenty of pictures interspersed with text. Keeping the book close to his chest, a weather-eye out for people who might see him, he started leafing through it.

The first set of pictures was disappointing, showing merely a number of barren landscapes with gnarled trees; groups of conical huts and herds of cattle with huge horns. He persevered. The second group showed a succession of black women milking cows, decorating their bodies and nursing fat black babies. They were more or less naked. Cheered, Benson turned the pages.

The first picture in the next section showed three warriors crouched around a camp-fire. The man on the left wore a pair of shorts and had been photographed from the side. The man on the right sat on the ground, his legs out in front of him, his thin arms supporting him, long hands splayed on the ground just behind his bare buttocks. But the photograph seemed to have been under-exposed and Benson peered anxiously, knowing that the man's penis must be there, but not quite able to discern anything in the dark haze that made up the region. However, the man in the centre crouched, facing the camera and staring stone-faced into the lens. Again, the under-exposure of the photograph blurred the man's pubic region but Benson could discern something hanging down between the man's feet. It was not clear and it seemed impossible that it could be what he thought it might be.

He brought the book closer to his eyes, forgetting altogether the people who might be around and might observe him. He adjusted the book to catch the light better. Yes, there could be no mistaking it. The stone-faced man was huge. He gazed at the picture, then, intoxicated, turned the page.

Photographs of other men, all nude, all beautifully proportioned, all huge, passed before his eyes. The library was suddenly as hot as Africa, the blood pulsed at his temples like an insistent drumbeat. He felt ill with pleasure and with pain. He found himself wondering if Brother de Porres had been like that under his cassock. Brother Michael had said as much. Was the singer in 'Missa Luba' like that? Was he carrying a penis of gigantic size beneath his trousers as he sang the 'Credo'? How wonderful it must be to be like that, or, if one could not be like that, to have a friend like that!

A man had approached the shelf and was bending down looking through South America. Benson, flushed and confused, snapped his book shut. He did not put it back on the shelf. That would have given him away. Instead he put it under his arm and started looking through The Benelux Countries.

The man crouched and took out a large picture book. He gazed for a long moment at the front cover: 'Savage Innocents', with its picture of a naked Indian family. Benson found himself looking down on to a small bald patch in the centre of the man's head.

He opened the book and looked at the photographs. Without any shame, he concentrated on each page much longer than Benson thought seemly in a public place. He pointed to one of the pictures, looked round and up at Benson and said, 'Look at that one!'

Benson looked everywhere but at the place where the man pointed. He saw that the man had a beaked nose, and was terribly tall and thin.

'Er . . . yes,' said Benson returning his attention to The Benelux Countries.

The man stood up. 'What have you got?' he asked.

'Oh, it's just a book. I'm studying "A" level geography, you see,' stammered Benson.

The man looked hard at Benson and worked his lips like Mum did when she wanted to distribute her lipstick evenly. 'Pull the other one, dear. It's got bells on. I've been watching you for ten minutes. I know what you like!'

'I er . . .' managed Benson.

The man reached out and took 'Tribes of the Southern Sudan' from Benson. He opened it and soon found the pictures of the tribesmen. He seemed to know his way around the book and confirmed this by saying, 'He's my favourite.'

He held out the book to Benson and Benson found himself looking at a very angry tribesman who seemed about to throw his spear at the photographer. The man's penis, caught by a fast exposure, arched like a rainbow in front of him; his face was relaxed, the narrow eyes hinting at great arrogance, arrogance which Benson thought was entirely justified. If he had one like the tribesman, he would be extremely arrogant too and parade it round the place. He'd never go into the cubicles at the swimming-pool to change. No. He'd towel his back and let it swing and bask in the admiring glances of envious less-favoured men; he'd enjoy medicals and not go crimson when told to lower his pants. He'd be able to satisfy girls then! It was clear that with what he had they would say to him 'You're no good!' and go away, but if he had one like the tribesman, they would fall at his feet. Gwen Watford, Lucy, and Rosalie Critchley would follow him around like puppies and stand at the front porch asking him if he could come out to play. And, best of all, he wouldn't have to chase other men. It would be so convenient! Everything he needed would be right there in front of him with no effort required on his part . . . like breakfast in bed. Oh, what a good time he'd have!

Then the man slapped the book shut and gave it back to Benson. He did this by taking Benson's arm, raising it, popping the book under it before placing it at his side and giving it a light squeeze. Then he said, 'You'll get a lot out of that, young man.'

'Yes. Er. Thank you.'

'Are you taking it out?'

Benson had not thought of that. 'Well I don't . . .'

'Oh, I should if I were you, dear,' the man replied. 'Any number of beauties in there to play Tonto to your Lone Ranger.'

Benson looked around fearfully and thought of Brother Michael. 'How do you mean?'

'I can see you're a coy one, dear. "How do you mean," she says!'

And the man walked away taking tight little steps. Benson watched his departure, mouth open. The man walked past the librarian at the counter who smiled and said something to her companion who giggled and said something back which made the librarian laugh a laugh which echoed through the quiet library. The man pushed the door of the library open, then, turning, flashed a smile back into the library. It reached Benson but passed the librarians who spluttered with giggles. Then, aiming an arched look at the girls, the man disappeared, leaving the door to swing to on its own behind him.

Benson fled from Travel and Anthropology to the safety of Local Interest. There he thought to himself, 'He knows! How does he know? Do I look funny? No, it must be because I was there looking at the books. He must do the same thing. But what cheek to come up to me like that! Just like Brother Michael!'

In order to compose himself, Benson browsed through 'Build Yourself a Bungalow!' and decided that he thought he knew why modesty had become important in the western world. It wasn't Adam and Eve, he decided. It wasn't the virtue that everyone said it was. No, it was just shame and fear at not coming up to the exacting expectations of onlookers. Women were modest because they didn't want the world to see that their breasts were floppy and that they had fat bottoms. Men wore pants because they didn't want people to laugh at the size of their penises. After all, it would be dreadful for a fellow to go into a grocer's and have the assistants giggle and whisper, 'I don't think he'd be much good in bed!' Yes, that was why people wore clothes.

When he had regained his composure he made his way to the counter and checked out 'Tribes of the southern Sudan'.

'You're not going to walk through the cemetery at this time of night are you dear?' It was the man from the library. He had been waiting for him.

'I prefer to go this way,' replied Benson flatly. He kept walking.

The man walked with him. 'Well suit yourself. I like a man who knows his own mind.'

They walked on. Benson wanted to ask the man what he wanted, though he knew. His erection was making it uncomfortable for him to walk.

'Haven't I seen you before somewhere? In the cottage. maybe?'

'The cottage?' asked Benson. 'Where's that?'

'Don't you know anything?' said the man archly. 'The toilet, the public convenience, the comfort station!' He effected an American drawl. Then he stopped dead in his tracks. 'That poor President Kennedy! What a waste. What a waste!'

'Yes, it's very sad.'

'Well have I?'

'Have you what?'

'Seen you in the cottage?'

'No.'

He took hold of Benson's arm. Benson stopped and turned towards the man. Then his hand felt through Benson's brown Beatles' mac and touched his erection. As he was doing this he asked, 'I wasn't wrong, though, was I?' And feeling him, he smiled and said, a feminine simper in his voice, 'No, I wasn't wrong.'

Quite suddenly, he removed his hand and started walking again. Benson followed and asked, 'How did you know?'

'Takes one to know one, dear.'

'How do you mean?' asked Benson for whom the cliché was as novel as a mango.

The man shrugged. 'I mean that I knew as soon as I saw you. When I saw you having a vada in the dinge section, I said to myself, Andrea – my name's Andy in real life actually, dear – Andrea, I said to myself, there's a gay one if ever I saw one.'

'A gay one?' asked Benson.

'A homo, a pouff, a queer, a gay boy. You really were born yesterday, weren't you dear?'

They were approaching the hedge that divided the non-Catholic from the Catholic side of the cemetery. Andy chose this place to suggest that he and Benson went off among the graves 'for a little grope'.

'Certainly not!' exclaimed Benson. 'I'm a good Catholic!'

Andy sighed noisily. 'Another one! Well you don't have to worry, dear. This isn't a mixed marriage.'

Andy headed off among the gravestones. 'Come on!' he hissed.

'No!' Benson replied in a whispered scream, but then he added, 'Not here. Let's go to the other side of the hedge.'

They walked along for a few more yards. 'Will this do you?'

'All right.'

And Benson followed Andy among the graves.

They got to a quiet place and Andy started to undo the buttons on Benson's mackintosh.

'I like your mackintosh. It's up to the minute is that.'

'Yes, my mum bought it for me in town. She wanted me to have a navy one but I insisted on this one. The Beatles wear ones just like it.'

'Very nice,' and he was undoing the buttons of his trousers. Benson stood frozen and forlorn. The bodies of non-Catholics turned in their graves nearby.

'St Andrew is the patron saint of fishermen,' observed Benson by way of polite conversation as Andy struggled to release Benson's erection from his underpants.

'You don't say? Well I bet St Andrew never fished out anything like this. You're a well-built boy! What's your name by the way?'

'Er . . . John,' lied Benson.

'Yes. Well built. Very nice indeed.'

'Do you really think so?' asked Benson, cheered.

'Yes, I really think so.'

'Can I see you please?'

'I thought you'd never ask.'

Andy quickly undid himself, reached for Benson's hand and pulled it to him.

Benson was rather disappointed to find that Andy was not hard, neither did he come up to Benson's exacting standards. As if divining what Benson was thinking, Andy said quite matter-of-factly, 'Sorry about that, dear. Still, what I lack in size I make up for in technique.'

Andy got down on his knees in front of Benson and kissed his erect penis. Benson put his hand over it and said, 'Don't.'

Andy pushed his hand away and spoke to Benson from a kneeling position. 'Look, dear, this is what I do.'

'How do you mean?' asked Benson.

Andy sighed, 'Oh for God's sake shut up and enjoy yourself!' And he took Benson into his mouth and began to suck on him in a way that Benson had always reserved for Strawberry Mivvies.

For a short moment Benson surveyed Andy in the gloom below him. But only for a moment. Soon he was intoxicated by the feeling Andy's mouth was giving to him and he let his hands stray down to the man's head. He took hold of his hair, gripped it tight and pulled Andy's head towards him and away. Andy moaned his approval of this and Benson, now a total stranger to himself, out of himself as he had never before been, moved his hands to Andy's ears. He grasped them gently and directed the other's head in ways which sharpened the pleasure-pain of each moment. He moaned and listened to Andy's muffled moans and the fart-like slurps he was making with his embrace. He felt that he was coming, but coming in a way that he had never managed in the past. It was as if his whole body and blood and soul would squirt itself through the tiny opening at the end of him. Opening his mouth wide, throwing his head back, he gazed up at the opaque, amber-tinged sky. He stopped breathing and tottered in ecstasy on the brink. Then, with a growl, he came and came and could not stop. Andy did not withdraw. Indeed he could not have withdrawn even had he wanted to, so tightly did Benson's hands restrain his head.

It was over. Cold flakes of regret began to settle on Benson's blank brain, but they did not stick. He let Andy go and watched as he stood up. But he did not feel revolted. Neither did he seek to run away. He even laughed when Andy observed, 'Now that wasn't too bad, was it?'

'No,' he managed. 'It was really nice actually.'

'You needed that. Christ, you needed that, dear!'

Benson frowned his disapproval at that mention of his ex-Friend in such a context.

'I must get on home. My mum and dad will be wondering what's happened.'

'Can I see you again?'

'Well er . . . I don't know,' replied Benson uncertainly.

'They all say that! Why do they all say that?' sighed Andy theatrically.

Benson thought for a moment. Once he'd been to Confession – what would he say? – Andy would become an occasion of sin for him. Still, he could always meet him again in order to convert him from his sinful ways. Yes, that was what he'd do.

'Do you know the back of the Prom?' asked Benson.

He got home. The new porch light had been switched on to greet him. It was only ever put on when a family member was out at night. This did not disturb Benson much. He was, in fact, rather worried because he was so unworried. This indeed was a new experience, a new twist in the puzzling conundrum of his life.

Keeping 'Tribes of Southern Sudan' hidden, he decided just to poke his head round the door of the lounge and tell them he was home. Then he'd go upstairs, wash, hide the book, and come back downstairs. By then, he reckoned he would have regained his composure completely.

His plan was foiled, however. There, seated in his dad's chair was the new curate at church, Father Hanlon. He cradled a cup and saucer, Mum's best, on his leg and held a plate with a scone on it in his left hand. Mum and Dad sat on the settee.

'Come on in and say hello to Father Hanlon,' said Dad cheerily.

'Er . . . good evening, Father. Will you excuse me for just a minute? I'll be back soon.'

'Don't be long!' Mum sang out.

Benson ran up the stairs and into the bathroom. He pulled out his penis and washed it thoroughly. It was red, blushing from all the attention. He washed it carefully and put it lovingly back into his trousers. He could not for the life of him understand why the usual pangs of guilt and depression had not descended upon him. It worried him strangely. What had just happened in the cemetery should have sent him desperately seeking absolution. He should be thinking how to accost Father Hanlon before he left the lounge and get down on to his knees in front of him. He should have started making promises of the 'never again' variety to the sky on his way home. He had not. Why, he had not even made an Act of Contrition!

He washed his face and brushed his teeth. It was all very peculiar. After leaving Andy at the gate of the cemetery he had skipped home with a spring in his step. He just rather resented the presence of the priest downstairs. He would have to postpone bedtime and the pictures in 'Tribes of Southern Sudan'.

His face was caught by Dad's shaving mirror. It magnified it hugely. He looked deeply at the face and thought it no bad sight all in all. He needed a shave, that was certain. Well, he'd get round to that all in good time. But, he decided, he really quite liked his face. Almost handsome.

'What are you doing in there?' It was Dad's voice.

'Sorry, Dad. Won't be long. Sorry.'

Dad went into the lavatory and Benson went downstairs to meet Father Hanlon. Unafraid.

'It's a bad time, Mrs Benson. A very bad time,' Father Hanlon was saying as Benson entered the lounge. 'It's nice to come and see you and know that there are some good Catholic families still around.'

'Well I don't know about that, Father. Still, we try, don't we, son?'

Benson nodded.

Father Hanlon placed his cup and plate on the coffee table and turned towards Benson. 'Are you settling down to your schooling again all right, young man?'

'Yes, I think so, Father.'

'And you don't miss the Brothers?'

'No, not really. Some friends there but I don't think the life was for me. I decided I didn't want to teach.'

'What do you want to do?'

'I don't know.'

At this point Mum stood up and started to collect together the dishes. She loaded them on to a tray and said, pointedly, 'I'll just go and wash these things up.'

She left the room and Father Hanlon slapped his

knees and leaned far back in his chair. 'Well, it was really you I came to see actually,' he said.

He seemed amiable enough but Benson found himself winding up again and had the distinct feeling that something was up.

'I thought we might have a little chat. I'll get to the point straight away. I received a letter from Father O'Callaghan at the Novitiate. In that letter he mentioned the circumstances that had caused you to leave St Finbar's.' The priest saw Benson's reaction and continued, 'Now it's nothing to be worried about. I shall not say anything to your mum and dad about it. The reason Father O'Callaghan wrote was, I think, because he felt a little guilty about you. He didn't go into the reasons, but that was the impression I got. Anyway, I was just wondering if I could be of any help . . .'

It was a question but Benson did not have the least idea what to say in reply. So he just shook his head slowly.

'What I mean is . . . are you having any difficulties in that direction?'

Benson knew what Father Hanlon meant. It struck him as slightly ironic that he should ask that because, only last week, Benson had been to him in confession and told him what the problem was. Then the priest had said that he must learn to master his flesh or his flesh would master him. And he must have known it was Benson talking to him through the grill.

Benson watched the priest's discomfiture. The anxiety had left him. He felt cool again. For a short moment he allowed himself to go back an hour in time to the cemetery and think of Andy on his knees in front of him and the feelings he had kindled there in the dark.

'I think I am growing out of that, Father. It was probably just a stage. I do have problems but that isn't one of them,' he said in a steady voice.

Father Hanlon looked relieved. 'Can I be of any help to you with these problems? I'm here to help.'

'No, you're not! You're here to mess me up!' thought

Benson. 'Well, yes. I do have some problems with some dogmas of the Church, Father.'

'And who doesn't? I know I do. Which dogmas cause you most trouble?'

'Hell, Father.'

'Ah, yes. Hell. And what is it about hell that you find particularly difficult?'

'I cannot reconcile the God of Infinite Love and the God of Infinite Justice, Father.'

Father Hanlon leaned forward in his armchair and nodded.

'You see,' continued Benson, 'if someone killed my mum I would be terribly angry. Were it in my power I would seek retribution from the killer. Perhaps I would throw him into fire. But in the end I would forgive my mother's murderer. Maybe after fifty years or five hundred years. Anyway, within some finite period . . .'

The priest stroked his chin with his left hand and frowned down at it, nodding.

'And I think that my eventual forgiveness of the murderer is a virtue, is good. Goodness in me I am taught comes from God. Yet God, who tells us to forgive "until seventy times seven" does not follow His own rules.'

'Well,' replied the priest, 'if you'll forgive me for saying so, you are not God. His ways are often mysterious. I would only say that hell is mentioned repeatedly in the Gospels. It cannot be ignored. Your Catechism says: "They who die in mortal sin will go to hell for all eternity." That is clear enough.'

'Yes, but that's the problem.'

The priest looked nonplussed.

'You see,' continued Benson, 'I see hell as a betrayal of the Love of God. It is my duty as a Christian to seek to make Christ my Friend. But how can I do that in a proper spirit if He will turn away His Face from me forever? We are told from our earliest days that we are prone to sin. But if we die in sin, that's it and He gives up our friendship and is content to live in the delights of heaven while

I languish forever enduring horrible torments! I just can't accept that.'

Father Hanlon looked stern. 'You must accept it! It will become clear when you die. Have faith.'

'But when I die it will be too late!' exclaimed Benson. He was articulating these thoughts for the first time and was amazed at how easily they slipped out and how convincing they sounded when given expression. He had thought somehow that they would sound silly but it was rather Father Hanlon who sounded silly. He did not have any answers at all.

'It's terribly difficult to commit a mortal sin, you know,' said Father Hanlon quietly.

'Is it? Tell that to all the people who thought they were committing a mortal sin by eating meat on Friday and died. Now the Vatican Council say it's all right to eat meat on Fridays.'

Father Hanlon laughed. 'I don't think that was ever a mortal sin.'

'But lots of people thought it was!' said Benson.

'Well I think it all comes down to faith in the end. You must pray about it.'

'But,' continued Benson, completely carried away and determined to articulate his complaints about his friendship with Christ and the way it seemed to be falling far short of what he had a right to expect from a Friend, 'I'm trying to make Christ my Friend! It is necessary that all friendships be based on complete trust and honesty. If I had a human friend who could send me to hell or let my house fall down without giving me a friendly warning, then that friend would cease to be my friend.'

'But God always sent warnings! All those prophets tried to warn those wicked cities to stay away from vice!'

'Yes, but that was the God of the Old Testament! I'm talking about His Son! It's God's Son who is supposed to be my friend!'

'But can't you see that They are one and the same?'

'No, I can't! Jesus is Love and the God of the Old Testament is all anger and revenge and acts of God! They cannot co-exist! They just can't!'

Father Hanlon gave up and just looked at his hands a little angrily. Then he said, 'Well, let's hope that the Third Member of the Trinity will descend to enlighten you. All I can suggest is that you pray about it.'

'But prayer won't change facts!' rapped back Benson.

Dad came in then carrying the whisky bottle and two glasses.

'Say goodnight,' he said.

'Goodnight.'

'Don't forget to clean your teeth!' shouted Mum from the kitchen.

'I won't. 'Night.'

In bed he opened 'Tribes of the Southern Sudan'. He gazed at the picture of the man with the spear for a long time, caressing himself under the bedclothes.

Then he looked at himself, held himself out and compared himself to the man in the picture. It was hard to tell. Probably the man in the picture was better off than he. But perhaps not. He was, anyway, better off than Andy.

He switched off the light and told himself the story of meeting Andy and going to the cemetery with him. As he came closer to climax, the man with the spear appeared from behind one of the graves. Andy ran away in terror but Benson stayed. He got down on his knees before the man.

A few minutes later he heard Father Hanlon bidding Mum and Dad goodnight and God bless.

Then he slept like a child.

Throughout the next week things went well for Benson. He managed to produce an essay on 'Hamlet' for Mr Stone which earned a large number of red ticks and a 'Much Improved! Keep it up'; he went to Confession in a new mood, mentioned his fall to the priest (at another parish) but told the priest that he did not think it was as serious a sin as the priest was making out; for the first time he got into conversation with a group of other students in his class and found they were nice and seemed to like him. And, whenever guilt and depression raised their well-known faces from the pond of unknowing, he was able to put them to flight by remembering the night with Andy and anticipating the next one.

One side of him saw the swift sex act which had taken place among the non-Catholic dead in the cemetery as dirty and unworthy. But, for once, this side did not predominate. He felt that something which had resulted in such a change of mind in him, such a conversion, could not be really bad. When he recalled it he felt a warm glow suffuse him similar to the feeling he had when he imagined himself eating two Mars Bars in a row followed by a quarter of sherbet lemons to refresh the palate. But the new memory was much more intense. Andy had freed him from his bondage. He could not wait to meet him again to thank him and he thought he knew how he could best thank him and this warmed him further.

The night arrived when he had arranged to meet Andy under the railway bridge near the back of the Prom. It was also the day of President Kennedy's funeral ceremonies. While the great of the world marched solemnly behind the dead President's coffin through the Washington streets, Benson rushed through his Geography homework so that he could be out of the house by seven. Dad was in the greenhouse and Mum alone kept vigil with the world in front of the television.

Then, while they lowered the President's body into the earth of Arlington Cemetery, Benson washed himself thoroughly upstairs and dabbed his face with Dad's Old Spice. He went in to Mum to say goodbye. Mum was dabbing the tears away from her cheeks. On the television the American flag was being folded and folded again by men in smart uniforms.

'It's so sad! Poor Mrs Kennedy!' exclaimed Mum.

'Yes. I'm off out Mum. I'm going to the library.'

'You should be watching this, son. It's history.'

'I've only got eighteenth-century European and nineteenth-century English, Mum. We don't do any American history.'

'What a waste!' said Mum, referring to the dead President rather than Benson's history syllabus.

'See you later. I won't be late.'

It was raining a thin drizzle as Benson made his way up the road. He turned up the collar on his mac and trotted off towards the back of the Prom.

Some of the houses he passed had their curtains open and in all he saw the blue flickering of televisions tuned to the funeral of the President.

He was not totally indifferent to these events; indeed, the death of the President had been one of the factors which had made the past week so spicy, had tinged it with an edge of unaccustomed drama and newness. Kennedy's death had been added to the exciting recipe, but it was an incidental flavouring only. The basic ingredient was Andy.

He arrived at the bridge under the railway track and stood beneath it to shelter from the rain which was increasing in intensity. He heard a train approaching and looked forward to the thunderous rumble it would make as it sliced the rails above his head. He was not disappointed and shouted loud as it passed, confident that no one would hear him.

Andy had not turned up but he was early. The track that led to the back of the Prom was deserted. The promenade lay a couple of hundred yards away. It was unlit but an occasional car could be seen, its headlights starkly contrasting with the gloom. Then, in the far distance, he could make out the lesser lights of ships entering and leaving the river on the high tide.

He remembered how, for a full month, he had gone down to the promenade ship-spotting with a group of other boys. But that had been many years ago. The expeditions had ended when one of the boys had dropped a pair of binoculars which had belonged to Michael O'Boyle's dad into the water from the pier that had been their spotting point. The group had walked home sorrowfully, trying to console Michael O'Boyle who had started to weep and would not be consoled. After that the ships had lost their attraction.

But now he would watch them enviously as they pointed their beautiful prows out towards the mouth of the river and the open sea. 'The Saxonia', 'The Corinthia', 'The Empress of Canada' nosed their way back to the wide world. Great ships on the move to the far corners of the earth along an endless watery road that led without interruption from his front gate to Accra, Sydney, Hong Kong and Bandar Seri Begawan. The thought of that intoxicated him. If he put his toes in the cold brown water of the estuary that toe was joined to the toes of people swimming on warm tropical beaches. They were just separated from him by millions of briny tears.

He thought of Bruno then too. Bruno had disappeared like those ships. Two old ladies now lived in the Tencer house. No one seemed to know what had happened to Bruno. He had disappeared just as the gun emplacements had disappeared.

'Well you came then.'

Andy had approached the bridge from the same direction that Benson had taken.

'Yes, of course. I said I would,' replied Benson.

'I'm glad you came. I've thought about you a lot since last week.'

'Same here.'

'That's nice.'

Andy and Benson walked off the path on to the sodden short grass of the back of the Prom. Benson thought of 'Camp on Blood Island'. They did not speak for a while. Both were wondering where to go.

Then Andy said, 'This is no place for us, John. It's a filthy night. You can come to my room if you like.'

'That would be nice! Is it far?'

'Not far,' replied Andy, 'but you mustn't ever tell any-body where I live even if we stop seeing each other. And you must never come there without phoning me first. Is that OK?'

'Yes.'

'Sorry to be so tiresome, dear, but you know what we're doing is illegal and I'm older than you. I'd get into more trouble than you, you know.'

'How old are you?' asked Benson.

'That would be telling! No, I'm twenty-seven,' con-fessed Andy.

'Are you? You don't look it.'

Andy snorted but said nothing.

They made their way back the way Benson had come only a few minutes before. As they walked Benson began to get a bit alarmed because their route was leading them frighteningly close to his own home. But then they turned to the right, towards the library.

Outside an old Victorian house whose back faced Albert Park, Andy said, 'I'm here.' And took out a set of keys.

He led Benson into an empty and very cold hall and up the stairs. They climbed three floors to the top of the house. A large skylight over the stairwell tapped to the rain.

Andy, looking around him, opened the door of his room. He went over to the window, drew the curtains and then returned to the door where Benson was stand-ing and switched the light on.

'Well, here's where it all happens, dear,' he said.

The room did not impress Benson greatly. Andy had a bed, unmade, in the corner. The walls sloped against the bedhead, forming an acute angle. Across the room, near the curtained window, there was a gas ring on a table along with a bottle of milk and some pans, crockery and cutlery. Next to this was a grimy washbasin. In the centre of the room were two bald easy chairs set on either side of a coffee table which had, under glass, a picture of a Spanish flamenco dancer.

'Let me take that wet mac,' said Andy. He motioned Benson to sit down in one of the easy chairs, and went over to the gas fire and turned it on with a lighter. Then, fishing about in a drawer, he produced a candle which he lit with the lighter. This he placed on the table and went over to the door and switched off the light.

He sat down in the other easy chair and moved the table to the left so that there was nothing between him and Benson.

'Well here we are,' he said.

'Yes,' said Benson. 'It's very nice.'

'It is thump!' exclaimed Andy. 'It's a bloody dump! Still, it's home.'

They did not speak then and Benson found that the silence caused him to become excited. His grey trousers bulged. He put his hand down to cover himself but Andy pushed it away.

'Is that a pickle in your pocket or are you pleased to see me?' he asked.

'How do you mean?' asked Benson.

Andy smiled, stood up and knelt down before him.

It was as good as the last time. Perhaps, if that were possible, rather better. They took longer than before and Benson was able to lie back in the easy chair, relaxing, taking the pressure off in order to keep his excitement from spilling over. Andy accepted the change in rhythm and seemed pleased whenever Benson enforced his desire on him.

When they had finished and both lay sighing in their easy chairs, Benson asked, more because he felt he ought than because of anything he wanted to do, 'Can't I help you at all?'

'Oh, no, dear. You've already done more than enough.'

'Yes, but you haven't er . . .'

'Come? No, I haven't. But don't worry your head about that. When you get to my age you don't need it as much.'

'Don't you?' asked Benson, incredulous.

'No. You acquire more sophisticated tastes. I'm happy to see you satisfied. You're a real man, you know that?'

'Do you really think so?'

'Oh, yes! And believe me I've seen a few in my time.'

Benson could hardly believe Andy was talking to him. 'Who, me? Are you sure you mean me?' he kept wanting to ask Andy. But it was obvious that Andy must mean him. Who else was there?

'How long have you been doing . . . er . . . have you been a ho . . . er?' asked Benson.

'I was born with sequins up me arse, dear,' replied Andy.

'Were you?'

'Never mind. I have been a homosexual for as long as I can remember. How about you?'

'Me too more or less,' replied Benson. 'But I've been fighting it.'

'I know you have. That's bloody obvious. You've stopped fighting now, have you?'

Benson was uncertain. 'I don't know. You see, it's a sin.'

Andy nodded knowingly. 'You're a Catholic too. I remember you shouting it out on our honeymoon!'

'Yes, and you?' asked Benson.

'I don't believe in it any more,' stated Andy. 'Fancy a coffee?'

'Er, yes, please. Thank you very much,' said Benson, wondering if he should. The bed-wetting was now only an occasional lapse but he still felt insecure when he drank anything in the evening.

As Andy filled the kettle and put the water on his gas ring, Benson asked, 'So you don't go to church?'

'No, never. Well, sometimes I go if something really bad happens or at Christmas or something.'

'But not every Sunday?'

'No!'

'And you don't go to Confession?'

'Never!' And Andy banged the coffee tin down on the table for emphasis. He turned towards Benson and said,

'I am a typical lapsed Catholic, dear. Well, perhaps not typical. I always think that "lapsed" is the wrong word for what happened to me. It makes you think that you just get too bloody lazy to do the necessary. But that's not how it was with me, dear. When I found out that I was a gay boy the whole bloody house of cards fell down. Yes, that's more how it is. I just collapsed. I'm a collapsed Catholic.'

Benson was shocked and puzzled. 'How do you mean?' he asked.

'I've just told you. It's a house of cards, the Catholic Church. You build it up slowly and you've got to keep your hands from shaking. Don't steal . . . don't lie . . . don't talk about people behind their backs . . . The house starts easily enough and you start getting really cocky so up you go to build the next floor. Don't eat meat of a Friday . . . don't go to Communion if you've eaten after midnight . . . don't use swear words.

'Then on to the next floor. Love Jesus and Mary and Joseph and Uncle Tom Cobley and all. Then you're up in the attic. Get married and raise a good Catholic family and don't marry a Protestant and don't commit adultery and don't use contraceptives and don't whatever you do go with a man even if it is the only thing in the whole world that you really want to do, the only thing that nature seemed to have made you to do . . . And in my case the fucking attic roof fell in, dear, and it brought the rest down. I'm a collapsed Catholic trying to make the best I can by searching through the rubble for something to call my own.'

'I see,' said Benson.

'I don't think you do, but you probably will. That's not my concern. I'm not going to make you a bloody apostate as well as a fully fledged queer.'

'But that's it, isn't it?' asked Benson. 'I mean it's one thing or the other. You can't be a Catholic and do what we're doing, can you?'

'Not easily, no. But some manage it, I had my first bit of real sex with a priest and he's still a priest as far as I

218

know . . . and not a million miles from where we sit neither.'

'No! Who?'

'My lips are sealed.'

'Go on, don't be a meanie!'

'Wild horses wouldn't . . .'

'Tell me!'

'Father Clarke at St Peter's.'

'No!'

'Yes.'

'You mean he really did . . . err?'

'Yes and I was in my altar boy's cotter at the time.'

'And he's still at that church?'

'Yes, he is. He's the parish priest.'

'He isn't.'

'All right, he isn't,' stated Andy, tiring of Benson's disbelief. 'I've told you what I know. Believe me or don't believe me. I don't care. Anyway, why are you so shocked? Priests are human beings too! If he can eat his cake and have it too, good luck to him I say. The more queers there are in places that count the better.'

Andy made the coffee and brought it over. He placed Benson's mug on the flamenco dancer's face.

Benson changed the subject and asked, 'Are your mum and dad living near here?'

'My mum lives in town, near the cathedral. I see her once or twice a week. My dad was a sailor and died in the Far East when I was little.'

'Do you have many friends who are er?'

'Some. What about you?'

'Me? No,' replied Benson, a part of him shocked at the idea. Andy pursed his lips and Benson added, 'Except you, of course.'

'Thanks.'

'Don't mention it. This is nice coffee.'

They drank their coffee and Benson said he ought to be getting back. Andy said OK but was once more kneeling in front of him.

This time it was more a labour for both of them but it was just as nice.

'Can I see you again?' asked Benson as he put on his mac.

'I'm not sure. You mustn't come here without giving me a ring first. You can have my number. I'm busy for a while and may be going away for a bit but give us a call in a fortnight.'

'A fortnight! That's a long time,' sighed Benson.

Andy shrugged and gave him his phone number.

Benson ran home, mulling over what had happened that night.

Mum had gone to bed when Benson got home. Dad was in his armchair reading 'Amateur Gardener'.

'Where's Mum?' he asked.

'She's gone off to bed, son. She said she wasn't feeling too bright,' replied Dad, looking up from his magazine, then closing it.

'Mum is all right, isn't she, Dad?' Benson asked. He had noticed that Mum seemed to have lost some of her energy. She no longer pulled out each strand of white hair that appeared, saying, 'Out you come!' They were spreading over her once-black hair like sherbet over a sideboard.

'Yes, I think so. She gets a bit out of sorts sometimes. She tires herself out, you know. I tell her to take it easy but you know what she's like.' Dad had opened the magazine again but he seemed restless. At last he threw it across the room on to the settee.

Benson tried to make his exit. 'I've got to do some learning work before I go to sleep,' he said, hanging on the door.

'Don't go just yet, son. Sit down for a moment, will you?'

Benson did so, wondering what could be on his dad's mind and fearing the worst.

Dad looked at Benson sitting next to the 'Amateur Gardener'. He looked uncomfortable to Benson and this increased his own agitation.

'Father Hanlon told me about the funny business at St Finbar's. It came as quite a fright, I can tell you, son,' said Dad, in a voice quite unlike his usual one.

Benson looked down at his hands and said nothing. He thought of Father Hanlon and that he had promised that he would say nothing.

'I er . . .' said Benson.

'What's done is done,' said Dad. 'I just thought I should warn you that you must fight to put all that sort of nonsense behind you. In my line of work we get all sorts of bent people arrested and brought in and sent off to prison. They're pretty pathetic for the most part, these homos. If I thought my son was that way, well I . . . I don't know what I would do.'

Dad did not sound angry. Benson sat with eyes downcast not knowing what was going on in his father's mind but knowing that he felt miserable and dirty.

'I'm not one of them, Dad,' he said.

'I hope not, son. If you were, well, it would kill your mother.'

'Well I'm not! Honest, Dad!' Benson managed. He had started to cry.

'Nobody's accusing you,' said Dad in his policeman's voice. 'We all make mistakes and Father Hanlon says it was probably just a stage and that you have grown out of it. I just thought I should warn you. That's all.'

At last Benson said goodnight to Dad and went up to bed. He did not look at 'Tribes of the Southern Sudan'. He lay in the dark wondering if he was adopted and hating Father Hanlon. He wished the priest would die and go to hell for he did not feel that he would ever be able to see his dad again without embarrassment and guilt welling up in him. For that the priest should pay and pay and pay. For all eternity.

The next day, because of the illness of their form teacher, Brother O'Toole, Benson's class had Brother Wood for their Religion lesson.

Nobody in the class liked Brother Wood. He refused to

give any respect to the Sixth Form students, respect they felt their age and status deserved. Brother Wood had been known to strap boys from the Sixth Form and seemed to take delight in humiliating them in front of boys from the lower forms.

Benson had unhappy memories of Brother Wood from the time before he went off to be a Brother. The boredom and fear of those Maths lessons had stayed with him, a bad memory at once activated by the sight of the cruel Brother.

Brother Wood came into a class already hushed by the knowledge of his imminent arrival.

'You can imagine with what joy I heard that I would have to take you irreligious so and so's for Religion during Brother O'Toole's unfortunate illness,' Brother Wood began in his usual tone. He took from the inside pocket of his cassock a little red Catechism. 'I don't propose to continue with the lesson that Brother O'Toole would have given you.' He held the little book high. 'Now I know that many of you will not have seen this Catechism of Christian Doctrine for some time. It seems to have fallen out of favour of late. However, I think some of you need reminding that what it contains remains, despite what the Vatican Council may have intimated to the contrary, the backbone of our faith. If you know this, you know the Church and that is all you know on earth and all you need to know, as the Irish poet said.'

Still the class sat on in silence.

'A question and answer session, I think. I shall choose questions drawn from random parts of the Catechism and quiz the class. Three failures and it's a strapping . . . to keep you on your toes.'

With that Brother Wood started at the front of the row on the right and worked his way back.

'O'Boyle, what do you mean when you say that the Pope is infallible?'

'When I say that the Pope is infallible, I mean that the Pope cannot err when, as shepherd and teacher of all Christians, he defines a doctrine concerning faith or morals, to be held by the whole Church,' replied O'Boyle with alacrity.

'Scott, what honour should we give to relics, crucifixes and holy pictures?'

'We should give relics, crucifixes and holy pictures a relative honour, as they relate to Christ and His Saints, and are memorials of them,' replied Scott.

'Muir, is it a sacrilege to contract marriage in serious sin, or in disobedience to the laws of the Church?'

'It is sacrilege to contract marriage in serious sin, or in disobedience to the laws of the Church and, instead of a blessing, the guilty parties draw upon themselves the anger of God,' replied Muir.

'Hepher, what do you mean by the flesh?'

'Let me see. By the flesh I mean our own corrupt inclinations and passions,' which are the most dangerous of all our enemies,' replied Hepher, in a monotone.

'Only just, Hepher. Only just.'

Then it was Benson's turn. Brother Wood searched through his Catechism to find a question for him. As he did so he kept saying, 'One for Benson. One for the lost sheep, Benson.'

He found what he was looking for and asked, 'What are the four sins crying to heaven for vengeance?'

Benson knew he was going to get that one, or one like it. He stood up, afraid and shaking slightly, though more shaking with barely contained dislike for the Brother than from fear. 'The four sins crying to heaven for vengeance are: 1. Wilful murder. 2. Oppression of the Poor. 3. Defrauding labourers of their wages,' replied Benson and sat down.

'You've forgotten one, young fellow-me-lad.'

Benson repeated the three he had said, then, wild and inspired, added, 'Giving a bad example to youth,' while he looked straight up at Brother Wood, making no attempt to conceal his dislike.

Brother Wood returned Benson's gaze for a long moment. Then with the hand that held the Catechism he hit out at Benson, catching him a stinging blow on his cheek. Benson reeled back but in a moment he was straight again and once more looking with contempt at Brother Wood.

'You're a nasty piece of work so you are, Benson,' he said between clenched teeth. Then he added, 'I'd have thought you of all people would have remembered the other sin that cries to heaven for vengeance: The Sin of Sodom.'

He hissed the words and moved on to the top of the next row, still looking at Benson hard. The Catechism shook slightly in his hand.

At the end of the first round of questions only Benson and Flynn had failed to answer their questions.

Benson looked at his watch. There was still twenty-five minutes to go. He hoped that he would be able to answer the next ones. At least he thought he hoped he could. Another part of him was saying, 'Let the beast do his worst! Let him hit me again and again!' He thought of Father Hanlon and his betrayal of him and hated.

Brother Wood came to Hepher again at last but looked all the time at Benson as he spoke the question. Benson looked back at him steadily. He felt a stillness inside which, coming as it did in stark contrast to his usual busy brain, he found remarkably pleasurable. Even the stinging in his cheek was nice, made him feel somehow detached, free from anguish.

'Hepher, are we bound to obey the Church?'

Hepher replied as meek as a lamb, 'We are bound to obey the Church, because Christ has said to the pastors of the Church, "He that heareth you, heareth me; and he that despiseth you, despiseth me".'

Then Brother Wood stood in front of Benson. He did not look at the little red book in his hand. His eyes looked straight into Benson's and then blinked and looked at an area of air about a foot above his head.

'Benson, what are the four sins crying to heaven for vengeance?' he asked.

'You asked me that one before, Brother.'

'Well I'm asking you again.'

'The four sins crying to heaven for vengeance are: 1. Wilful murder. 2. Oppression of the poor. 3. Defrauding labourers of their wages.' And he stopped.

'There's another, Benson!' said Brother Wood, between clenched teeth.

'I'm sorry, Brother. I've forgotten it again.'

Brother Wood gave Benson a look which made Benson think, 'He hates me! He really hates me!' But he smiled at the thought because he knew that Brother Wood was committing a sin by hating.

'Can any of you tell me what the fourth sin crying to heaven for vengeance is?' asked Brother Wood, still looking steadily at Benson.

'The sin of Sodom, sir,' volunteered Scott.

'That's right, Scott. Benson here has a selective memory, I'm thinking. He likes to banish from his mind what should be foremost in his mind.'

Benson, a stranger to himself, asked, 'What do you mean by that, Brother?'

But Brother Wood ignored him. 'That's two failures, Benson. Another one and you're for it.' And he departed up the row, his shaking nicotined fingers forming a V sign.

Benson was now the only one with two failures against his name. He knew that there would be a third and still he did not care. They looked at one another eye to eye and Benson hated Brother Wood back – tooth for tooth, tit for tat.

At last Brother Wood was back to Hepher.

'Hepher, what are the seven Corporal Works of Mercy?'

'The seven Corporal Works of Mercy are: 1. To feed the hungry. 2. To give drink to the thirsty. 3. To clothe the naked. 4 To harbour the harbourless. 5. To visit the sick. 6. To visit the imprisoned. 7. To bury the dead.'

'Very good, Hepher,' smiled Brother Wood, his voice shaking slightly.

And for the third time Brother Wood stood in front of Benson. The two looked at one another a long time. Then

Brother Wood looked away and Benson felt he had won, but, seeing the man's hands shaking violently, could not take much pleasure in the victory.

Quietly, Brother Wood asked Benson. 'Benson, what are the seven Spiritual Works of Mercy?'

'The seven Spiritual Works of Mercy are: 1. To convert the sinner. 2. To instruct the ignorant. 3. To counsel the doubtful. 4. To comfort the sorrowful. 5. To bear wrongs patiently. 6. To forgive injuries. 7. To pray for the living and the dead,' replied Benson, in a tone which he hoped, not knowing why, was conciliatory.

'Saved by the skin of your teeth, Benson,' said Brother Wood.

'Yes, sir,' replied Benson, triumphant.

The bell rang, much to the relief of everyone. Brother Wood left the room and the class turned to look at Benson.

Scott said, 'He's given you a black eye. Sue him.'

Hepher said, 'Well done, Moses.'

'Benson to you, Hepher,' Benson replied.

In the school toilets at lunchbreak Benson assessed his injuries. A livid red-black bruise, the shape of Australia without the Northern Territories, covered his right cheekbone. He bathed it with cold water, stood back and decided that, all in all, he liked it and found it a suitable addition to his already handsome appearance.

Some of his classmates gathered round him to admire and commiserate, then left to spread the news the length and breadth of the playground that Moses had been transfigured by a blow from Brother Wood, but, throughout, he had never once winced and who would have thought it?

Clitherow, a member of Benson's class who was terribly brainy and was often absent because he took special classes for Oxford Entrance, stayed with him.

'You did very well,' he told Benson. 'It was easy enough to see what Wood was trying to do to you and you beat him well and truly, the beast!'

This was a rare compliment, coming from Clitherow. Clitherow sailed through the Lower Sixth on a high intellectual cloud. He was excused the adolescent banter of the other boys because even the dimmest could discern that he was bright and heading for the heights. He had never once spoken to Benson, though they always nodded greetings. His manners were perfect.

'What are you going to do about it?' he asked Benson.

'Nothing,' Benson replied.

'Why not? You'd be doing a service for the whole school! That Wood is a worse than senseless thing!'

'No, really, Clitherow. It doesn't matter.'

'I suppose it's your outmoded belief in the Catholic Church that's holding you back,' stated Clitherow, in a patronising tone.

'No, it's not that . . .'

'What then?'

Clitherow was impatient of confusion. He did not have friends at school and seemed to drift round St Bede's like a superior lost ghost who should have been haunting a stately home but had somehow ended up haunting a council house. He did not speak like the rest of the boys, more like the people who read the news on the Home Service. His father was a consultant at a hospital and a Knight of St Columba.

'I don't want to make trouble,' said Benson.

'I see,' Clitherow sounded disappointed.

'I mean, I think I won my argument,' Benson continued.

'What argument was that? I wasn't listening.'

'Never mind.'

'No, tell me!'

'I wouldn't answer Brother Wood's question about the Four Sins crying to heaven for vengeance.'

'Why not?'

'Because I don't think it does.'

'You've lost me,' said Clitherow.

'To tell you the truth, I'm lost myself,' said Benson.

'Good,' said Clitherow and he shook Benson's hand.

Benson was flattered by all this attention from the Brain of the Lower Sixth. 'Do you want to go for a walk in the playground?' he asked, though he would have accepted a negative answer gracefully.

'I'd be delighted.'

The two walked out into the playground where every boy in the school seemed to be screaming and running around aimlessly.

'Do you ever feel out of place here?' asked Clitherow, surveying the scene.

'All the time. All the time.'

'Shake on it.' And he shook Benson's hand again.

Benson was as pleased as Punch. This was living!

'Have you read Sartre?' asked Clitherow.

'Er, no. Who's he?'

'You haven't read Sartre! Please do so as soon as possible. He has much to say about our situation. But tell me, where do you stand with regards the Myth of Rome?'

Benson felt he was drowning in his ignorance. 'How do you mean, the Myth of Rome?'

'It's my term for Catholicism. What do you think of Catholicism? They seem to have you down as a Holy Joe round here. That essay you wrote on Hamlet's character was a scream. I had to put my handkerchief in my mouth to stop the titters.'

'Well I have problems with hell.'

'That's a start, but is that the only thing you have problems with?'

Benson thought hard. 'I have problems with the way, say, Brother Wood acts towards us.'

'I would agree,' conceded Clitherow. 'There is a yawning gap between the spirit of the Gospels and the spirit prevailing at this institution. The problem is, you see, that Christianity just won't work. The Fathers of the Church realised that quite early on and they set about making the whole thing more worldly and comprehensible. I've nothing against Jesus per se. Quite a decent sort of fellow. He'd obviously read his Aristotle. But all the rest? A distraction.'

Clitherow had lost Benson and Benson told him so. 'How do you mean?' he asked.

'Right-ho. Let's just say that I am an agnostic.'

'But you do go to Church, don't you?' asked Benson, shocked.

'I do not.'

'How long . . . how long have you been like this?'

'Since I attained the age of reason. But that's enough about me. Where do you stand?'

'Well I still believe in the Church. I think. It's just that I do have problems with some details,' replied Benson.

'As I say, that's a start anyway. Once you've made a small hole in the dyke the water of unbelief will soon swamp the City of the Plains.'

'Oh, I don't think so. I can't imagine life without God. It would make life . . . well . . . silly somehow. A waste of time.'

'Absurd?'

'Yes, you could say that.'

Clitherow clapped his hands together and then turned and placed them on Benson's shoulders. 'Read Sartre!' he said.

'How do you spell it?'

Clitherow told him. Then he said, 'You're homosexual, aren't you, Benson?'

'Who me?' asked Benson. 'How dare you!'

'Please don't shy like that! I'm not Hepher. You are, aren't you?'

'I think I may be. Yes,' answered Benson after a pause.

'Good. That wasn't too difficult, was it? I am too, though I also have a fondness for women.'

'Are you really? Gosh.'

Clitherow held out his hand to Benson and shook it. 'I must be going now. I have my school dinner to eat. You see, I am not beyond doing penance. We must meet again soon. Read Sartre!'

And Clitherow weaved his way across the playground towards the dinner room leaving Benson in a state of cheerful confusion.

That evening Benson was quizzed about the bruise on his cheek. He lied and told Mum and Dad that he had got it while playing football in the playground. Dad seemed pleased that his son was indulging in rough physical pursuits. Mum was less convinced. However, after a short barrage of questions had been successfully rebuffed by her son, she let the matter drop. Benson went into the front room to do his homework.

Christmas came and went.

Benson went to midnight Mass as usual and fell in love with his Friend again under the spell of ritual and soft sermons full of love and sacrifice.

Although Dad did not mention anything more about his departure from St Finbar's, Benson frequently felt embarrassment and guilt when he was with him. He longed for the holidays to end so that he could go back to school and be around Clitherow again.

At school things were better. His classmates showed him a new respect; Clitherow became a fast friend. He went for long walks with him and discussed Sartre and a man called St Genet, who, Clitherow reckoned, was as alienated as Benson; his work was going well and he seemed to be getting the hang of the required method for writing essays; and there had been no repetition of the bullying tactics of Brother Wood. Life, on the whole, was definitely picking up.

Clitherow had been correct about religion. The hole in the dyke of Benson's faith was daily becoming bigger. On some days he felt it was large enough for him to see through it to a calm sea that stretched uneventfully towards the horizon. And there on the horizon there was a white town full of people like Clitherow who would help him make sense of his life. Jean Paul Sartre was there and told him to jump into the dark and take decisions, while his wise wife nodded and their friend, Genet, put his arm around him and said he understood; Joan Baez was there singing of lost loves and poor black people clubbed down in the Southern States of America; Bob Dylan was there singing about changing times and the lonesome death of Hattie Carrol. And among these luminaries walked Benson, expecting to find 'Dearest Him who dwells ... Alas! Away!' behind each palm tree. Benson took long walks with Jean Paul and told him of his sufferings. Sartre nodded and smoked the briar pipe he held on the back cover of 'La Nausée'. When Benson had finished his tale, Sartre said, 'Act!' and Benson said he would have a go. Then Jean Paul took Benson home for tea. His lovely wife, Simone, made wonderful jelly.

But at other times it seemed that the dyke of faith was intact. He would visit a church, kneel down and watch the altar. A feeling of being home and in the presence of God filled him up and made him weep. Then it would seem incredible that he could ever have doubted. He began, at such times, to see Clitherow as bad company; Sartre as a bad writer who wrote books that would pull poor souls like Benson into the pit.

But the arguments against Catholicism, Benson's stock of ammunition, were daily becoming larger. Before he knew it he had stockpiled a large arsenal, which, for good or bad, he would fire off whenever tempted back to the Church.

The sixth form at school was doing its prescribed job. It had started Benson on the path of thought. He questioned everything: bath and bath-water were subjected to great scrutiny and thrown out. For a while he held on to the baby, protecting it and singing it holy songs by way of reply to the arguments of his peers. But not for long. Soon he was holding on to the baby of faith more and more loosely. When he actually threw it away, he hardly noticed it was gone. He only knew that his arms were open to embrace, free at last, his own nature, needs and inclinations.

*   *   *

231

For some time Benson had not been able to get back in touch with Andy. He rang his number repeatedly from telephone boxes but it was never answered. He was always extremely disappointed when he heard the rings going on and on. There was a quality to them which told him the room was empty but it did not stop him from letting the telephone ring.

Then, on two occasions, he went and stood outside Andy's house hoping that he would come out. If he had, Benson would have pretended he had just been passing. He thought he saw lights in the attic window on one occasion, but did not dare to go up to the front door and knock.

One evening, about a month since he had last met Andy, he went to the library to find another book by Jean Paul Sartre. The two he had read since being introduced to him by Clitherow had mystified him rather. He read both diligently and gained some satisfaction from the fact that he could go back and tell Clitherow that he had done so, but he did not really understand what the author was going on about most of the time.

'Well look who it isn't!' It was Andy standing behind him.

'Hello, Andy! Where have you been?'

'I've been here.'

'I've called you a few times but you've never answered the phone. I was a bit worried.'

Andy flicked his left eyebrow. 'Well you know how it is, dear.'

'How do you mean?'

'I've had other fish to fry.'

'Have you?'

'Yes.'

Benson could see that Andy was restless and did not want to talk. 'Can I come and see you?' he asked him, quietly.

'No, I don't think so, dear.' He came closer to Benson and whispered, 'You see, it's a bit difficult. You're under age and I'd be for it if we were found out.'

'But that didn't worry you before!'

'That was before.'

'I see.'

Andy wandered away soon after that, leaving Benson to wonder what it could all mean. He tried to remember why he had come to the library in the first place but for a long time could not remember, his brain being so full of confusion brought on by Andy's rejection.

Then he remembered that he had read a review of a new novel by an American writer, James Baldwin. It was called 'Another Country'. He had decided then that he would try to find it on the library shelves.

He looked under B but found nothing. Then he went over to the catalogue drawers and saw that the library did indeed stock the book but that it had a red star, which meant that it was in the permanent reserve and had to be asked for, the book being considered too risqué to be put out on the open shelves.

Quaking a little, Benson approached the librarian and asked her for 'Another Country'. She disappeared through a door into a room at the back and then returned carrying a thick novel. This Benson took eagerly and checked out. He looked round for Andy but he was nowhere to be seen. He left and walked home through the cemetery.

'Another Country' opened Benson's eyes.

He read it closely at a slow pace. He rationed himself to a few pages a day in order to make the feast last as long as possible and then, when he had completed the book, he turned back to page one and read it again. He wept for the death of Rufus, the black hero, who jumped off a bridge in New York because he was unloved and messed up by America and had not been touched by Vivaldo, his white friend, who, though sometimes sharing a bed with Rufus, had been unable to reach across the divide of conventional morality and touch his friend when Rufus needed an embrace so badly. Had Benson been Vivaldo he knew he would have been able to reach out. If Benson had been Vivaldo then Rufus would not have leapt to his death.

One segment of the novel dealt with the relationship of Eric and his French friend, Yves. There was an idyll in which the two lived in Chartres and made love within sight of the spire of Chartres Cathedral and Benson read this part over and over again. The scales fell from his eyes and he realised that not only was he not alone but that love between men had possibilities for beauty. This was the first time he had ever seen such a portrayal and it completed the sea-change in him brought on by Andy.

He missed Sunday Mass for the first time, taking 'Another Country' to the cemetery and reading favourite parts. He went home and, bold as brass, made up an account of the sermon he had heard at Mass. He felt no guilt. He was intoxicated. He had jumped into the dark. He had made his decision. He was going to be a happy homo.

At school Benson joined the intellectual set, along with Clitherow and others. He was at the forefront of the group of sixth formers who argued about religion and questioned the rectitude of everything.

Clitherow introduced him to Bach's cello works and Tom Paxton and Benson introduced Clitherow to 'War Requiem' and 'Missa Luba'. It was a time when a new book made his heart race, when a song could change his perspective and beat away niggling doubts. His heart opened to everything and he dreamed of a famous future.

He and Clitherow would go into the city to study at the main library. Once over the ferry and on the city streets, both boys felt that they were at the centre of things, in the midst of all the possibilities that life could hold out.

The library itself was a distraction for Benson. There were lots of foreign students there, studying for their degrees at the university.

Benson would look at the studious African and Arab faces, wondering if one of them could be 'Dearest Him'.

Sometimes they would look up and notice him watching them. They might smile. They might not. But they did not give any look or recognition in the way that Andy had.

One night he followed an African student home from the library. The student carried a briefcase and walked across the city to a tenement near the Anglican Cathedral. He disappeared into the wretched place without once looking behind him. Benson went home and wrote his first poem.

And one day soon after, in the art gallery next to the library, Benson found himself face to face with his old friend, the soldier in 'Faithful Unto Death'.

He stood looking at the painting, amazed at how well he had remembered it from the brief look he had been allowed during Brother O'Toole's lesson all that time ago. But now he interpreted the painting in a different way. The guard was looking at life straight in the eye. He did not flinch from its cruel, burning realities. He saw the bubbling cauldron of wickedness. He saw the inquisitions of Catholicism; the death of Viola Liuzzo and Medger Evers in the South; the cruelty of war; the indifference of rich nations towards poor ones; the complications of life and man's ever-erring reaction to it all. The guard knew it all and stood to attention, steady and still. The guard was his own man, an individual who had taken his decision and was sticking by it, no matter what anguish resulted.

Benson bought a postcard of 'Faithful Unto Death' on his way out of the art gallery and kept it inside his paperback of 'Iron in the Soul' like a Holy Picture in a missal.

And so, as Catholicism ebbed out of him, new enthusiasms and guilts took up their places in Benson's soul. He shivered to Martin Luther King's sermons; wept at the sight of the American police brutality on the freedom marches in the South; ranted against George Wallace and the colonial sins of Britain; worried Mum and Dad to distraction by being either monosyllabic towards them or venting his spleen on aspects of Catholicism.

Mum went scuttling back to the psychology shelf at the library. Once again she was able to put a word to her son's ailment. Back home she went and announced, 'It's adolescence. He's growing up, becoming his own man. That's the problem.'

Dad looked at Mum through a haze of cigarette smoke. He listened to the Dansette in the front room playing 'Blowing in the Wind' too loud.

'I can't see what he sees in that fellow's voice. He sounds like a bull's death rattle.'

'That's Bob Dylan,' replied Mum. 'He dotes on him, he does.'

Mum had taken the time to ask Benson about the man whose records littered the front room. They mostly belonged to Clitherow.

'Well, I don't know which was worse, his religious mania or this. At least he kept a civil tongue in his head when he was religious. Listen to that racket!' said Dad.

Benson was now playing Britten's 'Missa Brevis'. He had bought the E.P. with his Christmas money and played it every day. He loved it loud. The boy's choir had a piercing edge to it and the organ echoed and amplified the shrieking quality of the choir and pierced Benson to the heart.

As he listened he was busily engaged on learning Matthew Arnold's 'Dover Beach' by heart. Arnold's poetry was one of his set authors. 'Dover Beach' was his favourite. He felt that his 'sea of faith' was withdrawing to the accompaniment of the 'long, withdrawing roar' of Britten's 'Missa Brevis'. He repeated the poetry and listened to the music and his spirits soared into a merry melancholy which was becoming his most abiding quality.

He shared his feelings with Clitherow alone. Clitherow understood. But the hapless parents in the kitchen were left, shut out. In the dark.

At school, Benson had managed to move from his place at the back to the desk next to Clitherow at the front.

Since the incident with Brother Wood, Benson found that he was treated by the rest of the class with a new respect. This was undoubtedly helped by the fact that he was Clitherow's friend and that his work was winning acceptance among the staff.

Both Clitherow and Benson considered themselves set apart in the school and did nothing to ingratiate themselves to either staff or fellow students. Several of the teachers were rather frightened of the sharp precociousness of the pair at the front.

Brother O'Toole had soon returned to teach them Religion and Benson, though sorely tempted to argue with everything the Brother said, could not bring himself to do so. He remembered Brother O'Toole with affection from the days when the Brother had taken him for English before he had gone off to be a Brother. And, since his return, Brother O'Toole had never been anything but decent to him, had never mentioned anything about his reasons for leaving the Brothers, though Benson knew that Brother O'Toole must have been privy to all the gossip.

But, if Brother O'Toole's Religion lessons kept Benson quiet, they did not inspire him to return to the Faith. The books and music and feelings that stabbed his heart daily and made him wild with excitement had far more power over him than anything Religion could offer.

Suddenly, it seemed that everything Benson touched added to the arguments against Catholicism. History books detailed the wickedness of Renaissance popes, newspapers told him about the world's population problems and the way the Catholic Church stood out firmly against all effective forms of contraception. Benson was confused by all this but he now took Hamlet as one of his heroes and saw him as a kindred soul, likewise confused by all the conflicting information that the world and circumstance had thrown at him.

But once a week Benson allowed himself to let his doubts about Catholicism have full head. A priest came to give the class a Religion lesson. The priest was so pious and traditional that he opened himself up to the contemptuous comments of the sixth form sophisticates.

One day, the priest came in and said that he wanted to talk to them about the saints as patrons and intercessors.

'The Church is all-embracing,' began the priest. 'There is a saint for everyone. Any job you take in life you will have a saint to help you out. For example, butchers have three saints: Adrian, Antony and Luke; barbers have Antony of Padua and Louis; bricklayers have Steven; hopeless cases have St Jude.' He looked up at the class. 'Now who is the patron saint of porters?'

The class was silent.

'St Christopher.' The priest answered his own question. 'And who is the patron saint of shepherds?'

The class was still silent. Clitherow yawned.

The priest noticed the yawn and frowned, 'St Drogo.'

Benson put up his hand. 'Who is the patron saint of women in labour, Father?'

'I don't know off hand, but I can look it up.'

'I know!' said Benson.

'Tell us then.'

'St Anne.'

The priest smiled wanly. 'Well, yes. I suppose that makes sense.'

'And who is the patron saint of women in difficult labour?' asked Benson.

'Not St Anne?' asked the priest.

'No, not St Anne. You'd be barking up the wrong tree if you were in difficult labour and went to St Anne for help. She'd direct you to St John Thwing.'

'Would she now?'

'Yes,' continued Benson. 'You've got to get the right one for the right job. You see, St Gabriel is the patron saint of television workers but St Claire of Assisi is the patron saint of television. You've got to be pretty accurate, you see.'

'Well I don't think you do. Our Lord understands and . . .'

238

Benson interrupted. 'So what's the point of it then. Who do you go to if you're a prostitute or a mother living on a rubbish tip in Lima with ten children to feed and no way of limiting your family? Who do you go to if you're being beaten and shot and lynched by wicked whites in Selma, Alabama, or if you are a tea-picker in Assam being exploited by Brooke Bond? Who do you go to if you are beyond the pale; if you are sexually different through no fault of your own? Who do you go to?'

'We're not talking about birth control or civil rights or sexual deviation today, young man. We're talking about patron saints.'

Clitherow put up his hand. The priest nodded to him. 'I think we should be talking about birth control, Father,' he said. 'At St Damien's Church yesterday a Catholic doctor who has started a birth control clinic near here was refused communion by the parish priest. I was there. He went up to the altar rails and knelt to receive the Host. When Father Coe saw him, he just passed him by, leaving the doctor with the communion plate in his hand. That is what we should be talking about.'

The priest reluctantly began to talk about the Church's policy to artificial methods of contraception. Benson whispered to Clitherow, referring to the withdrawal of communion from the doctor. 'It was a case of Eucharistus Interruptus.'

Clitherow exploded with a sneeze of laughter.

The priest stopped. He looked at Clitherow hard. Then he picked up his books and left the room.

The class remained silent, wondering what would happen next. A long five minutes passed. Then the priest returned with Brother Hooper. He pointed to Clitherow and Benson, saying, 'Those two. Every time I take this class, those two disrupt it. I'm tired of it!'

Brother Hooper, stony-faced, pointed to them. 'Come with me, you two,' he said.

Clitherow and Benson followed Brother Hooper along the bottom corridor of St Bede's to his office.

He sat at his desk while motioning Clitherow and

Benson to stand across from him. He looked at them closely, distastefully. Then he sighed, and, fondling a paper-knife, said, 'This is not the first time I have had complaints about you two. Brother Wood came to me some time ago to tell me that you, Benson, had refused to answer catechism questions and insulted him at the same time. I decided to let that pass because Brother Wood had already administered his own form of punishment to you.' He turned to Clitherow. 'You, Clitherow, I am very disappointed in. You should know better than to behave as you have just behaved. It is up to you to give a good example to the other pupils . . .' and he turned his gaze back to Benson.' . . . pupils who may not be as gifted as you are. You must understand that, while you may be able to handle these problems of faith and still come up smiling, it is not given to all so to do. You may be the cause for them to fall into disbelief.'

Clitherow said, 'But, sir, I was only trying to talk about issues which are important.'

'And I know what that issue is! But this is a Catholic institution. You have been sent here by your parents to receive a Catholic education. That is the given. To question that faith in the way that you do is just not acceptable. I warn you both that if this occurs again I shall strap you both in front of the whole school.'

'But, sir . . .' began Clitherow.

'Keep silent!' shouted Brother Hooper. 'I shall strap you both in front of the whole school and then you will be suspended to encourage the rest. Never in all my years in education have I come across a year like this one! It is a poor future for Mother Church if it is chaff like you that she will inherit.'

They stood silent in front of Brother Hooper. Benson had adopted his 'do your worst' look. The headmaster noticed it, opened his mouth to remark, but, instead, waved his hands at them dismissively. 'Get out of my sight!'

They walked back towards the classroom.

240

'Did you notice how he played with that paper-knife?' remarked Clitherow.

'Not really, why?' asked Benson.

'Doesn't matter. Anyway, it beats me why they're called Brothers,' said Clitherow.

'What makes you say that?'

'Because they're not like any fucking Brothers that I'd be prepared to acknowledge,' replied Clitherow.

Turning the corner of the corridor Clitherow gave a V-sign to the statue of the Founder of the Order. The statue, taking Clitherow's rebuff in the right spirit, continued to smile seraphically.

'I'm feeling iconoclastic,' Clitherow announced.

'How do you mean?'

But Clitherow could not reply as they had reached the classroom door.

Quietly and modestly they took their places in time to catch the priest telling the class that the patron saint of skin diseases was St Marculf.

That Friday Clitherow invited Benson to come to his home the following day to have tea, stay the night and 'do something iconoclastic'. Benson said he would be delighted and told Mum. Mum said she was pleased he had made a friend.

He had found Mum sitting in the lounge when he got home. She was not reading or doing anything else that Benson could discern. She looked a bit tired to him.

'You OK, Mum?' he asked her.

Mum smiled and nodded. 'Yes, a bit tired, that's all.'

'Can I make the tea?' Benson asked.

'That's nice of you, son, but I've made a salmon salad. It's less work.'

Benson nodded and retired to the other room. There he got down to doing all the homework he had for the weekend in order to leave himself free for fun and intellectual stimulation with Clitherow. He disposed of his work without much difficulty and set about writing a poem.

Then, carrying a small suitcase and a copy of his poem, Benson went back into the lounge to say goodbye to Mum.

'Be a good boy,' she told him, as she always had done. Then she added, 'You going to give your mum a kiss?'

Benson had been about to protest that he was too old for that sort of thing but thought better of it. He darted across the room and planted a dry kiss on Mum's cheek.

'Well, it's better than nothing I suppose,' Mum observed.

'Right-ho, Mum. Bye!'

He rushed out of the house and ran up the road.

Half an hour later he was walking with Clitherow from the bus-stop near Clitherow's home. Clitherow had been waiting there for him.

'I've got a surprise for you!' he exclaimed as soon as Benson was off the bus. 'How do you fancy going to an orgy?'

'How do you mean?' asked Benson.

Clitherow sighed: '*How do you mean*?' he mimicked. 'You always say that! Such a cliché! Look, an orgy is an orgy. One of my homo acquaintances has fixed us up. There's a house he knows not far from here. You go there and pay some money and strip off. It's all dark and you have an orgy.' Then, seeing Benson's miserable expression, he added, 'Or you can drink beer or talk or look at dirty pictures. It's up to you.'

'Where is this place?' asked Benson.

'Near,' replied Clitherow, guardedly.

'Isn't it expensive to get in?' asked Benson hopefully.

'Don't worry, I'll pay.'

'When are we going?'

'This evening. After tea. We'll say we're going to the pictures.'

'I'm not sure,' said Benson.

'Look, it's about time I found out what it's all about. You had a good time with that chap in the cemetery. You said it was the best feeling you'd ever had. Now I want to go.'

242

Benson regretted that he had ever told Clitherow about Andy and what he had done to him. It had seemed right at the time because Clitherow had been telling him stories of his adventures with women. He had told him that he had cornered a girl who worked at Woolworths behind the settee at a party. The girl had let him put his hand down her dress and up her skirt. He had not liked what he had felt. It was like having one's hand trapped in an over-used teapot, he said.

'I want to try everything, Benson! I want to open myself up to every experience, and drink deep!' Clitherow shouted, startling a pair of old ladies they were passing. Benson tried to smile at the old ladies reassuringly.

'Life is for living, Benson! You and I, we have spent too damned long seeing life as a preparation for death, as a vale of tears! We've got to get out of that bog-Irish attitude to life! The only sin, Benson, is not to live! The only sin is to turn away from experiences! We must read every book! See every country! Use our time well! We must not merely "measure out our lives in coffee spoons" . . . have you read Eliot yet?'

'No, not yet,' replied Benson. In truth he had tried but had thought it all a bit lengthy. He had turned page after page after page and kept sighing to be confronted with a seemingly never-ending wasteland of words leading nowhere.

'Well maybe you aren't ready for him yet. Everything to its season, my friend. An orgy! I can't wait!'

But Benson was already wondering whether his towel would be big enough to go round him and cover his nakedness during the orgy and whether he would be able to put one leg in front of another when in such a stressful situation.

But he said nothing and soon they had turned into the long drive that led up to Clitherow's house.

The house had been built for cotton brokers in retreat from the city and had a commanding position over the estuary. The garden was huge but largely untended.

'What do you do with all these rooms?'

Clitherow shrugged, 'Live and partly live.'

There was a black Rover outside the front door. Benson and Clitherow went round the back and into a huge kitchen with a stone floor. An Aga took up a lot of the floor space and a grey-haired woman sat on a stool by the cooker reading 'The Tablet'. The woman looked up.

'Hello, young man,' she said. 'You must be the friend I've been hearing so much about.' She turned to Clitherow. 'Show him to his room and then bring him down here straight away. I want to hear about his time with the Brothers.'

'He's trying to forget it, Mother,' said Clitherow, laughing.

'Well as soon as he's told me all about it he can forget it.'

'I'll be glad to tell you anything I can,' said Benson helpfully.

'Good lad.'

Clitherow took Benson up a carved, curving staircase to his room. There were old paintings of ships on the panelled walls. Benson's room looked out over the sea. He could see the funnel of a ship sitting on the horizon.

'Gosh, this is super!' he exclaimed. 'If I had a room like this I'd never want to leave it.'

Clitherow shrugged and said, 'The view does have a "certain seedy appeal". That's Auden.'

'Is it?'

They went back to the kitchen where a tray of tea and some scones awaited them. As Benson ate, Mrs Clitherow quizzed him about the Brothers.

'Were they very hard on you?' she asked.

'Well, it wasn't easy, Mrs Clitherow. But then it wasn't supposed to be easy.'

Mrs Clitherow nodded. 'It's always seemed to me that they're a sadistic lot. Did you find that?'

Benson munched on a scone while considering a

reply. At last he said, 'Some are and some aren't. There are good and bad everywhere.'

'But it isn't a natural sort of life. Don't you get a lot of perverts there?'

'Er,' said Benson.

Mrs Clitherow continued. 'I expect you do. You must have been lucky. I'm of the opinion that sex really cannot be sublimated. What do you think?'

'Well, er, I think you're probably right. They do say that cold showers . . .'

'I must get you to have one every day,' she said to Clitherow.

Clitherow winced. 'I don't intend to sublimate anything.'

'No, we Clitherows are not good sublimators. I've got ten children, did you know that?'

'No, I knew it was a big family but . . .'

'He's the last,' she said, pointing to Clitherow. 'Totally unplanned. A bit of a shock, I can tell you. I thought I was well past the age. He just slipped through. Lucky to be here, the young rascal.' She winked at her son and Clitherow pulled a clown's face at his mother.

Benson thought what fun it must be for Clitherow to grow up with this mother. She was as sharp as a razor. There seemed to be nothing Clitherow could not say to her. Gosh, that must be marvellous! And all the books everywhere! How wonderful, he thought, to have intellectual parents with a house overlooking the sea.

Then Dr Clitherow came in. Benson was introduced and called him 'Doctor', but he just said, 'Call me Paddy.'

Paddy did not talk as much as Mrs Clitherow. He sat listening sagely to everything that was said, a smile on his face, a pipe just like Jean-Paul Sartre's in the corner of his mouth.

Clitherow was explaining why they had laughed during religion.

'So he said "Eucharistus Interruptus" to me and I just burst out laughing.'

Doctor and Mrs Clitherow laughed hard and long. 'Sure that's a good one!' laughed Dr Clitherow. 'That reminds me of the one about Jesus walking through the wilderness and coming on this woman tied to a stake. There was a big crowd of people all around and the Pharisees came up and said to Jesus, "This woman is an adulteress and the law says that she must be stoned to death. What do you have to say about that?" Well, Jesus had a look at the woman and then had a look at the crowd and then he bent down and started writing in the sand. He said, "He who is without sin cast the first stone!" There was a silence and then a big red brick was lobbed through the air from somewhere back of the crowd and biffed the poor woman tied to the stake on the bonce. Jesus stood up and peered over the crowd to see where the brick had come from. Then he frowned and said, "Mother! Really!" '

The kitchen rocked with a gale of laughter. Benson, shocked and delighted, laughed louder than the others, amazed and full of wonder that the Clitherows could share such a joke. He wished for a moment that he could be adopted by the Clitherows and spend his life in this kitchen talking.

'Still, it is wicked what's happening to that doctor over his clinic,' said Mrs Clitherow. 'It can't be long before the Church sees the light over contraception. Until they do I shan't darken the doors of St Damien's. That Father Coe is a reactionary bugger.'

'The Church will never change,' said Clitherow.

Dr Clitherow took his pipe from his mouth and looked hard at the bowl as he spoke. 'It's a pity. The Church has so many beautiful qualities. It's a great institution, but seriously flawed.'

'Look at Papal infallibility!' exclaimed Benson, confident.

Dr Clitherow nodded.

'I mean they made it a doctrine in, was it 1870, and the only thing they can find to be infallible about is the Immaculate Conception and the Assumption. It's as if they want to put stones on the path to trip everyone up.'

'Yes, the Assumption is an assumption,' said Clitherow, unfairly, Benson thought, because he had told that one to Clitherow.

Much laughter again and the laughter and good talk lasted through tea with Benson confessing about Brother Michael and P. F.s and even his own feelings, though he was careful to place all dubious revelations in the past tense.

They left the house at six and took a bus to get to the house where the orgy was.

Benson had not wanted to leave and had had to be prised out of the kitchen by Clitherow.

'They like you. I can always tell.'

'Do they really?' asked Benson, immensely flattered. 'I like them too. Gosh, you are lucky!'

'I suppose I am. They're not bad all in all.'

'Not bad! They're wonderful! There's nothing you can't say to them. Oh, I wish they were . . .'

He did not finish the sentence. He had been going to say that he wished they were his parents. He did too but it seemed like a betrayal of Mum and Dad at home.

'Do they like Bob Dylan?' he asked instead.

'Mum does but Dad can't stand the voice. But they both dote on Joan Baez.'

'Gosh!' said Benson.

They sat on the top deck of the bus in the very front seat and watched the scenery.

'Cigarette?' asked Clitherow.

'I don't mind if I do.'

Benson only became apprehensive again when the bus left them in a leafy street and Clitherow led the way saying, 'It should be the first street on the left.'

Five minutes later they turned into the drive of a house rather like Clitherow's. Clitherow went straight up to the door and rang the bell.

A middle-aged man dressed in a P.T. kit came to the door.

'Can I help you?' he asked.

'Yes. Tim Edgar said we could come.'

'You know Tim Edgar well?' asked the man in a simper like Andy's.

'Yes. Very well.'

'Come in then.'

Benson followed Clitherow into the hall of the house. There were piles of clothes on the floor.

'That'll be twenty-five shillings, please.'

'For both of us?' asked Clitherow.

'Each.' The man saw the look of surprise from Clitherow and added, 'Look, if I had my way, dear, chickens like you would be let in for nothing, but rules are rules. Still, it covers the price of two beers. Everything else is free.'

Benson had been about to whisper, 'Let's go!' but didn't because Clitherow took out a five pound note and handed it to the man who gave them each a towel. 'You leave your clothes here. Don't worry, I'll be here to take care of them.'

They started undressing. As they did so, an old, fat man passed through the hall. He was naked and the flesh fell around him like bags of flour. He pursed his lips when he saw them and said,'Hello boys!' Then he disappeared through the door on the right.

Clitherow looked at Benson and snorted.

Benson put his towel round him before he took off his shirt and vest. This was his custom and he was mildly shocked to see Clitherow strip himself bare and put his towel nonchalantly over his shoulder. Benson noticed that Clitherow was very well built and had black, straight pubic hair. It occurred to him that he had never even had a glance at Clitherow in the nude before.

Clitherow watched Benson taking his socks off while keeping the towel around himself. He reached over and ripped the towel away, revealing Benson in an erect state.

'Goodness me!' he said.

Benson replaced the towel and gave Clitherow a withering look.

Clitherow, still naked, made his way to the door on the right and Benson followed. They came into a room where upwards of twenty men in various stages of disrepair stood around naked drinking beer from bottles. The hubbub of chatter faded as the men saw the newcomers. Clitherow went over to the table and asked a young man for two beers. He gave one to Benson who was the only one in the room with his towel on.

'Take that towel off, for God's sake!' he whispered.

'I . . . I can't,' Benson whispered back.

He drank down the warm beer and then he did so.

He noticed that there was a door through which men kept going. Clitherow had seen the door and nudged Benson towards it.

'Don't go in there unless you're serious,' said the fat man they had seen earlier in the hall.

Clitherow did not reply. He opened the door and pulled Benson through.

When Benson's eyes had become adjusted to the semi-darkness, which was relieved only by the light of a single candle, he saw that the room was full of shadowy figures. Most of these figures were either standing against the walls or walking slowly about the room. He tried to follow Clitherow across and as he did so a man felt his penis and squeezed it. He nearly panicked then but was saved by the relaxing effects of the beer and the dim sight of other men in a similar state of erection. He let his hands fall at his sides and found that men were placing themselves in range for him to touch. Soon he had lost sight of Clitherow and was on his own, both hands full and hands touching him all over.

He turned round to say no to the men but felt hands on him, stroking him, admiring him, whispering flattering phrases into his ears. For a moment, Benson wondered, 'How can I find Dearest Him in this darkness?' But before he knew what was happening a man had knelt down in front of him.

'Mind your teeth!' he told the man.

Then he had a vision of the handsome soldier in 'Faithful Unto Death' turning and seeing the scene he was standing guard over. His expression changed to one of anger and contempt for Benson, 'Is *this* what I sacrificed my life for?' And the guard aimed his spear . . . but Benson's penis was straining with excitement and he wanted to concentrate on his pleasure. 'Turn around and do your job!' Benson commanded the soldier. 'You watch the molten lava if you want to! I've got other fish to fry!' He concentrated on the shadowy view of the wet serpent, the most troublesome part of himself, pulling itself from the man's mouth – burnished and growing – and back into it again and again and the soldier vanished from his mind. And Benson thought, 'I am a sexy bugger! I – with my head full of Jean-Paul Sartre and catechisms of Christian doctrine and Saints' Feast Days and Matthew Arnold and ideals and historical dates and Ordnance Survey map symbols and the Latin names for wild flowers and beautiful works of art like "Faithful Unto Death" and the complete songbook of Bob Dylan and Simon and Garfunkel and Joan Baez and Judy Collins – am a sexy bugger.' And he loved the feeling that that thought gave him for it banished all other thoughts but that one and left him empty to receive his molten pleasures purely.

Too soon it was over.

The man below him withdrew into the crowd of men all around. Benson caught sight of his face. He knew that face and smiled knowingly to himself. Then he strode arrogantly around the room, glorying in the reaction his still-tumescent penis was having on the other men. They would do anything for him, he thought.

He met Clitherow in the other room a few minutes later.

'Are you having a good time?' asked Clitherow.

'Mmmm, yes,' said Benson.

'Let's have another beer. I'm having my eyes opened tonight. I know what you mean! Some of these men are real experts. The fellow I had took his teeth out.'

'No!'

'Yes! I don't think I'd like to do it to anyone though, do you? It's lovely to have it done, but I think it's a bit perverted to want to do it.'

'I thought you said you should open yourself to everything in life?'

'Yes,' conceded Clitherow, 'but there are limits.'

They drank their second beers.

'Well, I'd like to do it to you, if that's all right,' said Benson quite coolly.

'Would you, really?'

'Yes, I would. You're my best friend after all.'

'Then come with me. There's another room which is quieter.'

And Benson followed Clitherow into the room. There was one couple on a mattress to one side. Otherwise it was empty.

Clitherow lay down on his back and Benson lay down beside him. They played with one another for a while and Clitherow kissed Benson on the lips. Then he said, 'Show me you're my best friend.'

Benson knelt down over Clitherow and did his best.

The bus home was, naturally enough, a different world. Benson could not believe he had experienced what had just happened. He told Clitherow his feelings.

'That was living! I feel wonderful!'

Clitherow held Benson's hand, but discreetly. 'You're quite an expert. I hope we can do that again,' he said.

'Me too.'

'I said it would be an iconoclastic weekend. It has been, hasn't it?'

Benson nodded.

When they got back to Clitherow's house Dr Clitherow was at the front door.

'Where have you been? We've been looking for you everywhere!'

Then he turned to Benson and said, 'Your dad phoned earlier in the evening. Your mum's been taken to hospital. He's there with her.'

'What's the matter?' asked Benson.

'She was taken poorly and your dad came home and found her in a bit of a state. I don't know what the problem is but I'll run you to the hospital now. I think your dad would like to see you.'

Then Dr Clitherow turned his attention to his son, 'Where did you go? You weren't at the pictures. I rang the place. I do wish you'd tell me where you're going. I've been worried sick.'

'We went for a walk instead,' replied Clitherow.

Dr Clitherow ran Benson to the hospital. They found Dad sitting alone outside the ward. He looked glum and did not cheer up when he saw his son.

Dr Clitherow introduced himself.

'They're operating on Mum,' Dad told Benson.

'I'll go and see if I can find out something,' said Dr Clitherow.

Benson sat down beside Dad but didn't say anything.

'I found her unconscious on the hall floor, son. She must have been trying to get to the telephone.'

'It isn't really serious is it, Dad?' asked Benson.

'I don't know. She'll need all our prayers.'

Benson felt suddenly dirty. His mouth tasted of old beer and a memory of sex. 'I've got to go to the bathroom, Dad.'

In the bathroom he washed his mouth. He pushed a finger round the inside of it, trying to clean it. He gagged and retched and started to cry.

When he got back Dr Clitherow was standing next to Dad looking solemn. 'Its looking bad. I can't understand why it wasn't noticed earlier.'

'Mum was never one to complain,' said Dad.

Dr Clitherow left them alone. Dad did not speak, but just sat and smoked and gazed at the linoleum floor.

At last a nurse came up to them. 'Your wife's through the operation but she's very weak.'

'Can I see her?'

'Just for a moment.'

Mum was lying in bed with tubes up her nose and down her throat. Her breathing was slow and came in heavy sighs with dreadful silences between. Dad and Benson looked down at her for a long time. Then the nurse came over and said that she would keep them informed about her progress.

Dad nodded and wandered out of the door of the ward without a word. He did not look back to see if Benson was following.

Mum never regained consciousness.

A week later Benson found himself, dressed in an altar boy's surplice and cotter, standing by her grave as Father Hanlon recited the prayers for the dead.

Clitherow, his mother and father, Brother Hooper and many of Mum's friends and neighbours, stood ranged round the grave. When the time came they all poured some earth on to the coffin. Benson noticed that the gravediggers stood, leaning on their spades, beyond the hedge that separated the Catholic and the non-Catholic sides.

The service ended. He heard a loud motor bike pass on the nearby road and wanted to shout obscenities at it for not understanding what was taking place. How dare it continue as if nothing had happened! How dare it not show more respect!

Dad walked back to the big funeral car with the priest. In the five days that had passed since Mum's death he had been even more silent than usual and had spent a lot of time in the bedroom upstairs packing up Mum's clothes.

Benson had caught him coming down the stairs with a parcel of her things. On top of the clothes, all of which Benson could recognise and see Mum wearing, was the Stratton powder compact with a Chinese crane on the front which he had given to Mum for Christmas, only a month ago.

'What are you doing with Mum's things, Dad?' Benson had asked.

Dad had not looked at him. He stared unhappily at the pile of things in his arms. He had tied the bundle together with green garden twine.

'I'm taking them to the Sisters, son. They'll be able to use them.'

'Yes,' said Benson and he had started to cry.

Dad did not stop to say anything to his son, but brushed past him, opening the front door and banging it behind him. Benson could see him through the mottled glass of the door, lifting the boot of the car.

Benson had followed Dad out to the car and opened the boot just as Dad was starting up. He picked up the powder compact and rushed back into the house with it, ignoring Dad who asked him what he was doing.

That night he had slept with the powder compact cradled against his cheek. He spoke to Mum through it and asked her to understand what was happening.

'Now you know everything, Mum. Help me! Are you happy? Please be happy! You were the best mum in the world. You know me now! Help me to be honourable and faithful unto death.'

After the funeral there was a wake at Benson's house. He passed round sandwiches that Mrs Brown had made.

'Your dad will need you now,' said Mrs Brown.

'Yes,' replied Benson.

'But don't you worry, your mum is happy now.'

'Yes.'

The plate of sandwiches shook. Mrs Clitherow relieved him of them. She held his hand and said, 'You're always welcome at our house. Always. My son needs a good friend. We'll all enjoy having you around at any time, son. You're a real tonic for us. And I know your dad is proud of you. You should have heard him talking about you just now!'

Benson tried to smile at Mrs Clitherow but instead his

mouth turned downwards, his chin quivered like a child's and the tears gushed from his eyes.

'Come here, son!' exclaimed Mrs Clitherow and she took him to her and hugged him tightly.

Some time later, Brother Hooper said that he wanted to leave but could not find Dad. Benson excused himself and went out to the front room. Dad was not there. He went upstairs but there was no sign of Dad.

On his way downstairs he met Clitherow.

'Have you seen my dad?' he asked him.

'No, I haven't. Not recently anyway.'

Clitherow accompanied Benson to the kitchen. Dad was not there. They looked through the kitchen window at the winter garden and at a watery sun which seemed to be setting before it had properly risen.

'There he is,' said Clitherow, pointing towards the greenhouse.

Benson saw Dad, alone and hunched in the greenhouse, muttering to the flowers.

That evening when everyone had gone, Dad announced that he was going out for a walk.

'Would you like me to come along, Dad?' Benson asked.

'No, son. Thanks all the same, but I'd rather be alone.'

Then, seeing his son's crestfallen expression, he added, 'We'll have plenty of time for walks soon. But now I need to be by myself. You'll understand one day, Martin.'

'I understand now, Dad,' Benson replied, his voice breaking.

Dad nodded and took out his coat from the hall cupboard.

Benson stood at the dining-room window as Dad walked up the road in the amber light thrown out by the new street lamps. Then he turned back to the room and caught himself in the wall-mirror over the sideboard. He gazed at his reflection for a long time, wondering who was looking back at him so steadily, with such a sad, sober expression.

'I'll show you,' he told the stranger.

Martin Benson placed 'Missa Luba' on the Dansette, turned the volume to maximum and danced his way through the African mass.

He danced for Mum and Brother O'Toole and Ninian and Novvy and Clitherow and Brother Michael and Bruno and Mrs Brown and Eric and for the calm wild creature he saw in the octagonal mirror who had not drawn the curtains and who, for the moment at least, did not care.

THE END